Fleece Navidad

Fleece Navidad

Maggie Sefton

BERKLEY PRIME CRIME, NEW YORK

THE BERKLEY PUBLISHING GROUP
Published by the Penguin Group
Penguin Group (USA) Inc.
375 Hudson Street, New York, New York 10014, USA
Penguin Group (Canada), 90 Eglinton Avenue East, Suite 700, Toronto, Ontario M4P 2Y3, Canada
(a division of Pearson Penguin Canada Inc.)
Penguin Books Ltd., 80 Strand, London WC2R 0RL, England
Penguin Group Ireland, 25 St. Stephen's Green, Dublin 2, Ireland (a division of Penguin Books Ltd.)
Penguin Group (Australia), 250 Camberwell Road, Camberwell, Victoria 3124, Australia
(a division of Pearson Australia Group Pty. Ltd.)
Penguin Books India Pvt. Ltd., 11 Community Centre, Panchsheel Park, New Delhi—110 017, India
Penguin Group (NZ), 67 Apollo Drive, Rosedale, North Shore 0632, New Zealand
(a division of Pearson New Zealand Ltd.)
Penguin Books (South Africa) (Pty.) Ltd., 24 Sturdee Avenue, Rosebank, Johannesburg 2196,
South Africa

Penguin Books Ltd., Registered Offices: 80 Strand, London WC2R 0RL, England

This book is an original publication of The Berkley Publishing Group.

This is a work of fiction. Names, characters, places, and incidents either are the product of the author's imagination or are used fictitiously, and any resemblance to actual persons, living or dead, business establishments, events, or locales is entirely coincidental. The publisher does not have any control over and does not assume any responsibility for author or third-party websites or their content.

PUBLISHER'S NOTE: The recipes contained in this book are to be followed exactly as written. The publisher is not responsible for your specific health or allergy needs that may require medical supervision. The publisher is not responsible for any adverse reactions to the recipes contained in this book.

ISBN-13 978-0-425-22360-4

PRINTED IN THE UNITED STATES OF AMERICA

Acknowledgments

First, I want to thank Jean Utley for suggesting the marvelous title for this holiday mystery. Jean is the manager of the charming bookstore, Book 'Em Mysteries, at 1118 Mission Street in South Pasadena, California. I stopped in the cozy bookshop in May of 2007 to sign books and chat with readers. While I was there, I mentioned to Jean that I was going to write a holiday-themed mystery which would follow *Dyer Consequences* in the Kelly Flynn mystery series. I confessed I was having a hard time coming up with a "cute" title. Jean immediately started suggesting funny titles. When I heard her say *"Fleece Navidad,"* I laughed out loud.

I hope readers will enjoy this holiday visit with Kelly and her friends, because I had a whole lot of fun writing it.

Next, I want to thank a dear friend, Claudia Edwards, for her friendship and support over the years. She always believed in me as a writer, even when my earlier books weren't selling. Claudia and I met in West Lafayette, Indiana (home of Purdue University) when we both lived there raising our families. We struggled together through the rigorous accounting regimen at Purdue's Krannert School of Management and became CPAs. We then "suited up" and joined accounting firms. We may have looked like sober, serious accountants, but our fun-loving natures always gave us away.

So, imagine my surprise when a new character "walked onstage" in this book and introduced herself as Claudia

ACKNOWLEDGMENTS

Miller. I realized she resembled my old friend Claudia in many ways—until she opened her mouth. Oh, my. Character Claudia may share my friend's vivacious, lively personality and her delightful sense of humor. But—Character Claudia also has some other character traits that are . . . well, less than admirable, shall we say. But I'll leave it to the readers to discover Claudia Miller themselves and come to their own conclusions.

I also want to mention that the idea for Annie, the Celebrity Lamb, came after meeting the "real" Annie, an adorable lamb who is owned by sheep breeder Mary Ann Cothren of Gill, Colorado.

Finally, I want to thank Natasha York of Fort Collins, Colorado. Natasha is a knitter as well as an officer with the Larimer County Police Department, and she was kind enough to advise me as to the correct police procedures and terminology that are involved when crimes are committed and people are arrested. Natasha and I went over the entire manuscript one cold December afternoon. It may have been cold outside, but it was warm inside Jay's Bistro, where we had a delightful and delicious four-hour "working lunch."

I wish all of my readers a wonderful Holiday Season filled with Joy, Peace, and Love. Happy Holidays!

Cast of Characters

Kelly Flynn—financial accountant and part-time sleuth, refugee from East Coast corporate CPA firm

Steve Townsend—architect and builder in Fort Connor, Colorado, and Kelly's boyfriend

KELLY'S FRIENDS:
Jennifer Stroud—real estate agent, part-time waitress

Lisa Gerrard—physical therapist

Megan Smith—IT consultant, another corporate refugee

Marty Harrington—lawyer, Megan's boyfriend

Greg Carruthers—university instructor, Lisa's boyfriend

Pete Wainwright—owner of Pete's Porch café in the back of Kelly's favorite knitting shop, House of Lambspun

LAMBSPUN FAMILY AND REGULARS:
Mimi Shafer—Lambspun shop owner and knitting expert, known to Kelly and her friends as "Mother Mimi"

Burt Parker—retired Fort Connor police detective, Lambspun spinner-in-residence

Hilda and Lizzie von Steuben—spinster sisters, retired school teachers, and exquisite knitters

CAST OF CHARACTERS

Curt Stackhouse—Colorado rancher, Kelly's mentor and advisor

Jayleen Swinson—Alpaca rancher and Colorado Cowgirl

Connie and Rosa—Lambspun shop personnel

Fleece Navidad

One

"**Is** Marty going back for seconds already?" Kelly Flynn asked her friend Megan as they stood in the doorway of Curt Stackhouse's ranch house kitchen.

"Hey, slow down, there's plenty of turkey and stuffing left," Megan called after her boyfriend, who was headed toward the serving dishes that covered the counters.

"Already met my turkey quota," Marty said, balancing two cups of eggnog on an empty plate. "Now I'm after sweet potato casserole and creamed onions and cranberry sauce and . . ."

Kelly feigned shock. "*You* have a quota? I thought you were a bottomless pit."

"That's a fact," Curt Stackhouse said as he stood in the middle of the sunny kitchen. The tall, burly, silver-haired rancher sipped a Colorado microbrew. "I swear, I don't know where you put it, boy. You're as skinny as a rail."

"Nice of you to have us over for Thanksgiving, Uncle Curt," Marty said, piling a large helping of creamy sweet potato casserole onto his plate. "We need a big house for all this food."

"Got that right. This hungry crew needs a lot of room," Jayleen Swinson said as she ladled more eggnog into her cup.

"Didn't I tell you, Steve?" Greg's voice sounded in the doorway behind Kelly. "Ol' Marty is back again. You hold him off at the stuffing while I grab some mashed potatoes."

"Too late. They're gone," Jayleen said with an engaging grin as she leaned against the wood-grained counter. "I just watched Marty finish them off."

"*What?* I haven't had seconds yet," Steve Townsend complained as he stepped beside Kelly and slipped his arm around her waist. "I'm going to save Greg the trouble and pound Marty myself."

Kelly leaned against her boyfriend, while she listened to her friends insult the amiable redhead. For his part, Marty simply smiled between mouthfuls of sweet potatoes and creamed onions, uttering loud sounds of enjoyment which only egged on Greg and Steve to further insults.

"I knew we should have strung him up with the lights last Christmas," Greg said as he scooped hot gravy over a huge mound of stuffing. "I've had to fight with him over desserts ever since he showed up. It's all I can do to grab seconds."

"You mean thirds, don't you?" Kelly teased.

"Still, I think I should pound Marty for good measure. For all those missed desserts," Greg threatened.

"Like I always say. Ya gotta catch me first," Marty replied with a grin.

"I will, after I have more sweet potatoes."

Jayleen chuckled deep in her throat as she tossed her graying blonde curls over her shoulder. "You boys couldn't catch a three-legged billy goat, let alone each other. You're so full right now, you'd barely make it to the pasture."

Nearly sixty, and Jayleen still didn't show her age, Kelly observed. Colorado Cowgirl, in boots and blue jeans.

"Damn straight. I'd have to send the dogs out to find 'em," Curt said.

"Three-legged billy goat?" Kelly tried to picture the scene. "Have you got one of those, Curt? I'd like to see Greg and Marty have at it. I'll bet on the goat."

"Me, too," Megan said, laughing.

"Maybe we should ease up on him, Greg. After all, Marty did help us win the baseball tournament last summer," Steve said as he surveyed the remains of Thanksgiving dinner.

"And don't forget it," Marty said before wiping the last of the gravy on his plate with the last of Megan's biscuits.

"Yeah, yeah, yeah." Greg checked the empty biscuit basket. "Gone. I can't believe it. You ate all the biscuits."

"And you're surprised at this?"

"Dude, you're so dead."

"Why don't we keep him away from the pies?" Steve suggested, serving himself some turkey and stuffing. "That's fitting punishment."

"What about cutting off the eggnog?" Kelly said with a sly smile. "I swear he must have finished a gallon since we got here."

"Way more," Megan said. "You should see our fridge. You can barely find the food for the eggnog."

"Hey, it's a seasonal specialty. And you can't keep me away from the pies. I know the cook." He winked at Megan.

"I assume that's 'know' in the biblical sense?" Jennifer said as she strolled into the kitchen, empty plate in hand.

Greg snickered, and Kelly tried not to laugh too hard while Megan threw a wadded paper towel Jennifer's way.

"Whoa, good thing I need to go on a diet, because you guys have finished everything." Jennifer scooped a dollop of cranberry sauce onto her plate. "I suggest we all wait a couple of hours before we attack Megan's pies. Besides, Lisa and Mimi can use help finishing the tree. So we might as well be useful while we're working up an appetite again."

"Did you sort the ornaments?" Kelly asked as she reached for the coffeepot on the counter behind her. A fragrant plume of black nectar wafted toward her nostrils. Her taste buds started to wake up from the carb-induced stupor that was Thanksgiving.

Jennifer brushed her auburn hair over her shoulder. "Yeah, I figured we didn't want Megan anywhere near them. Not after last year, when she went ballistic."

"Hey, that wasn't my fault," Megan protested. "It was Marty's. He was the one breaking everything."

"Good Lord," Jayleen mused out loud. "It seems like only yesterday when ol' Marty stumbled into our lives."

Greg snorted. "Stumbled is right."

"I couldn't help myself," Marty declared, hand to heart. "I lost all control after tasting Megan's blueberry pie."

"Hey, you guys!" Lisa's voice commanded from the doorway. "Enough slacking off. Mimi and Burt and I need help. And no pie until the tree is finished and all the decorations are up. I'll hide those pies if I have to." With her long blonde hair twisted into a bun atop her head, Lisa looked like a fussy schoolteacher.

"Whoa, we'd better get back out there," Marty said as he rinsed his plate. "She sounds serious."

"Sorry, Lisa. Didn't mean to disappear on you," Kelly said. "I came in for coffee then got sucked into watching the guys finish off the leftovers."

"Well, you heard the trail boss," Curt ordered. "Go on, everybody, git!" He shooed the unruly group out of the kitchen, Jayleen bringing up the rear.

"We ought to grab a tree for the cottage on the way home. Small ones go fast," Kelly said to Steve as they walked back into Curt's high-ceilinged, expansive family room. Like last year, every nook and cranny, wall and window was filled with colorful Christmas decorations, both homemade and store-bought.

"You didn't have a tree last year."

"Yeah, I did. On the dining room table."

"That little thing?" Steve scoffed. "That wasn't a tree. It was a plant. Why don't we get a real tree?"

"And where would we put it?" Kelly countered as she paused at the edge of the family room, where Mimi and Lisa were hanging ornaments on the branches of a huge

Colorado spruce. Retired cop Burt Parker sat on the floor, untangling strings of lights. "There's not enough room in the cottage. We can't plop it in the middle of the living room."

Steve sipped his coffee and stared at the Christmas tree dominating the room. "Now, there's a tree." He lifted his mug in salute.

That it was. The Stackhouse Spruce was imposing. Fully twelve feet high, it nearly grazed the top of the sloping cathedral ceiling. Every branch was laden and dripping with ornaments. Heirloom and homemade, children's paper cutouts, glistening glass, hand-stitched bears, painted metal bells, crocheted angels, and carved wooden nutcrackers. Strung with rows of twinkling lights, the tree was aglow.

"It's beautiful," Kelly agreed.

"We have to find room for a tree. Even if it's in the middle of the living room."

Kelly chuckled. "You say that now. . . ."

"Hey, Steve. I've replaced all the broken bulbs, so you and Greg can put up the outside lights." Burt held up two large strings of colored lights. "Why don't you get Marty to help you this year? It'll take less time."

"Yeah, but what if he trips and breaks them all?" Greg said as he headed for the front door.

"Then we'll string *him* up, like you suggested," Steve said, following after Greg. "Hey, Kelly, when is my alpaca scarf going to be finished? It's cold out there. Do I really have to wait for Christmas?"

"Yes, you do. You don't want to anger the Knitting Sages," she warned.

Greg snickered. "Knitting Sages, my ass. Why don't you take Kelly's scarf? She owes it to you for being so slow. Lisa's made me at least a dozen scarves."

"Good idea." Steve snatched Kelly's tweed alpaca scarf from a nearby peg and wrapped it around his neck. "I thought you said you'd have it finished by winter. It's almost December."

Marty wagged the end of his dangling emerald green scarf, taunting Steve. "I have two. Megan's working on a third."

Steve pulled on his gloves. "Marty is in a law office or the courthouse all day. Greg's in the computer lab at the university. I'm the only one who works outside in the cold. What's wrong with this picture?"

Kelly took a sip of coffee before she took the bait. "I promised it by winter. But it's not snowing yet, so it's not officially winter. Besides, I got distracted by autumn froufrou yarns. Couldn't help myself."

"Blame Mimi. It's all her fault. She's the one who puts those scrumptious yarns out there. Tempting us," Jennifer said, sipping her coffee.

Burt spoke up. "Don't apologize, Mimi," he said, still on the floor, untangling decorations now.

"I don't intend to," Mimi said with her musical laugh. "Yarns and fiber are my passion."

"I thought Burt was your passion," Jennifer said with a wicked smile.

Kelly watched the good-natured owner of their favorite knitting shop, House of Lambspun, blush as she laughed.

"Mimi's got a ton of scarves hanging by the doorway in the house, Steve. You can borrow one until Christmas," Burt offered.

"I'll take you up on that, Burt. Meanwhile, don't start the pie until we're back," Steve said as he followed Marty and Greg out the front door.

"Poor Steve, freezing to death out there on his building sites. Can't you knit faster, Kelly girl?" Curt barbed as he settled into a worn leather armchair.

"Hey, I can't help it. I'm slow. Lisa, Megan, and Jennifer are fast. And Mimi is warp speed. Me, I provide the balance." Kelly adjusted a twisted ornament. "Guys, I think this tree is finished. If you put any more ornaments up there, it'll fall over."

"I need more coffee. That turkey sleepiness is setting in, and I have to finish my shopping list tonight." Megan headed for the kitchen.

The thought of crowded holiday stores and shoppers reminded Kelly she hadn't bought a thing. "Boy, I haven't even made a list yet."

"Well, I've finished completely," Lisa bragged as she hung a painted star on a branch. "I started in September, and I've bought everything on my list."

"Everything? You're kidding."

"Nope. Every present is bought and stored in the closet. All I have to do is wrap them."

"But I haven't told you what I want yet," Jennifer countered as she draped silvery metallic strands onto a tree branch.

"Too late. I've already bought your gift."

"What if I don't like it?"

"You'll love it," Lisa said confidently. "Trust me. You know I have good taste."

"And you're efficient, too," Mimi added from the other side of the tree.

Jennifer sighed. "I hate efficiency. All that planning takes too much time."

Mimi added a tiny angel to the end of a branch. "There, now. Every ornament has a place. We're all done."

"Many hands make light work, my mom used to say." Jayleen settled into a maple rocking chair and stretched out her denim-clad legs. "I reckon you'll need a lot of hands for that charity bazaar, Mimi, so if there's any way I can help, let me know."

"Thank you, Jayleen, I'm going to need all the help I can find to finish those knitted items on time." Mimi glanced toward Kelly and her friends. "All you girls were good to sign up. I know you're busy with your own knitting projects. Especially Kelly. Poor Steve needs his scarf."

Kelly laughed. "Don't worry. I'll still have time to knit a Hat for the Homeless. Steve's scarf isn't in serious jeopardy."

"I may have to ask another favor," Mimi said, looking apologetic. "Saint Mark's Catholic Church's youth groups have all volunteered to knit hats, too. And their leader asked me if I could send her some knitters to help out this Saturday. She'll be teaching the kids in small groups. I wondered if a couple of you could volunteer. It would only be Saturday morning."

Kelly reviewed her mental daytimer. "I don't know how good I'll be at teaching knitting, but I'll give it a try."

"Count me in," Jennifer offered. "I used to be a summer camp counselor, so I've got an advanced degree in kids' crafts."

"That's great, girls! Thank you so much. We've got a ton of donated yarns and needles, so you'll have lots to choose from."

"Good Lord, woman, how many hats do you need?" Curt asked, balancing the bottle of beer on his knee.

"Well, it's not just hats. We're also knitting gloves and mittens, and they take longer. In fact, I've got people knitting all over Fort Connor. We're trying to knit up over a hundred sets of hats, mittens, and gloves to sell at the bazaar. All proceeds go to the homeless shelter." She gave a sigh. "Now I've learned I have to run the holiday bazaar fiber crafts booth, too. The organizer had promised someone else would do it, but I guess not."

Jayleen chuckled, crossing one booted foot over the other. "That's what happens when we volunteer to organize something, Mimi. It keeps growing and growing. I'll be glad to knit some hats and gloves for you."

Megan approached with coffeepot in hand. "I figured everyone needed a refill."

Mimi settled into a chair beside Burt. "Kelly, I wanted to ask you something. There's an antique booth at the bazaar and the woman running it is taking furniture on consignment. Would you like to sell any of your cousin Martha's things? I mean, you took everything out of the house when you sold it last summer, didn't you?"

"Actually I gave a lot of the everyday furniture to the Wyoming agency that bought the house. But I kept all of Cousin Martha's antiques." Kelly held out her mug for a refill, nodding her thanks to Megan.

"Why don't you sell some of the furniture, Kelly?" Lisa said as she stacked empty ornament boxes on the table. "Isn't it just sitting in a storage locker in Wyoming?"

Kelly took a drink of coffee. Deep, dark, and delicious, just the way she liked it. "Yes, it is, and that's where it's going to stay until I decide what I want to keep and what I don't. I won't know that until I buy a bigger place, and who knows when that will be."

"Are you sure you don't need the money, Kelly?" Mimi asked, looking concerned. "I know you were short earlier this year."

"I'm fine, Mimi. Thanks to Jayleen's help selling my herd of alpacas in the canyon, I had enough money to pay off that investor loan in June. And thanks to Curt, I've got money in the bank." She winked at her mentor and ranch adviser, Curt Stackhouse.

"Now that those Wyoming gas wells are producing, you should be all right," Curt said, tipping his bottle of beer. "Royalty checks will be coming regularly."

"Boy, I could use some royalty checks right now," Jennifer said as she sank into the love seat beside Kelly. "Actually, some new real estate clients would be better. I may be plundering my stash bag for Christmas presents. I hope you all like pot holders."

"Weren't you looking at canyon properties this summer, Kelly? Did you see any that caught your eye?" Burt asked as he stuffed unused lights into another box.

"Nope. Jennifer showed me what was available, but nothing gave me a buzz."

"Don't worry, Kelly," Jayleen said, leaning back into her chair. "There are plenty of pretty places in that canyon, and every year some of them come on the market. You just have to wait and see what shows up."

Lisa perched on a chair arm. "Why don't you buy one of those gorgeous lots that are available up there? Then Steve can build a house. You two must be tripping over each other in that cottage. Greg and I daydream about building a house up there one of these days."

"Yeah, Kelly. You know Steve is itching to build a house for you. He's an architect, for heaven's sake," Megan added.

Her friends weren't telling Kelly anything she didn't already know. "You're right. He'd love to build a house. Problem is, where? I don't know if I want to build in the canyon. Last year, I was certain I wanted to live up there, but now I'm not so sure. I've gotten used to living in town. Plus, I'm spoiled—I like to walk across the driveway to Lambspun every day for a knitting and coffee break."

"Well, I'm glad you're addicted to us and to Pete's coffee," Mimi teased.

"Speaking of coffee, I think I'd better make another pot," Jennifer said, rising from the love seat. "I hear the sounds of Big Guy feet outside on the porch."

Sure enough, two big guys and one tall, skinny redhead came stomping into the house, still exchanging insults as they shed their coats. A frigid breeze followed them in as well.

"Whoa, close that door. You're letting in the cold," Kelly called out.

"What was that you said about slacking off, Lisa? I don't see any pie, and I don't smell any coffee," Greg said, running his hand through his short blond hair.

"You can't possibly be hungry again." Lisa looked askance.

"Yeah, we are," Steve said, tossing Kelly's scarf over her coat. "We've been climbing up ladders and hauling around lights. Builds up an appetite."

"Did you catch that goat?" Kelly joked as Steve plopped his muscular frame onto the sofa beside her.

"Naw, we caught Marty instead."

Marty bleated on cue.

Megan sank her forehead into her hand, jet black hair falling about her face. "Please don't encourage him with animal sounds."

"Why-y-y-y-y nah-ah-ah-ah-ahttt?"

"That's it. I'm going to warm up the pie," Megan said, heading for the kitchen. "No barnyard animals allowed."

Kelly laughed. "Was that a sheep or a goat? I couldn't tell." Her laughter was cut short when Steve suddenly pulled her close.

"My nose is cold, and you're nice and warm," he said, burying his cold face into her neck.

Kelly shrieked at the shock of icy nose against warm skin. Her warm skin. "*Yeow!*" she yelled, laughing and pushing Steve away at the same time as she leaped off the sofa.

"Wait, it's not warm yet," Steve protested, playfully reaching for her.

"No, you're freezing. I'm going to start cleaning the kitchen. Who's up for a run after we've stuffed ourselves with pie?"

"Good idea, Kelly," Lisa said. "We'll need it after this feast."

Marty raised his hand. "I'm in. Megan, too, if we can talk her into it."

Jayleen chuckled. "How on earth can you run after everything you've eaten?"

Curt gave a snort. "I told you. That boy has a hollow leg."

"Hey, the pie helps everything settle."

"We can use the river trails. It won't be dark for a couple of hours," Steve said, glancing toward the window.

"You're coming, too, aren't you?" Lisa asked Greg as she followed after Kelly.

"You guys go ahead. I'm still cold," Greg said.

Lisa stared incredulously at her boyfriend, who had claimed her cup of coffee as well as her chair. "What? You ride your bike when it's below zero. It's only twenty today. That's positively balmy. What's up?"

Greg smiled from behind the mug. "Nothing. I'm just going to stay here and get warm. And see if Curt and Jayleen need any help."

Marty grinned. "He's up to something. He's got that look."

"Well, if you really want to help, you can start rinsing dishes," Lisa said, beckoning.

"Actually, I was thinking more along the lines of helping wrap the leftovers."

Kelly and Lisa headed for the kitchen, the sound of laughter following after them.

Two

Steve pulled Kelly closer to him, her body curving into his beneath the covers. Bare skin warming bare skin. Warm. Getting warmer.

"Ummmm, what time is it?" she asked in a sleepy voice.

"Time to get up, unfortunately."

Kelly squinted at the bedside clock. Six ten. "Oh, it's early yet. You don't have to be at the Old Town site till seven thirty."

"Today I've gotta be there by seven."

Kelly made a soft noise as she wiggled against him. "Ummmm, let your new supervisor handle it."

Steve's body responded against hers. "That's who I'm meeting at seven. Dutch and I have to check some plans." He ran his hand down her hip. "Why don't we continue this in the shower?"

"But then I'd have to get out of bed, and it's soooooooo warm here." She wiggled against him again.

"You are dangerous, woman," Steve said before kissing her neck.

Kelly thought there would be more, but instead Steve threw back the covers and climbed out of bed.

"I'll turn on the hot water and let it steam the room," he suggested as he strode toward the bathroom.

Kelly drew the covers up to her chin, snuggling into their warmth. She heard the sound of the shower, and Steve appeared in the bathroom doorway. His interest was still evident.

"Hot water, steam, c'mon . . . join me." His eyebrows wiggled suggestively.

Kelly snickered beneath the covers. "But I'd have to walk across the cold room. Why don't you warm me up first," she tempted as she pulled back the covers and patted her side of the bed.

"C'mon . . . the water's hot."

Kelly just smiled in reply and continued to pat the bed beside her. The empty bed.

Steve grinned. "You sure you don't want a shower?"

"Afterward." She wiggled her brows in imitation of him.

"Let's see if someone else can change your mind," he said, striding to the bedroom doorway.

Kelly sat up. He wouldn't.

He would, and he did. Steve flung open the bedroom

door and called out, "Carl! Come here, boy. Kelly wants to play."

"Steve, don't you dare!" Kelly protested, but it was too late.

Kelly's Rottweiler, Carl, came bounding into their bedroom and leaped onto the bed—all one hundred pounds of him.

Kelly squealed and dove under the covers as Carl charged forward, long pink tongue ready to slurp.

"Here, boy, let me help you," Steve offered, lifting the covers for Carl to climb beneath. The better to slurp.

"*No*! Steve, no! *Yieeee!*" Kelly's squeals turned to shrieks as Carl found lots of bare skin to slurp.

Kelly squirmed and squealed while Steve laughed. Finally, Kelly rolled into a ball and fell off the bed to escape. Carl's nose was a lot colder than Steve's.

Kelly flipped the electronic door lock for her car as she and Jennifer approached the street corner across from Saint Mark's Church. The century-old spire towered over them.

It was a brilliantly sunny morning, as bright as a summer's day. Temperatures had climbed, surprising everyone including forecasters. All the holiday shoppers Kelly had seen walking about Old Town had their coats unbuttoned, their wool scarves dangling uselessly. Capricious Colorado weather at work. Change was the only constant.

"I love your new car, Kelly. I'm glad you went sportier," Jennifer said as they waited for the traffic light to change. "I'm sure I couldn't afford it, but it's nice to ride in."

"It was an impulse," Kelly admitted, glancing back at the sleek red car parked along the street. "First time I've ever done anything like that. I surprised myself."

"Impulses can be good, at least in your case. Me, I have to be careful when those impulses strike. They usually have names."

Kelly laughed, watching the light change. "Now that you mention it, how are things going? Romance-wise, I mean?"

Jennifer snorted. "I gave up on romance a long time ago. I settled for having fun."

Having fun was Jennifer's specialty, Kelly knew that. But she heard something else in her friend's voice. She wasn't sure what. "Any new guys on the horizon?" she asked as they crossed the street.

"Nope. In fact, the bar scene isn't what it used to be. A lot of my friends have either moved, gotten married, or gotten sober. It's depressing, actually."

Kelly recognized the teasing sound returning to Jennifer's voice. "Why don't you join Steve and me some night at the Jazz Bistro?"

"Maybe I'll take you up on that offer, sometime." Jennifer stopped at the foot of the steep concrete steps leading to the weather-beaten church doors. "Good Lord. I haven't been here since last Christmas."

Kelly looked up at the stone church as she climbed the steps. "That makes two of us. I hope nobody's keeping track."

"That's why I always check the font of holy water. If the walls start shaking, I'll see the ripples," Jennifer said, following behind.

A huge Christmas wreath adorning the double doors

announced the holiday season as they stepped inside the church vestibule. The scent of evergreen beckoned Kelly forward, and she stopped inside the sanctuary. The decorating committee had been working overtime.

Evergreen boughs and branches were everywhere. Tied with red ribbons, they dangled from the metal chandeliers, draped around the altar rails, and framed the stained-glass windows. The fresh evergreen scent brought back memories—lots of them. They rose in a wave, ready to engulf her in nostalgia—bittersweet and poignant. Christmas always meant Fort Connor to Kelly.

Memories of Christmases Past danced in front of Kelly's eyes. Her father, Aunt Helen, and Uncle Jim opening presents around the tree, sleigh rides across the snowy pastures, sledding down the foothills, Christmas dinner in the farmhouse. Scenes from her childhood when her father, Jim, and Helen were still alive. They were all gone now. Cancer, heart attack, and murder had taken them away.

Jennifer's voice broke through Kelly's thoughts. "Good. Nary a ripple," she said, staring into the font. "Clearly the Powers-That-Be don't know I'm here yet. Better not say my name too loud."

Kelly had to smile, as all twinges of sadness from the past were chased away by the warmth of the present. Friends. Good friends. She'd created a new family when she'd returned to Fort Connor. And she'd never been happier.

Glancing about the sanctuary, Kelly spied another familiar face. Two familiar faces, in fact. "Look, there's Hilda and Lizzie. They'll point us in the right direction," she said, waving to catch the elderly women's attention as they stood in a side doorway.

The two spinster sisters couldn't look more different. Hilda, tall and raw-boned and gangly, and Lizzie, short and round and as plump as a dumpling.

"Perfect timing, girls," Hilda von Steuben said, checking her watch. Still the schoolteacher keeping track. "Come along. The youngsters will be due in a few minutes. This way you'll have time to meet Juliet and get situated. I believe she wants each of us to instruct a group of ten." Hilda beckoned them through the doorway.

"Burt brought the box of donated yarns and needles this morning. Juliet was so pleased," Lizzie added, bringing up the rear.

"Is Juliet the youth group leader?" Kelly asked as Hilda led them down a spiral staircase to a lower level. Classrooms jutted out from a narrow, linoleum-lined hallway. Scuffed linoleum. Many feet had passed through these halls.

"Actually she's a librarian at the city library, but she volunteers to lead the church youth groups."

"Volunteer Extraordinaire," Lizzie said. "She's so good with the children. I always envied her ability to handle all age groups. It was all I could do to handle rowdy high school students."

"It was a good thing you two didn't have me in your classes," Jennifer said as she peered into an empty classroom. "I was one of those rowdy ones. You probably would have smacked me."

"Nonsense, my dear, one never needs to resort to corporal

punishment," Hilda said with a hint of a smile. "There are far more effective ways to rein in the rowdier ones."

"Here we are, Juliet," Lizzie chirped as she ushered Kelly and Jennifer into a brightly lit classroom. "Juliet, I want you to meet Kelly Flynn and Jennifer Stroud. Two of our finest young knitters from Lambspun. Girls, meet Juliet Renfrow. She is a master knitter and a weaver, too." Lizzie beamed as she gestured, almost as if she was pointing to exhibits at the state fair.

"Nice to meet you, Juliet, but I'm afraid Lizzie exaggerates my abilities," Kelly said, extending her hand to the slight woman who approached.

Juliet appeared to be in her sixties or so, judging from the amount of gray streaked through her chin-length brown hair. She had an old-fashioned hairstyle, cut straight at the chin and across the bangs. No makeup, either, as far as Kelly could tell. And no jewelry. She was plain and un-adorned.

But it was Juliet's clothing that really captured Kelly's attention. Juliet was dressed entirely in brown. A chocolate brown long-sleeved sweater reached to Juliet's hips. A beau-tifully knitted sweater, too. Beneath it she wore a café au lait tunic over a long molasses-colored skirt that covered dark brown leggings. Knitted leggings. Kelly wondered if Juliet had knitted the entire ensemble.

Juliet shook Kelly's hand in a surprisingly firm handshake. "So nice of you two to help us this afternoon," she said, her light gray eyes smiling into Kelly's. "We'll need lots of help keeping these young ones focused."

"Well, I hope I'm up to the task, Juliet. I've never taught

kids before. Except on the ball field. I've coached baseball and softball, but this is way different."

"Not as different as you would think," Juliet said with a quick laugh as she shook Jennifer's hand. "I'll get the kids situated and settled, and start the instruction. They're used to me telling them what to do, so they won't give me any grief. And I'll be watching to make sure they don't try it on you." She winked.

"Don't worry about me," Jennifer said with a dismissive wave. "I used to teach kids at summer camp. They can't mess with me."

Juliet laughed, and the smile transformed her face.

"What can we do?" Kelly asked.

"You can help me put out these yarns and needles." Juliet lifted a large box from the table beside her and headed toward the long, rectangular tables Hilda was cleaning.

"Ohhhh, wait'll you see all the yarns Mimi collected from the shops in town. They're beautiful," Lizzie enthused.

"Everyone was so generous," Juliet said, tipping the box over a tabletop. Out scattered colorful balls of yarn.

"This is perfect for beginners," Jennifer said, examining a ball of yarn. "Not too thin, not too thick. It'll be easy to work with."

"Jennifer, could you please fetch those paper towels on top of the cupboard for me?" Hilda called. "I'm afraid my old knees are a bit shaky on a stepladder."

"Hold on, Hilda, I'll get them," Jennifer said, hastening across the room.

"About forty children signed up, so we'll have our hands full," Juliet said as she headed to another table.

Kelly helped scatter the yarns this time. Lizzie appeared with a box of circular knitting needles and arranged them in clusters beside the yarns.

Remembering her own experience knitting a hat for the first time last winter, Kelly wondered out loud. "Do you think the kids will be able to finish at home? It gets a little tricky at the end. What with those double-point needles and such."

"Oh, I'll be around to help them. I thought I'd have a knitting workshop twice a week so the kids could have extra help." Juliet smiled at Kelly. "I remember my first hat, too."

"Make sure you don't volunteer all your time away, Juliet," Lizzie said, a twinkle in her eye. "You want to make sure to have enough time for Christmas parties and such."

Kelly recognized the look in Lizzie's eye. It appeared every time something aroused Lizzie's interest, especially her interest in male-female relationships. *Romantic* relationships, in particular.

Juliet's smile disappeared. "Oh, I never go to parties. I'm much too busy preparing for the holidays."

"But that was before your Romeo started courting you," Lizzie continued to tease as she glanced at Kelly. "Juliet has been seeing a lovely gentleman this year. A widower. They'd seen each other for years at the library. Then one day . . ." Lizzie gestured like an aging Tinkerbell. "Poof! Magic happened."

"How romantic," Kelly replied obligingly. She noticed, however, that Juliet seemed uncomfortable. Juliet made no reply. She simply kept scattering colorful balls of yarn on the next table.

Lizzie, however, continued to fill in the silence. "Surely you and Jeremy have some special holiday plans."

Juliet's lips pursed together. "I'm afraid we don't. Jeremy's been busy lately—"

"Surely not too busy for you," Lizzie teased again.

Juliet's discomfort was palpable now, and Kelly wished there was some discreet way she could get Lizzie to keep quiet short of stuffing a ball of yarn in her mouth.

Juliet shook the box, emptying the remaining yarns on the last table. "I've heard he's seeing another woman," she said softly, her cheeks aflame. Then she turned and hurried toward the classroom doorway. Children's voices could be heard in the hallway.

Lizzie stared after Juliet with an expression of embarrassment and contrition as a noisy group of elementary students burst into the classroom.

Three

Kelly looked up into the Colorado blue sky as she crossed the driveway between the beige stucco, red tile–roofed knitting shop and her lookalike cottage. Another bright, sunny morning. Balmy temperatures, too. Balmy for December, that is. Was this another Indian summer? No rain in sight and no chance of snow, according to the weatherman.

She glanced over her shoulder at the Colorado Rockies in the distance. Snow-capped peaks glistened. The High Country had snow. She and Steve, Greg, Lisa, Megan, and Marty had gone skiing the day after Thanksgiving. All the mountain ski resorts had snow.

Denver had snow. Colorado Springs had snow. Even Greeley had snow. But nary a flake in Fort Connor so far. Maybe that was the Cheyenne Ridge effect. She'd heard since childhood that the Cheyenne Ridge in Wyoming protected Fort Connor from severe winter snowstorms. Denver and Boulder would be dumped on, but Fort Connor would only get a couple of inches. However, every few years a blizzard would roar through the Front Range, and all bets were off.

Kelly paused to admire the Christmas greenery that adorned the Lambspun front door. Jewel-like beads wound through the evergreen boughs, and tiny ribbons dangled. Balancing her coffee mug and knitting bag, she pushed open the door and stepped inside the winter wonderland that Mimi and her elves had created. Kelly paused in the tile foyer, the skylight above flooding the area with sunlight.

The colors of autumn had been cleared away after Thanksgiving. Soft golds and browns, burgundies, deep purples, and forest greens were once again stored downstairs awaiting the inevitable turn of the seasons. Now, the old Spanish colonial farmhouse was alive with bright holiday colors, as each room opened and flowed into the next. Vibrant reds, greens, yellows, and blues were everywhere.

Fat, fluffy balls of jellybean-colored yarns tumbled from an old steamer trunk. Silky skeins of vermillion hand-painted silk beckoned from an antique cabinet. Gossamer fibers draped along the walls waiting to be spun by holiday elves or fairies. Christmas green wools were wound in skeins piled high. Whites, so bright they sparkled. Royal blues, hand-dyed and wrapped in soft bundles of mohair and silk.

Kelly drank in the color surrounding her as she wandered from the foyer into the adjacent room. Gloves, hats, and mittens dangled from the ceiling. Scarves were draped across an antique dresser. Plump skeins of royal blue merino wool spilled from bins along the walls, tidy balls of cotton and silk were piled high atop tables, scrunchy multicolored ribbons tied in bundles were stacked on shelves, luscious soft skeins of baby alpaca overflowed baskets.

Everything begged to be touched. As usual, Kelly obliged and sank her free hand into a bin of soft, puffy balls of jellybean-colored cotton and silk. Next, she stroked a variegated green twist of mohair, then caressed the vermillion hand-painted silk, coiled tight as a woman's braid.

She was fingering an unusual combination of bamboo and cotton when Jennifer's voice called to her from the next room.

"Join me, Kelly. I've got a few minutes of break left."

Kelly strolled into the main room, the largest in the shop, and plopped her knitting bag and coffee mug on the library table that dominated the room.

Shelves lined the walls, alternating with overflowing yarn bins. There were books and patterns for every kind of fiber imaginable. Kelly found all those choices confusing and usually wound up asking Mimi's friendly shop staff.

"I thought you'd be out with your new real estate clients. Didn't they come in Saturday afternoon?"

Jennifer's circular needles worked a bright green yarn quickly. Kelly recognized a charity hat coming into shape. Way faster than her own project.

"Oh, yeah, and are they eager. They're from Nebraska, and they're looking for land where they can build their retirement home. They've been vacationing in Colorado for years. I swear, they want to see every mountain property be-

28

tween Fort Connor and Wyoming, starting with the farthest and most remote. So I took them up Cherokee Park Road to some of those building sites yesterday. You know, waaaay out there."

"You mean out past where the electric poles stop? I remember those sites. Talk about wide-open spaces." Kelly chuckled as she pulled out her circular needles, blue-green yarn dangling from them. The charity hat. Only two inches knitted so far. She eyed Jennifer's hat, which had at least six inches completed.

"Yeah, emphasis on *open*. I told them they'd have to rely on solar energy out there. In fact, they'd have to have a whole array of solar panels. They both do consulting, and they're on their computers all day."

This time Kelly laughed out loud. "Whoa! They'll need more than one solar array. What'd they say when you told them?"

"Their faces fell, because they really liked that prairie-type look to the land. So they're modifying their search closer to town where there are still electric poles on the building sites. But nothing has caught their fancy yet."

"Have you taken them up into the canyons yet?"

"I'm taking them into Poudre Canyon this afternoon. They're speaking with lenders and such this morning, which gives me the chance to work here at the café. Pete was sweet to let me off the last two morning shifts. I told him I'd make it up by catering some of his evening functions."

"Sounds like his catering business has really picked up. That's good."

Small business success stories made the accounting lobe

of Kelly's brain go warm all over. It brought back memories of her first years in the Washington, D.C., CPA firm where she used to work. Her first year there, she'd had to intern in the small business division. "Shoebox" clients they were called, because they often kept their records in a shoebox and would dump them on Kelly's desk. She'd been glad when her time in the trenches was finished and she could move up to corporate accounting, which was her goal.

"Yeah, Pete's doing really well. I'm proud of him."

"Good morning, girls! How lovely to see you here this Monday morning," Lizzie announced as she entered. She was dressed in her traditional Christmas outfit—bright red winter coat with knitted green wool scarf, topped off with a red bow adorning her silver hair, which was swept into a bun. "It was wonderful working with you two on Saturday, and Juliet was delighted with your help. We handled thirty-eight students, all told."

"I'm not sure who handled whom," Kelly said. "That was a heckuva lot harder than teaching baseball. I'm not sure my students will be able to finish their hats on time."

"Nonsense, dear, you did a splendid job." Lizzie slipped off her coat and perched on the chair next to Kelly. She reached into her bulging knitting bag, and lemon yellow froth appeared.

"Baby blanket, right?" Kelly guessed. "I swear, every one of your nieces and nephews must be swaddled in blankets by now."

Lizzie laughed. "This one is destined for Lucy. I thought she could use another. Her little boy is growing by leaps and bounds."

"How is Lucy doing? I haven't seen her since the baby was born," Jennifer asked.

"She's doing quite well. Her spinning business is picking up, and she's teaching more classes. And the baby is a healthy little rascal. Yes, Lucy has really turned her life around." Lizzie's fingers moved swiftly as she stared at the yarn. "Actually the person I'm concerned about now is Juliet. She looked so sad and despondent Saturday, not her usual cheerful self at all."

Kelly wanted to reply but didn't. Juliet had appeared in good spirits until Lizzie started prying into her social life. Clearly, Juliet was a private person.

"Break's over. Gotta get back to the café," Jennifer said, putting away the holiday green hat. "Maybe I'll see you folks tomorrow. It depends on my real estate clients," she said as she hurried out.

"Who is this man Juliet's seeing? Where'd she meet him?" Kelly asked, switching the focus of the conversation.

Lizzie perked up. "Jeremy Cunningham is a lovely gentleman, a retired university professor and a widower. And he would be an excellent match for Juliet. Shy and bookish, just like Juliet." Lizzie's busy needles paused as she stared off into the bookshelves along the walls. "Juliet told me they had known each other at the library for years. Historical research is Jeremy's hobby. They shared their love of books and began having long discussions. Then, he began asking Juliet out in late spring." Lizzie looked up as Hilda and Megan entered the room.

"Hey, there," Kelly greeted them. "Were you two taking a class?"

"Yes, indeed. Megan and I have progressed to Mimi's intermediate spinning class. I confess, I'm beginning to have hope that I will master the wheel at last."

"Don't listen to her," Megan said, giving a dismissive wave. "Hilda's doing beautifully."

Lizzie picked up her sad musings, like a dog chewing a favorite bone. "I just don't understand what happened with Jeremy. Do you, Hilda? He and Juliet were perfect for each other. They looked so sweet together. Juliet adored him, too, you could tell. He was her heart's desire. How could he simply stop seeing her?"

"Inconstancy, thy name is Man," Hilda decreed as she settled at the head of the table. The better to supervise a discussion.

"Who's Juliet?" Megan asked as she pulled out a chair across the table.

"She's the librarian who's running the kids' knitting project at Saint Mark's," Kelly answered before Lizzie could launch into another long description. "She's a really nice lady. A little shy. Kind of a plain Jane—"

"We call her the 'little brown wren,'" Hilda finished, her lined face smiling. "She loves brown."

Kelly laughed. "You can tell. Does she ever wear any other color?"

"Only in December." Lizzie answered, her needles returning to the lemon yarn. "That's when she wears her Christmas capes. They're beautiful. Juliet's a seamstress as well as a knitter and a weaver."

"Oooo, is she the one who makes those capes Mimi sells every holiday?" Megan looked up from the tangerine mittens she was knitting. Project or present? Kelly wondered.

"Indeed she is," Hilda said. "Juliet brings several to the shop, and they're usually gone within a week. And she donates all the proceeds to charity."

"In that case, I'm going to tell Marty that's what I want for a Christmas present. They're gorgeous, and it's all for a good cause."

"Juliet's so talented and so sweet." Lizzie picked up the sorrowful tale again, barely missing a beat from where she left off. "I cannot understand why Jeremy would start seeing another woman. Who *is* she, and where did he meet her?"

Clearly, Lizzie was determined to worry about this unfortunate love affair. Out loud, too. "Who knows, Lizzie? Maybe he met someone at his church or at a social function," Kelly suggested in an attempt to bring closure to the subject. "I've heard Fort Connor is awash in seniors. Everyone wants to retire here because it's so nice. Great weather—"

"Not after last winter," Megan interrupted. "I heard some of them went scurrying south after they learned how quickly Colorado winters can turn brutal."

The click-clack of high heels against wood floors sliced through the quiet then, as a woman's voice called out from the adjoining room. "Yoo-hoo, I think I found the knitters."

A slender, well-dressed woman with frosted blonde hair approached the long table, lacy knitting bag over her shoulder. Kelly recognized the woman's designer suit from her former life in the corporate CPA world. Wardrobe was a part of the business. Now those suits hung in her closet and only came out for business meetings with the company that drilled her gas wells in Wyoming.

The woman, who appeared to be in her fifties or so, pulled out a chair beside Lizzie. "Good morning, ladies. My name's Claudia Miller, and I've recently moved to Fort Connor. I've been asking about yarn shops and heard this one mentioned many times." She glanced around the room admiringly. "I must say, there is a wonderful selection here."

"Welcome to Fort Connor, Claudia. I'm Hilda, and this is my sister, Lizzie. We both taught school here in Fort Connor for over thirty years."

"It's wonderful to meet you," Lizzie chirped.

"Nice to meet you, Claudia. I'm Kelly and this is Megan," she said, gesturing. "And you definitely came to the right place if you want to find beautiful yarns and meet new friends."

"Kelly came only a year ago last April for her dear aunt's funeral, but she's here to stay now." Lizzie beamed.

"Well, thank you, ladies, for your warm welcome. I appreciate it," Claudia said as she removed a deep violet and magenta shawl from her knitting bag. "You say you taught school here for thirty years? Goodness, that's quite a spell. I taught school years ago when I was just a green little thing. Barely knew what I was doing. But that's where I met my first husband, Frank. He was the principal."

Kelly noticed Lizzie's bright gaze fix on Claudia, like a robin eyeing a worm. Anything that verged on male-female relationships stimulated Lizzie's considerable curiosity. Kelly took a drink of coffee, waiting for Lizzie's interrogation to begin, glad that her attention had been diverted from "poor Juliet" stories.

"Your first husband?" Lizzie probed in a sweet voice. "I take it you've remarried since then."

Claudia gave a wave of her hand before returning to the shawl in her lap, needles moving swiftly and surely. "Oh, heavens, yes. That was years ago. I was still young when poor Frank crashed into a tree and died. And wrecked our brand-new Cadillac convertible, I might add." She tsked loudly. "It never ran the same after it was repaired. I had to trade it in. Such a shame, too. It was a jewel of a car."

Kelly had to smile watching the von Steuben sisters' reactions to Claudia's nonchalant description of her husband's demise—as well as the car's. Hilda stared at Claudia as if she'd sprouted another head. Lizzie, however, leaned over her knitting, clearly eager to hear more. Kelly exchanged an amused glance with Megan.

"And Frank? Was he a jewel?"

Again, the airy wave of her hand. "Oh, he was all right. Kind of dull and plodding, but a good provider for our daughter and me. Certainly not very exciting in the bedroom, if you know what I mean," Claudia said with a small smile.

Lizzie's eyes lit up, and a flush colored her round, dimpled cheeks. "Actually, I don't. Neither Hilda nor I have ever been married."

Claudia gazed at Lizzie with astonishment. "Don't tell me two fine, handsome women like yourselves have never married! I don't believe it. What is the matter with the men around here? Are they too busy with their ranches and such?" She shook her head in disapproval. "I married a rancher once. Fred, my second husband. I swear he spent more time with the cattle than he did with me. It was almost a blessing when he fell out of the barn and broke his neck."

Kelly nearly choked on her coffee. Megan ducked her head and stared at the yarn in her lap, knitting even faster.

"Where was that?" Kelly asked when she could speak.

"In Texas. I'd moved there from Missouri after I lost Frank. To tell the truth, after Fred died, I was happy to leave Texas. Too many bugs. Scorpions in your shoes, centipedes three inches long crawling on your sofa." She gave a little shiver. "My daughter, Krista, was leaving for college, so I moved to Florida. That's where I met Nathan." Needles busily worked the varicolored yarn. "Of course, Florida is filled with bugs, too. Horrible flying things."

"Nathan is your third husband, I take it," Lizzie probed, clearly enraptured by Claudia's soap opera life.

"*Was*," Claudia said in that matter-of-fact, pass-the-butter tone. "He died in the bathtub when the radio fell into the water. I told Nathan he shouldn't have that radio so close to the tub, but would he listen? *Noooo*."

Hilda stared at Claudia. "Good Lord, woman! How many husbands have you had?"

Kelly had to hide her laughter behind her mug and noticed Megan's shoulders shake as she bent over her knitting. Lizzie, however, seemed spellbound by Claudia's tales.

Claudia glanced up from her knitting, clearly oblivious to Hilda's concern. "Three. I guess I've just had bad luck with husbands. In fact, that's why I'm here. I'm on the lookout for husband number four. Fort Connor is rated as one of the best places to retire in the whole United States, so I figured there ought to be a fair share of eligible men in town."

Hilda did not deign to reply, sending Claudia a disapproving stare before returning to her pink wool charity hat. Lizzie, however, fairly wiggled with delight at this outspoken woman's stories.

"How do you intend to meet your next, uh . . ."

"Victim," Hilda muttered.

"Don't mind her, Claudia. She's only teasing." Lizzie waved at her elder sister. "It sounds like you've never had trouble meeting men before."

"Lord, no. I'm not shy, as you can see. So I don't wait for men to come and find me. I go out and find *them*."

Hilda gave a loud sniff, but said nothing this time. Kelly decided to get in on the conversation, curious as to Claudia's strategies. "Sounds like you could teach a class."

"Ohhhh, you bet I could. You have to have a plan. When I arrived in town, I joined the senior center, the newcomers' club, travel club, three book groups, a fit-for-fifty exercise class, and a financial discussion group. And most important of all, the senior singles' group at the center. That is one of the most active seniors' groups I've ever seen."

"Really? I've only gone to the center for bridge club and sewing circles, but I've heard friends talk about going to other events." Lizzie's expression turned wistful. "I confess, I've been curious. It always sounded so . . . so interesting."

Claudia sent her a sly smile. "Why don't you come with me to the senior center tomorrow? You'll enjoy it, and"— she paused dramatically—"you'll meet some eligible men."

Lizzie blushed, her face coloring all the way down to her dimples and beyond. "Oh, my . . . I don't know if I should."

Kelly watched Lizzie glance to her elder sister and saw Hilda's disapproving scowl.

Claudia didn't seem to notice. "Why shouldn't you? You're an adult. And a resident of Fort Connor for what sounds like forever. Why don't you come over and see your city's tax dollars at work? You helped pay for the senior center, so you should use it."

That argument seemed to capture the former math teacher's attention, Kelly noticed. Megan must have thought so, too, because she spoke up. "She makes a good point, Lizzie. You may like it. Why don't you give it a try?"

Lizzie's bright blue eyes lit up. "Well, I suppose I could—"

"Ah-*hem*," Hilda's loud voice interrupted.

Lizzie's smile disappeared as she glanced warily at her sister. Stern and disapproving didn't begin to describe Hilda's expression. Kelly sensed Hilda had spent a lifetime reining Lizzie in. After witnessing Lizzie's excessive curiosity firsthand, Kelly understood why. But there couldn't be any harm in letting Lizzie check out the senior center. She couldn't get into any trouble with all those people around. Lizzie had friends all over town. Surely, she wouldn't do anything embarrassing.

The little voice in the back of Kelly's head whispered, *You want to bet?* Kelly ignored it and offered her encouragement anyway. "Go ahead, Lizzie. If you don't enjoy it, then stop going. Simple as that."

Lizzie glanced from Kelly to Megan to Claudia, her smile returning. "Well, I suppose I could. . . ."

"Absolutely. I won't take no for an answer," Claudia said. "You deserve to step out a little, Lizzie. And who knows? You may meet a wonderful gentleman like I did."

Lizzie's eyes began to dance. "Oh, goodness, I don't know. . . ."

"You wouldn't mind a fine, upstanding gentleman caller, now would you?" Claudia tempted.

Lizzie clearly wouldn't, Kelly could tell from the excited look of anticipation on the spinster schoolteacher's face.

"Well . . ." Lizzie demurred, glancing at her knitting.

Hilda simply rolled her eyes and didn't say a word. Letting Lizzie off the leash at last, Kelly figured.

"You'll have a wonderful time," Claudia said. "And I promise you'll meet lots of eligible men. I mean, that's how I met the fine gentleman who's courting me now. He's a widower and an excellent catch. A retired university professor. Very quiet and reserved. But I'm loosening him up." Claudia smiled complacently. "We've been seeing each other for over a month now, ever since he came to the book group to discuss the Spanish Civil War. Apparently that's his research hobby. Anyway, I was so taken with him, I went up to him after club and invited him to lunch."

Kelly had to smile. "You certainly don't waste time, Claudia."

"Indeed I don't, Kelly. I know exactly what I'm looking for, and Jeremy fits the bill to a tee. An attractive widower who's financially well-off. My mama always said, 'You can love a rich man as easy as a poor one.' I've taken those words to heart, ladies." Claudia nodded in emphasis.

Kelly barely heard Claudia's mother's advice. The name

"Jeremy" had captured her whole attention. She glanced around the table and saw her own thoughts reflected. Lizzie stared at Claudia with a stunned expression. Hilda looked appalled.

Jeremy. Juliet's Jeremy. It had to be. An eligible widower, retired professor, who loved research. The Jeremy who no longer had time for the "little brown wren," because he was seeing another woman.

Claudia had to be the Other Woman. Kelly noticed Hilda's scowl had frozen on her face, while Lizzie stared at her knitting.

"Jeremy's getting serious about our relationship, too. I can always tell. He's got that *look*," Claudia continued to gush. "In fact, I'm expecting a little surprise by Christmas."

Despite her reluctance, Kelly couldn't stop herself from asking. "You mean a present?"

Claudia cast a beaming smile toward Kelly which showed off her pretty face. She looked much younger. "Not just any present. A small, square-box type of present."

Kelly forced a polite smile in return. Poor Juliet.

Four

"**Out** you go, Carl," Kelly said, holding the patio door open for her dog. "It's warm outside. Go take a nap in the sun."

Carl obligingly raced onto the patio, then surveyed the scene for a second until he spotted what he was looking for. A lone squirrel was perched atop the chain-link fence, paws holding something.

"Go for it, Carl. He's having lunch. Maybe you can out-run him this time."

Carl didn't need encouragement. He was already across the cottage backyard, barking ferociously as if a mountain lion had invaded their yard instead of Saucy Squirrel.

Kelly grabbed her knitting bag and empty coffee mug and headed for the cottage front door. After spending all morning categorizing alpaca revenues and expenses, she needed a coffee and knitting break. Sometimes the repetition of her rancher clients' work began to wear on her. Part of her still missed the challenge of corporate accounting. But then she'd look at the Rockies in the distance, and she'd reconsider.

Afternoon sun reflected off the snow-glazed peaks as she crossed the driveway and wound through the café's outside patio. It was so warm, the tables were still filled with people lingering over lunch. Temperatures had been in the sixties or seventies for a week. After last year's brutal cold and blizzards, this extended fall was a welcome change. Winter was still waiting in the wings.

She scampered up the steps into the café and held out her mug to one of the waitresses. "Hey, Julie, can you fill 'er up, please?"

"Sure, Kelly. Your timing is great. Jennifer is over in the shop now, celebrating a real estate sale."

"Wow, good for her." The aroma of Eduardo's heady brew drifted to Kelly's nose as a black stream filled her cup. Caffeine. Dark and rich. "I was hoping those Nebraska clients would decide to buy," she said before heading down the hallway that led to the shop.

Rounding a corner, Kelly carefully wove her way through the crowded rooms. Holiday fiber fever was in high gear. Customers were everywhere, pawing through yarn bins, poring over patterns, studying yarns, examining labels. It was still early December, but the holiday clock was ticking. There were presents to be made. Handmade presents took time.

"Congratulations, Jen," she said as she entered the main room, noticing all her friends were already around the table. "You nailed that deal. That's a big load off your shoulders."

"You bet. I was sweating bullets, because they were agonizing up to the last moment. I was so afraid they'd throw in the towel and wait until spring," Jennifer said, as she tapped knuckles with Kelly.

"Do we still get pot holders for Christmas?" Lisa asked, smiling over the navy blue gloves she was knitting.

"I'm afraid so. There'll be no money till the closing in January, so it's still pot holders. Or washcloths. I can afford some of that French chenille," Jennifer said, returning to the purple mittens dangling from her needles.

"You'd better give Kelly her pot holder early," Megan said, glancing up from the red gloves she was creating. "She's going to need them. I want everyone to bake cookies for that holiday bazaar booth. Mimi begged me to find bakers."

"Boy, you have to be desperate to ask me, Megan. You know I don't cook, let alone bake."

"You can slice, can't you?" Lisa teased when the laughter died down. "You can buy a roll of cookie dough in the store."

"Slicing, I can manage," Kelly said, settling into the chair beside Jennifer.

"Well, if you get adventurous, why don't you check in your garage? I packed up a box of Helen's cookbooks and recipes when you moved into the cottage last year. She used to make scrumptious gingersnap cookies every holiday."

"Oh, yeah, I remember those," Jennifer said, closing her eyes and emitting a loud sound of enjoyment. "Boy, were they delicious."

"Well, if I find the recipe, maybe one of you guys can make them," Kelly suggested, pulling out the nearly finished charity hat. "Meanwhile, someone has to help me finish off this hat. I haven't worked on these double-point needles since last winter when I made my own hat."

"Sure, let's get you started," Jennifer said, the purple wool dropping to her lap. "You remember how to switch from the circular to the double points?"

"Uhhhh . . . I have to count stitches then divide into four sections and transfer them onto four shorter double points, right?"

"That's right. Have you got the double points you used last time?"

Kelly dug into her bag and produced the packet of five wooden needles. Approximately eight inches long, the needles were the same size in diameter as the circular needle she was using. However, these needles were tapered on both ends. "Here they are."

"Okay, so start counting and divide by four. Next, you'll hold your circular needle with your left hand, then use one of the double points to knit with. Once you have the amount you need for one section knitted onto that needle, then take another double point and start knitting with that one. Make sure you keep your yarn snug and connected to the stitches on the first needle. Then, you just repeat the process. Knit the next amount onto the second needle, then the third, then the fourth. Once all the stitches are transferred onto the four needles, then you'll use the fifth double point to knit with. That's when you'll start decreasing."

"It's beginning to come back now," Kelly said, staring at the needles.

"Okay, then get busy. I'll be right here if you get stuck." Jennifer returned to her purple yarn.

Kelly examined the edge of the blue-green hat and started counting. Sixty-six stitches. Okay, that's sixteen stitches on three needles and eighteen on the last needle. A faint memory surfaced from the back of her mind. *You've done this before.*

"Okaaaay . . . wish me luck," Kelly said, picking up one of the shorter needles. Hopefully knitting memory would kick in.

"You'll do fine."

Jennifer was right. After knitting only five or so stitches from the circular to the shorter needle, Kelly remembered the process. Within a few minutes of quiet knitting, she'd completely transferred the hat to four double-point needles. Ready to shape the crown.

"Good job. Now you're ready to decrease the rows. Here's a stitch marker, so you can mark the end of the row. You'll use the fifth needle to knit." Jennifer dropped a small plastic circlet on the table.

"Refresh my memory. What's the pattern again?"

"For the first row, you knit one, then knit two together, and repeat that pattern until the end of the row. Then you knit three rows regularly. Then after that, you really start to decrease. You knit two together for one row, then knit regularly for the next row. Then knit two together for one row, then knit regularly another row. All the way until you only have about six stitches on your needle. Then you'll use your tapestry needle and pull those stitches together and weave them inside the hat. Ta-da."

"Got it," Kelly said, feeling confident at last. She'd done this before. She could do it again. "Okay, here goes," she said, taking the fifth needle and beginning the process. Knit one stitch, knit two together . . . knit one stitch, knit two together. . . .

"You know, Kelly, I bet you could make Helen's cookie recipe. If you can follow a knitting pattern, you can surely follow a recipe. It's just another form of pattern."

Knit one, knit two together. "I don't know, Megan. You know how many mistakes I make with knitting. Can you imagine what I could do to Helen's recipe?"

Lisa chuckled. "You can do it, Kelly."

Arguing voices sounded in the classroom doorway. Politely arguing voices.

"You are being much too harsh, Hilda," Lizzie said as she flounced into the room, her sister right behind. "Claudia's not a loose woman. She's simply lively, that's all."

"She's a common gold digger," Hilda decreed in her deep contralto, dumping her tapestry knitting bag at the head of the table for emphasis. "I've seen scores of women like that, and they're consummate actresses. They're all smiles and wiles on the outside, while inside they're scheming to trap a rich husband."

Kelly exchanged glances with her friends. Lisa and Jennifer smiled. Megan rolled her eyes. They'd been listening to Hilda complain about Claudia and her "shameless behavior" for several days now. Clearly, Hilda wasn't pleased with Lizzie's new social companion. The "Merry Widow," as Lisa called her.

"Sounds like you've been out on the town again, Lizzie," Jennifer interjected. "I swear, you go out more than I do. Maybe I should join the senior singles."

Jennifer's lighthearted comment brought Lizzie's smile

back as well as soft laughter around the table. "You're too young, dear," Lizzie said as she withdrew the lemon yellow baby blanket.

It was still unfinished, Kelly noticed. Apparently Lizzie's social schedule had interfered with her knitting time. "Let's see, Lizzie . . . you've been to the senior singles' dinner and the movie club and the lunch club and a wine-tasting group and—"

"And the travel club and the book discussion group and the knitting group of course," Lizzie picked up the list, cheeks flushed with pleasure. "And last night I joined the square dancing club."

"Lizzie, I'm so proud of you," Megan enthused. "You really did take our advice. And now you've met all sorts of new friends."

"Oh, yes, and picked up friendships with people I'd lost track of over the years." Her fingers worked the stitches rapidly.

"Is the Merry Widow coming with you to all these groups, too?" Lisa asked.

Hilda made a disgruntled noise as she worked the azure blue yarn in her lap. More mittens.

Lizzie didn't even glance at her sister. "Claudia comes to some of them, but she has her own interests. So she introduced me to several of her friends and got me launched, so to speak. Frankly, once I discovered all the fascinating activities that are happening there . . . well, I couldn't wait to get involved."

Claudia had obviously opened a whole new world to Lizzie, and Kelly was pleased. She couldn't resist asking, "I take it some of Claudia's other interests include the widower Jeremy. Is she still seeing him?"

"Ohhhh, yes. In fact . . ." Lizzie paused and glanced at her sister before leaning over the table to whisper, "She spent the night with him."

Jennifer smiled. *"Now* it's getting interesting."

"I told you she was a loose woman. Using her wiles to trap poor Jeremy." Hilda wagged her head, a frown etched into her lined face.

"Poor Jeremy?" Jennifer cackled. "It sounds like he's having the time of his life being trapped."

"Face it, Hilda, Claudia is lively, funny, and pretty," Megan added. "Most men Jeremy's age would be interested."

"She's still a schemer and a gold digger," Hilda declared. "Look at that list of husbands. She's looking for a meal ticket, that's all."

"Maybe she's just lonely," Jennifer said without looking up from her needles. Hilda simply sniffed and didn't reply.

"I think you may be right, Jennifer," Kelly ventured, hoping to lower the temperature around the table. It didn't feel right to have Lizzie and Hilda arguing.

"We loose women have to stick together," Jennifer said with a wink before sipping her coffee.

Lisa snickered. "I've never met this librarian you guys told me about, but I have a feeling Jeremy's forgotten her."

Lizzie wagged her head. "I know, I know. I confess I'm torn. I've known Juliet for years, and I was so happy she'd found someone. But now—"

"But now, that brazen hussy has stolen him away," Hilda

declared, fingers working the yarn so fast the mittens danced on her needles.

Here we go again, Kelly thought, about to interject another moderating comment, when the familiar click-clack of high heels sounded in the next room. The Brazen Hussy herself. Kelly sneaked a peak at Hilda, who looked as though she'd just bitten into a sour apple.

"Well, well, well, we've got a full house this afternoon," Claudia announced as she sashayed into the room. "How lovely to see everyone."

Claudia settled into a chair beside Kelly and removed the magenta shawl she was knitting. Kelly noticed Claudia was wearing one of the two designer suits Kelly recognized. Not the latest fashion, but stylish nonetheless. "Lizzie has been filling us in on her latest senior center excursions. Sounds like her social calendar is getting full."

"Oh, my, yes. Lizzie took to the senior club scene like a duck to water," Claudia said with a little laugh. "I'm delighted—"

"If you ladies will excuse me, I must speak to Mimi about my yarn order," Hilda announced as she gathered her knitting and stalked from the room.

A noticeable silence descended for a few seconds, then Claudia spoke in a quiet voice. "I'm sorry that Hilda doesn't like me, but I seem to irritate a lot of women. I guess I'm too outspoken for their tastes."

"Don't mind Hilda," Lizzie said, glancing over her shoulder. "She'll come around."

Claudia shook her head with the air of someone used to

these encounters. "Noooo, I don't think so. It happens all the time." She gave a little shrug. "I can walk into a room and feel it. There's something about me that annoys the living daylights out of most women." The multicolored yarn formed into neat, lacy rows on her needles.

Jennifer chuckled. "I know what you mean, Claudia. A lot of women don't like me, either. But that's okay. I kind of like rattling cages."

"We've noticed," Lisa said.

Kelly held up her coffee mug. "From one cage rattler to the next," she saluted both Claudia and Jennifer. Claudia seemed to relax after that. Her shoulders were no longer hunched.

"Lizzie tells us you and your new boyfriend seem to be getting more . . . how shall I say it? . . ." Jennifer paused dramatically. "More involved."

Kelly stared at her double-point needles, wondering if Claudia would take the bait.

She did. Claudia gave a sly smile. "You might say that."

Jennifer briefly glanced over her shoulder at the browsing customers. "So, how's ol' Jeremy stack up? Compared to your other husbands, I mean."

"*Jennifer* . . ." Megan rasped, nodding toward the customers prowling the shelves and yarn bins in the room.

"What?" Jennifer said innocently. "Hilda's gone, so I thought we could talk."

Kelly chuckled over her coffee and watched Lizzie eye Claudia expectantly with that bright-eyed robin look.

"Jennifer, you are too much," Claudia said after she finished laughing. "Let's just say that Jeremy is a good student, and I'm an excellent teacher."

Lisa hooted out loud at that, which elicited several smiles from the nearby customers who had been obviously eavesdropping.

"Still waters run deep, as my mother always said," Megan offered.

Jennifer grinned at Megan. "What would you know about still waters? You've got Marty. He's a veritable fountain."

Megan choked on her coffee, she started laughing so hard, as did everyone around the table.

"Waterfall is more like it. Never stops."

"No, a Jacuzzi. It comes in bursts."

"Stop, you guys, I've spilled my coffee," Megan pleaded between laughs.

"I bet Megan is the still water in that relationship," Claudia said.

Kelly noticed a woman who was browsing in the corner yarn bins suddenly turn and survey the table. Her stern gaze fell on Claudia. "I see you've already ingratiated yourself with the locals. You don't waste time, Claudia. You've been in Colorado less than two months."

Claudia stared back at the woman and blanched, her busy needles dropping to her lap.

A hard smile appeared on the woman's thin, pinched face. "Surprised to see me, I take it."

Who the heck is this? Kelly wondered, as she stared at the woman and at Claudia's reaction. Claudia was clearly shocked speechless, her blue eyes huge.

"How . . . how did you know where—" Claudia stammered.

"You mean, how did I *find* you?" The woman's smile

hardened at the corners of her mouth. "I tracked you here from Florida. It took a while, I admit. You were very clever, slipping away in the middle of the night like that. Not telling anyone. Everyone at the retirement home thought you'd simply moved out."

Claudia stared stricken at the woman, not answering.

"But stealing that old woman's car was a masterstroke, I must admit."

"I did no such thing!" Claudia protested. "Mary Ann Howard gave me that car, so . . . so . . . I could—"

"So you could escape, right?" The woman's gaze narrowed. "You forgot about the credit card bill. All those travel expenses you ran up on that stolen card. That's how I tracked you."

Two customers glanced apprehensively over their shoulders and moved their browsing to another room.

Claudia stared, horrified. "I didn't steal her credit card. Mary Ann gave it to me so I could come here. I was going to pay her back."

More heads turned from the adjoining room, and Kelly glanced at her friends. Each of their expressions mirrored her own. *What is going on here?*

"Sheila, why have you come here? All you had to do was ask Mary Ann. She'll tell you." Claudia's voice contained an uncharacteristic tone of pleading.

Sheila's mouth twisted. "Mary Ann had a massive stroke and died right after you ran off."

Claudia gasped, then stared at Sheila, mouth hanging open.

Lizzie placed a hand on her friend's arm and asked in a tremulous voice, "Claudia . . . who is this woman?"

Color rushed back into Claudia's face. "She's . . . she's my stepdaughter, Sheila Miller."

"*Was* her stepdaughter." Sheila bit off the words. "Until she killed my father."

Five

Lizzie's horrified gasp hung in the air. Kelly stared at Claudia, who was visibly shaken, blue eyes tearing up, and Kelly's protective instincts rose up full force. She leaned back in her chair and fixed Sheila with a cold stare of her own. Corporate skills were always useful.

"Ms. Miller, you might want to be careful what you say to someone in public. That last comment would be considered slander in a court of law." She held her stare until Sheila blinked.

Sheila glanced away. "His death was no accident, I'm sure of it."

"Still, you cannot go around accusing people like that," Kelly continued, her voice in the cellar. "That's for a judge to decide—"

"Excuse me, ladies, is there a problem here?" Mimi's anxious voice sounded from the classroom doorway. "Several customers have told me there's an argument going on. Kelly? Lisa? What's happening?" She approached the end of the table, her face revealing her concern.

"Sheila got a little tense for a minute, Mimi, but I think she's calmed down now," Kelly reassured her.

Mimi settled into Hilda's empty chair. "Sheila, I'm Mimi Shafer, and I own the shop. I like to think this is a nurturing place for people to gather. So if there's a problem of any kind, maybe I can help." She glanced at Claudia's red face and back to the visibly angry Sheila standing at the other end of the table.

Sheila crossed her arms tightly across her chest and glared at Claudia again. "No one can bring my father back," she said in a tight whisper.

"I'll leave," Claudia said softly. Grabbing her knitting bag, she withdrew a red pom-pom with keys attached. "It's me she's after . . . she's been harassing me ever since her father's death . . . saying terrible things . . . awful . . ."

"Telling the truth," Sheila snapped.

Claudia turned a tearful gaze around the table. "Don't believe what she says, she hates me!" She fled from the room, her knitting bag clasped to her chest.

"You can't run away from the *police*! They're right behind me," Sheila called, stepping away from the table as if to follow Claudia.

Kelly immediately jumped to her feet, blocking Sheila's path. "I don't think that's a good idea, Sheila. Why don't you sit with us for a while?"

"Yes, please." Lisa spoke up in her calm therapist voice. "We want to know what's caused this trouble. Tell us, please."

"Yes, Sheila, please tell us, help us understand," Mimi pleaded in her soft maternal tone. "Let me get you something warm to drink." She motioned to one of the shop girls hovering in the doorway, eyes wide.

Kelly also noticed someone else hovering in the doorway. *Hilda*. Watching and listening with obvious interest.

"Please sit, Sheila. It looks like you need to talk." Kelly gestured to a chair at the other end of the table.

Sheila hesitated for a minute before sitting. "I'm . . . I'm sorry if I disturbed your customers. It's just that I've been tracking Claudia for two months and to finally find her laughing and talking as if nothing ever happened . . ." She stared at the bookshelves. "It just tears me up inside."

"When did your father die, Sheila?" Lisa asked, her fingers busy.

Sheila's thin lips pursed. "Almost a year ago. I was out of town on a business trip when it happened. I'm a research consultant with a legal firm so I travel regularly. I had to hear about my father's death over the phone from that . . . that *woman*," she said bitterly. "I was devastated." She crossed her arms tightly under her breasts as she sat ramrod-straight.

Kelly felt a twinge of sympathy for Sheila. She'd lost her own father years ago to cancer. But at least she had been with him until the end. And she'd been able to say goodbye.

"I'm sorry, Sheila. I lost my father several years ago, too.

I still miss him," she said. "I'll bet you were really close to
your father."

Sheila darted a wary look to Kelly, but her stiff pose
started to relax slightly. "Absolutely. He was my best friend.
My mother died years ago, and ever since it's been just my
father and me."

"Do you have any other family, Sheila?" Mimi probed
gently.

"My father and I were family. We didn't need anyone
else. We were so close. I was his closest confidante until *she*
came along." Sheila's body tensed up again. "Claudia seduced my father away with sweet talk and lies. It would
never have happened if I hadn't been away on a three-month
research trip abroad. She never would have gotten past me."
Sheila gave a stiff nod.

"Maybe he was lonely, Sheila," Mimi said. "I know what
it's like to live alone."

Sheila shook her head several times, as if she was trying to
convince herself as well as Mimi. "No, no, Claudia seduced
him away. My father was old and in poor health. That's why
she chose him, I'm sure of it. She probably thought she'd get
a large inheritance, but I took care of that."

"How?" Lisa asked.

Something resembling a smile tweaked the corners of
Sheila's mouth. "Fortunately all of my father's estate was in
a trust, and I was still the sole beneficiary. All of it went to
me. And I made sure Claudia didn't get a dime."

Kelly exchanged glances with her friends. "Well, at least
you have all of your father's things."

"That's not enough!" Sheila snapped. "She needs to *pay*! Claudia stole my father twice and I'll never forgive her, ever!"

"Twice?" Jennifer echoed, looking at Sheila.

"Once when she tricked him into marriage, and again when she killed him."

"Careful, Sheila," Kelly warned.

Sheila turned an intense, dark gaze around the table. "She did it for the money. I *know* she did. His death was no accident. Dad always listens to the radio when he's bathing. It relaxes him. She must have dropped that radio into the water. I'm sure of it."

Kelly caught the quick, astonished glances of her friends. It was clear that Sheila was focused on Claudia. She hated her for splitting up the cozy little family arrangement she had with her dad. But deliberately dropping a radio into the water to electrocute someone . . . whoa.

Sheila continued, her voice as intense as her expression, clearly trying to convince her audience. "She married him for his money. That's what Claudia did before. I've searched into her past and those other two husbands of hers. They were both older men, and they both died under strange circumstances." She gave a righteous nod. "She got away with it those other times, but she's not getting away with it now. I'm seeing to it that justice will be done."

The table fell silent while the café waitress brought a tray with pots of tea, coffee, and hot chocolate. Mimi busied herself with pouring cups for everyone. Meanwhile, Kelly considered what Sheila said.

Strange circumstances. True, it was unusual for a widow to lose three husbands in a row to accidental deaths, but to assume that Claudia had played a part, well, that was a stretch.

Noticing that Sheila chose a mug of hot chocolate, Kelly hoped the warm milk would mellow out the woman's mood. Hot chocolate had a wonderful calming effect. Instead of challenging Sheila on her assumptions about Claudia, Kelly decided to keep her questions to a subject that was less inflammatory—and give the hot chocolate a chance to work.

"You said you'd been tracking Claudia for two months? How did you manage that? Did you hire an investigator?" She allowed admiration to fill her voice.

Sheila brightened, her pinched face relaxing. She appeared to be in her forties, but it was hard for Kelly to tell. "Oh, no, I did it all myself," she said proudly. "I'd been checking into Claudia's past for several months after my father's death. I even went to the towns in Missouri and Texas where she'd lived and interviewed anyone who remembered Claudia or her former husbands."

Kelly caught the incredulous gazes of her friends and gave them a spare nod, hoping they'd pick up her line of questioning. "Wow, that must have taken months," she said. "How'd you manage your job and all that interviewing at the same time?"

Sheila shrugged and took a drink of her hot chocolate. "It wasn't easy. I was driving around all day talking with people and working practically all night. But it was worth it. By the time I returned to Florida, I'd compiled an entire file of damning evidence."

"What kind of evidence?" Lisa picked up the thread.

Sheila's body relaxed even more as she leaned forward and rested her arms on the table. "Well, Claudia's first husband, Frank Morgan, died in a car crash, and there was no sign of drinking or anything else. It was unexplained. Happened in broad daylight on a road that wound around the river. I kept asking everyone who knew the gentleman if they remembered the accident. He'd been the beloved school principal for years. Most everyone I interviewed didn't remember a thing. But one man was the mechanic who worked on Morgan's car, and he recalled that he'd told Claudia the car's brakes were bad and needed service. He told her the week before the accident." Sheila looked around the table for emphasis.

"Whoa . . ." Jennifer said in a dramatic tone.

"What about her second husband?" Kelly prodded.

Sheila drained her cup and Mimi immediately hastened over to refill it. "Claudia moved to Texas after Morgan's death, and the ladies of Tyler, Texas, still remember Claudia, indeed they do." Something resembling a smile softened Sheila's mouth for a moment. "They were most forthcoming. According to them, Claudia dated every eligible bachelor in town before settling on Fred Baxter, who was a prosperous rancher. Or so she thought. He lasted five years." Sheila took another deep drink of chocolate.

"How did this man die?" Megan asked in a soft voice.

"He was found in a heap in the farmyard, right beneath

the barn's hayloft. Claudia's story was that Baxter, an experienced rancher for over sixty years, had somehow fallen out of the hayloft door above and dropped twenty feet to his death. He broke his neck."

"Merciful heavens," Mimi drew back, looking shocked.

Sheila looked around at her entranced audience. "Turns out Baxter wasn't as prosperous as everyone thought. Once he died, the ladies said Claudia was more distraught that most of Baxter's ranch was tied up with creditors than she was at losing her husband. She only received a small insurance annuity. So, you can see that by the time Claudia settled in Florida she was on the lookout for a wealthier target. And that was my father."

Kelly nodded. "Well, I can understand your concern."

Lizzie's trembling voice spoke up then. "Kelly, how can you say that? You know Claudia. Why . . . she's a gentle person. She couldn't kill anyone. Why isn't anyone speaking up for her?" Lizzie cast a frantic gaze around the table.

Kelly felt slightly disloyal, but her encouragement had enabled everyone to hear the past history of Sheila's resentment of Claudia. They also could understand better how Sheila had come to her conclusions. Rash as they appeared to be. Kelly was about to say something reassuring to Lizzie, when Sheila spoke first.

"I'm sorry to bring you bad news, ma'am. I can tell you're one of Claudia's friends. But sometimes people are not what they seem." Sheila's tone was markedly changed, more deferential and polite. Clearly respectful of her elders.

Kelly noticed Hilda still stood in the classroom doorway. Still listening with obvious interest to the dramatic tale. Her face fairly radiated "I told you so."

"But I'm sure those men's deaths were . . . simply unfortunate accidents," Lizzie said plaintively. "They couldn't possibly be deliberate. I've been with Claudia every day for a week, and I've never seen her angry or even raise her voice to a single soul. She could never harm someone. She's sweet-natured and kind."

Sheila's smile turned scornful at the edges. "Claudia's an excellent actress. She can be very charming. In fact, that's how she ingratiated herself into that elderly woman's good graces at the Sarasota retirement home. My informant at the home said Mary Ann Howard was old and in poor health and clearly her mental faculties were slipping. Obviously that's why Claudia targeted the woman. I'm told she started spending a great deal of time with Mary Ann. Then one day, Claudia suddenly disappeared, and so did Mary Ann's car and credit card."

Lizzie looked crushed, and her pale blue eyes turned watery as she ducked her head and stared at her yarn. "Oh, my . . ."

Kelly, however, couldn't ignore the word that had dropped out of Sheila's mouth. "You had an 'informant' in the retirement home? How did you manage that?"

Sheila drained the mug of hot chocolate. Mimi motioned to pour more, but Sheila waved her away. "I went to the home and started discreetly asking questions of the staff. I made friends with one of them, and she kept an eye on Claudia for me. That's how I learned she'd suddenly disappeared.

Claudia gave notice one afternoon that she'd be moving out, and the next morning she was gone."

Sheila ran her fingers over the edge of a pink crocheted baby blanket that lay on the knitting table. "Apparently Mary Ann's family didn't even discover the missing car for a couple of weeks after her death. And they didn't learn about the stolen credit card until the credit company's bill came in the mail." She stroked the pink yarn. "Imagine their shock at seeing credit charges on their dead mother's account. Of course, when I heard about the missing car, I put two and two together and came up with Claudia. She already knew that I was checking into her past and had found out about her previous husbands' deaths. I'm sure that's why she ran off."

Lisa exchanged a glance with Kelly. "Wow, you're one heck of an investigator, Sheila. How did you track Claudia to Colorado? Gas receipts?"

Sheila continued to fondle the baby blanket. Kelly noticed Mimi observing Sheila's motions with great interest. Seductively soft fibers could tempt even the thorniest person.

"The gas receipts showed she was driving west, but it was the phone bill that gave her away. When it came in, there was a collect call from Fort Connor, Colorado, to Mary Ann Howard the day before she died. I figured that had to be Claudia."

Lizzie's head bobbed up again, and she looked absolutely petrified. "Do the Florida police think Claudia stole the car?"

Sheila frowned as she reached both hands into the baby

blanket this time, slowly stroking the fibers. "They should be contacting the Fort Connor police any day now, I'm sure of it. I mean, I called them four days ago when I tracked Claudia to that seedy little motel near the interstate. I told the Sarasota detective that I'd located Claudia and the car in Fort Connor, Colorado, and gave him the exact address where to find her. All the Florida police have to do is start the process. They said the stolen car report would be entered into a national computer database with the car's VIN number and description." A self-satisfied smile appeared.

Kelly had to hand it to Sheila. Sheila's sleuthing efforts matched her own. Her previous sleuthing efforts, that is. Last winter, Kelly promised all her friends she would put her investigatory instincts on hold, and she had. Kelly hadn't done any snooping around for months. Nine months, to be exact. But who was counting?

"What will happen to Claudia?" Megan asked in a quiet voice as she knitted. "Stealing a car is a serious crime."

"A felony," Sheila supplied helpfully. "It was a 1999 Taurus and was definitely worth over five hundred dollars."

"You said the Florida police haven't charged her yet. Why do you think they're waiting?" Kelly probed.

Sheila hunched her shoulders and frowned. "I don't know. I check with them every morning. I'm sure it will be any day now. That's why I'm keeping track of her. I don't want Claudia slipping away again."

Mimi shot Kelly an anxious look. Sheila was calling the Sarasota police every morning? Kelly was about to zero in on that admission when Sheila suddenly pushed the soft blanket away and rose from the table.

"I have to go back to my hotel. I've got tons of computer work waiting for me. Here's my card with my cell phone number. Please call me if you learn anything, anything at all." Sheila pulled several business cards from her pocket and dropped them on the table.

"Why don't you drop by again tomorrow, Sheila? I've got a class in crochet that's working on those very same blankets," Mimi said with a big smile. "I think you'd enjoy it."

Sheila turned in the archway and glanced back at the blanket, then to Mimi. "Maybe I will. My mother used to crochet." Then she was gone.

Kelly wondered at Sheila's abrupt departure, but couldn't voice it because Hilda's booming contralto filled the silence as she steamed through the room on the way to the door. "It's time for us to leave, Lizzie. Good afternoon, ladies."

Lizzie stuffed her knitting into her bag and meekly followed after her elder—and righteous—sister without a word.

"Whoa," Jennifer said softly when the spinster sisters had left. "I wouldn't want to be Lizzie tonight. Hilda will be haranguing her for hours, I'll bet."

"Oh, yeah."

"For sure."

"Poor Lizzie."

"Poor Lizzie, hell. Poor Claudia."

Kelly caught Mimi's worried gaze. "Mimi, would you

and Burt like to join me for breakfast tomorrow morning? I'd like to ask him some questions."

Mimi nodded. "I'm sure Burt would be glad to join us for breakfast, Kelly. Meanwhile, I'm not going to wait. I'll start asking him questions tonight."

Six

Kelly lifted a forkful of cheesy scrambled eggs and devoured it, followed by a bite of crispy bacon and a homemade biscuit. She voiced her enjoyment with a loud "yum."

"It's a good thing I don't come over for breakfast every day, Pete," she said to the café owner as he refilled her mug. "I'd weigh a ton."

"One little breakfast every now and then won't hurt you, Kelly," Pete said with his genial smile as he filled Burt's cup as well. Mimi waved Pete off with a smile.

Kelly glanced at Burt. "So, did Mimi fill you in on yesterday's shop melodrama? She said she was going to grill you last night."

Burt chuckled. "She sure did. I have to admit, that is one weird story Sheila told. I've only seen Claudia occasionally around the shop, so I don't know her. But I respect your opinions. Both of you are good judges of character. What do you think?"

Mimi toyed with her empty cup. "I don't know, Burt. I've spoken with Claudia several times at the shop, and she seems to be a genuinely open and friendly person. A little flighty and flirtatious from what I've heard about her dating activity, but good-natured and kind. I cannot imagine her doing all those terrible things Sheila accuses her of. And yet, Sheila's account of Claudia's actions are . . . well, they make me wonder."

Kelly took a deep drink of Eduardo's black nectar before answering. She caught the grill cook's glance and held her mug high in salute. Eduardo grinned behind the grill, flashing a gold front tooth.

"I'm with you, Mimi. I don't know what to believe. I can't agree with Sheila's conclusion that Claudia murdered her two previous husbands or Sheila's father. But she does paint a damning picture of Claudia's activities at the Sarasota retirement home. That leaves a lot of unanswered questions. Since the elderly woman is no longer alive, she cannot corroborate Claudia's version of the story. Did she lend Claudia the car and the credit card? Or did Claudia steal them?"

"That's the issue," Burt said, swirling his coffee. "It'll come down to Claudia's word against the family's."

"What would happen then?" Mimi asked.

"The police would go with the family's version of events. After all, they know their mother. If she didn't tell them about lending the car, they'll make a reasonable assumption that Claudia stole it. And the card. After all, she's been located in a state two thousand miles away in possession of a car and a credit card that belong to someone else." Burt gave a sigh. "She looks guilty as hell."

Mimi bit her lip. "I'm afraid you're right. What if she's innocent? How would Claudia prove it?"

Burt shrugged. "I don't know, Mimi. She may not be able to prove it. And if she can't, she'll be charged with auto theft and theft of an electronic device. That's the credit card."

"Oh, my, oh, my, oh, my . . . I feel so sorry for her," Mimi murmured as she rose from the table. "I have to get back. Holiday hours, you know." She hurried off.

Kelly mulled over what Burt said. "What *would* happen if the Florida police charged Claudia with stealing the car? Would she be arrested here? Sheila mentioned the report would be placed on some national database."

"Yeah, that's exactly what happens. Once Florida officially charges Claudia with auto theft and files a warrant, then the Fort Connor police can locate the car and arrest her."

"Would she be jailed?"

"It all depends. After she was arrested, she'd be taken to the jail to be booked. If a judge is in court, then there'd be a hearing. That's when the judge would state the charges and set bond. For most out-of-state warrants, the bond would be ten thousand dollars. If she can't post bond, she'll go to jail."

Kelly pictured the flirtatious Claudia standing before a judge. If the sight of her stepdaughter Sheila scared Claudia, what would happen in front of a judge?

"Whoa, that sounds pretty scary to me, Burt. I'm wondering if Claudia has enough money to post bond. Apparently she has insurance policies from her previous two husbands, but thanks to Sheila, Claudia got nothing from her last husband."

"Mimi mentioned that. I gotta tell you, Kelly, that story makes Claudia out to be one desperate woman."

"Yeah, it does. But when you hear Sheila tell it, you also pick up her intensity loud and clear." Kelly wagged her head. "Listening to her talk about spending months investigating Claudia's past, tracking her from Florida, I swear that reminds me of when I used to go searching for clues."

Burt smiled. "Well, at least you didn't track anyone state to state."

"Did Mimi tell you that Sheila said she calls the Sarasota police every day to see if Claudia's been charged?"

"You're kidding." Burt's bushy gray eyebrows shot up.

"Nope, I'm not. She said so yesterday. I mean, Sheila's not even *involved* in that case. It's not her family, and Mary Ann wasn't her mother. Sheila's got spies or informants at the retirement home. I don't know, Burt. . . ."

"You know, that makes me curious." Burt stared off into the busy café. Pete and staff bustled about serving platters of breakfast.

"Curious enough to check with the Sarasota cops?" Kelly tempted with a conspiratorial grin.

"I have some old friends from the force who retired to Florida a few years ago. I could give them a call."

Kelly stared out the café window at the Rockies in the distance. Snow-capped and sparkling in the early morning sun. But nary a flake in Fort Connor. Milder temps—fifties, sixties, and sometimes seventies—still held sway. At least Steve no longer complained about needing his winter scarf.

"Well, I'll be damned. Look who walked in," Burt said.

Kelly glanced up and noticed Claudia standing beside the café's front door. Scanning the room with an anxious look, Claudia spotted Kelly and Burt and headed straight for them.

"May I sit with you two?" she asked, already pulling out a chair. "I don't want to be alone in case that dreadful woman shows up. I saw her outside in the motel parking lot this morning, sitting in her car watching me."

Burt and Kelly exchanged glances. Since the Merry Widow was right there in front of them, it only made sense to ask a few questions. Kelly started off, confident Burt would pick up her lead. "That must have been very upsetting for you."

Claudia dropped her gaze to her lap and withdrew her magenta shawl, nearly finished. "I've gone way past upset, Kelly. I'm scared now. Sheila has been spreading lies about me ever since Nathan died. She blamed me for his death. As if I could stand there and deliberately kill Nathan. It's . . . it's beyond belief."

"When you say 'spreading lies,' exactly what do you mean, Claudia?" Burt asked in a quiet voice. Kelly recognized his gentle questioning style.

Claudia looked at both of them. "It started right after Nathan's death. She whispered awful things to his friends at the funeral. I overheard them. Blaming me for his death." She returned her attention to the wool. "It was clear to me from the start that Sheila resented me. I tried countless times over the two years Nathan and I were married to reach out to her, but she always rebuffed me. Unfortunately, things got worse after his death. When she left town I breathed a sigh of relief, hoping that a long trip away might help her sort through her feelings. I assumed she was away on business, but not so. I soon learned she'd been to Missouri and Texas, where I'd lived previously, and had been interrogating anyone who knew me or my former husbands. I was shocked when she showed up at the house, making all these wild accusations."

"What sort of accusations?" Burt continued.

Claudia released a sigh. "Sheila was convinced that both Fred's and Frank's deaths were not accidents but murder. She kept waving a folder. 'Evidence,' she called it. Evidence that proved my guilt." She shook her head. "I was stunned. Shocked speechless. I just stood there and stared while she vilified me, then she stalked out."

Kelly watched Claudia's eyes grow moist. "Did she make these accusations to anyone else?"

Claudia nodded. "Ohhhh, yes. To anyone who would listen. She tried to get the local newspaper to instigate an investigation into her 'charges,' as she called them. Of course, the newspaper refused to print her accusations. But she did convince a sleazy gossip rag to print an interview with her where she said all those terrible things." A tear trickled down her cheek.

Kelly reached out and patted Claudia's arm. "I'm sorry, Claudia. That must have been truly awful."

"Awful doesn't begin to describe it. Sheila kept appearing everywhere I went. I had to stop going to the senior center during the daytime because she would show up. I was practically a prisoner in the house."

"It sounds like you didn't receive a dime after your husband's death." Kelly started a new line of questions. "That doesn't sound right. After all, you had rights as his widow."

Claudia gave a wry smile. "I may have had rights, but I had no money to hire an attorney. I was trying to live on what money remained in the checking account. I was still staying in our house, waiting for the estate to be settled. Then, after six months, I came home from errands one day and found Sheila standing there, a legal document in her hand. She had inherited everything, and I was left with nothing. Sheila announced she was taking over the house and told me to gather my things, leave, and never come back. She was changing the locks. I . . . I was dumbfounded. I just stood there at first, staring at her. Then I ran upstairs and threw what things I could into a suitcase and left. I was so devastated I didn't even realize I'd left most of my clothes and belongings behind until later."

"That's pretty harsh," Kelly said. "What did you do then?"

"I didn't know where to go at first. Fortunately the minister at a nearby church recommended a state-subsidized retirement home. Thank goodness, my little income covered the monthly bills."

"I'm surprised someone didn't suggest a lawyer who took pro bono cases. You know, free legal help."

Claudia shrugged. "After all those accusations of hers, I felt so beaten down, I didn't have the heart to pursue anything. To tell the truth, I was so demoralized and humiliated, I just wanted to crawl in a hole and die. I didn't have the energy to pursue another settlement, so . . . I just let Sheila have her way. Meanwhile, I tried to start my life over again. Fortunately, I made some friends at the retirement residence."

Kelly heard an opening and followed it. "Is that where you met this other woman, this Mary Ann Howard?"

"Yes, Mary Ann had been at the residence for five years. She was a lovely woman," Claudia said, her fingers deftly working the deep violet stitches. "Mary Ann was in poor health, and her vision was failing so she had great difficulty reading. Reading had been her great joy. She loved novels. Mystery novels, adventure novels, fantasy, science fiction, everything. I felt sorry for her and started visiting every afternoon to read to her. Oh, how she loved that. We became close friends. I could talk to Mary Ann." Claudia sighed. "Mary Ann was the only one I could talk to about Nathan's death and Sheila's harassment. Most of my other friends had dropped me like a hot rock once Sheila began spreading her lies."

"What about your daughter? Did she help you at all? Could you live with her?" Kelly asked.

Claudia rolled her eyes. "I'm afraid my poor Krista cannot be counted on. She's in another state and has her hands full with three small children. Plus, her husband is not very supportive. She's unable to help me. It's all she can do to help herself."

Burt signaled a nearby waitress for coffee refills and offered a mug to Claudia. He clasped his bear-paw hands together on the table and leaned forward. "Claudia, I've heard about Sheila Miller's version of how you came to Fort Connor with someone else's car and credit card. I have to admit, it doesn't sound good." Claudia's head came up at that. "Why don't you tell me *your* version of that complicated story, okay?"

Kelly sensed Claudia's hesitation and placed her hand on Claudia's arm. "You can trust Burt. He was a former detective with the Fort Connor police."

The change in Claudia's expression was immediate. Apprehension vanished, and her pretty face spread with a dazzling smile. "Really? Oh, my goodness, yes. It'll be a relief to tell someone in authority."

"Well, I'm not in authority anymore," Burt said with his good-natured smile. "But I can listen and give advice."

"Oh, yes, please," Claudia implored, hand to her breast. "If there's any way to stop Sheila from spreading those lies, I'll do whatever it takes."

"Why don't you start by telling me what happened, okay?" Burt coaxed.

Claudia let the yarn and needles fall to her lap. "Well, it all started when we received notices at the retirement residence that the monthly rents were being raised sharply. I confess I looked at that letter and my heart sank. My two little annuity payments didn't cover the higher amount, and I had no extra funds in the bank. I . . . I was just heartsick because I knew I would have to move, and there was nowhere else to go. Nowhere safe, that is."

She stared out into the café. "I fell apart. I just hid in my room and cried and cried. Mary Ann found me there and let me cry on her shoulder. I remember telling her that I needed to start over again, away from Florida and Sheila and all her lies. Find a new place to live and start fresh, somewhere far away. Dear Mary Ann suggested I take her car. It had been sitting in the residence garage for over a year, ever since her vision failed."

Claudia took a sip of coffee before continuing. "She handed me the car keys. Then she told me to take them and leave Florida, make a new start. She even offered me her credit card to pay for expenses until I could get settled." Claudia gave a little sigh. "I told Mary Ann I couldn't accept her offer. It was too much, and I didn't know when I could pay her back. But she insisted, saying that both the car and the credit card were sitting there unused. They weren't doing her any good. So she might as well use them to help someone else."

"That was extremely generous of her," Kelly said, still amazed at the story.

Claudia sent Kelly an earnest look and nodded. "Oh, that was Mary Ann. She was a sweetheart and a saint. I swore to her that I'd repay her every cent and return the car as well. Once I became situated, that is. And I promised I would stay in touch."

"Did you call her from Fort Connor?"

"Oh, yes, as soon as I found a motel and settled in. I called to let Mary Ann know. She sounded fine on the phone. I cannot believe she died the very next day."

Burt rubbed one hand over the back of the other in a gesture Kelly had witnessed many times. He was pondering Claudia's amazing tale. "Did you tell anyone at the residence about Mary Ann's offer?"

Claudia pursed her mouth, evidently pondering as well.

"I think I mentioned it to the sweet little lady who sat beside me at dinner. But she's so forgetful, I doubt she would remember. I learned not to share too much about my private life with people there, because gossip spreads so easily, you know. And I had a feeling that Sheila had a friend working on the staff. I'd often catch one of them watching me."

"Sounds like it's going to come down to your word against Mary Ann's family," Burt said gently. "And if that happens, the police will most likely side with the family. You realize that, don't you, Claudia?"

Claudia drew back, clearly aghast. It was obvious to Kelly that Burt's sensible scenario had never entered Claudia's head.

"What . . . what does that mean?"

"If the family files a stolen car report with the Florida police, then they'll investigate the crime and enter the vehicle into the national database as stolen. Then the Florida police would contact the police here to help them investigate. That's when the Fort Connor police would get involved. They would locate the car, and then they would contact you."

Claudia blanched. "They'd *arrest* me?" she cried.

"Yes," Burt said softly. "I'm sorry, Claudia. But once an

arrest warrant is filed, then the legal system takes over. Crimes have to be investigated."

Kelly placed her hand on Claudia's arm, patting reassuringly. "Don't panic, Claudia. I know a very good lawyer with a local firm, and I'll ask him if he does pro bono work. That way, you'll have someone to represent you."

"You mean they'd take me to the *police station?*" she squeaked.

"Yes, at first," Burt continued gently. "Then they'd take you to jail, where you'd be booked, and then you'd go before a judge—"

"Ohhhh, noooo!" Claudia wailed, both hands fluttering at her breast now. "They'd drag me in like a common criminal! Oh, my Lord! I couldn't bear it! *Oh, no!*"

"They wouldn't drag—" Burt tried to reassure her, but Claudia interrupted with another anguished wail.

"Ohhhh, noooooooo! Thrown into a cage with . . . with *criminals*! I'd die on the spot. I haven't done anything wrong! Please believe me!"

"Claudia, you're upsetting yourself," Kelly counseled, noticing concerned customers turning around in their seats in the café, curious as to the disturbance.

Claudia refused to be consoled. She grabbed Burt's hand and squeezed it between hers. "Oh, please, Burt, *please*! I beg of you, please help me. Don't let them throw me in jail, please! I'll perish. I won't survive. I'll *die!*"

Burt placed his other hand atop hers. "I promise I will do whatever I can to help you, Claudia," he said, his face reflecting his concern at Claudia's emotional outburst.

"Oh, thank you, thank you, thank you, Burt," she murmured. Leaning forward, she kissed his hand.

Burt looked surprised, and patted her hands before removing his from her grasp. "Don't worry, Claudia." The insistent ring of his cell phone interrupted then. "You have friends here," he added as he left the table, cell phone still ringing.

Kelly observed Claudia, concerned about the intensity of her outburst. Clearly, Claudia was "high-strung," as her aunt Helen would have said. Maybe some quiet knitting time would help.

"Claudia, you need to calm down. No one's coming to throw you in jail," Kelly declared, not entirely sure she was correct. "Why don't you sit here alone for a while and knit? I find that knitting quietly orders my thoughts and helps me make decisions. It's relaxing and settles my mind."

Claudia looked up, color coming back into her face. "You're right. I need to calm down. Yes. I'll try," she said, chewing her lip. She resumed knitting the magenta shawl.

"Do you have any activities scheduled at the senior center this morning?" Kelly asked as she left the table. Client accounts were calling. She had to get back to the cottage and back to work.

Claudia shook her head. "No, I'm afraid I won't be going to the senior center as much," she said forlornly. "Sheila's been talking to some of the group leaders there, and people look at me strangely now." She released a dramatic sigh. "Besides, it's another two taxicab fares. I've stopped using Mary Ann's car, so now it's much more expensive for me to get about town."

Kelly couldn't help feeling sorry for Claudia. Alternating her two nice suits, living in a seedy motel by the interstate while she tried to start a new life. *Good Lord.* Claudia's life was really the stuff of soap operas. She gave Claudia's arm another pat before she turned to leave. "Try not to worry, Claudia."

Grabbing her coffee mug, Kelly headed down the hallway that connected the café to the knitting shop. If Megan was there, she could check out Kelly's finished hat. If it met Megan's exacting standards, Kelly would turn it over to the charity collection. Then she could finish Steve's alpaca winter scarf—at last.

Kelly slowed as she rounded the corner into the shop. Holiday shoppers were everywhere—plundering yarn bins, digging into chests, and comparing fibers as they made their buying decisions. She wove her way carefully toward the front of the shop where a line had already formed at the cash register. Kelly spotted Lizzie and Juliet, who were talking beside the Mexican tile fireplace.

Kelly almost didn't recognize Juliet. The little brown wren was not attired head to toe in her favorite shades of brown. Instead, Juliet wore a dramatic crimson red cape that reached her knees.

"Goodness, Juliet, is that one of those Christmas capes I've been hearing about?" Kelly asked as she approached.

"Indeed it is, dear," Lizzie answered, pointing to Juliet like a proud mother. "Isn't it simply beautiful? Mimi sells every cape that Juliet brings."

"You certainly weren't exaggerating, Lizzie," Kelly said

as she admired the graceful drape of the fabric. The gently rounded and curved edges were bordered with two-inch green braid as were the pockets and hood. "It's gorgeous."

Juliet beamed, her pale cheeks coloring with obvious pleasure. "Thank you, Kelly. I've been making these for several years." She held a neat stack of folded capes in her arms.

Kelly reached out and touched the fabric. "Juliet, this is so soft and fine. It's scrumptious. You wove this?"

"Yes, I weave the fabric, then I make the capes. They've been selling very well. And it's such a worthy cause. All the money goes to the Separated Moms and Kids Fund."

"What's that?" Kelly asked, still fondling the fabric. It was soft enough to have been woven by angels.

"The county police department collects money to buy toys for mothers who are incarcerated and away from their children during the holidays. Then they throw a big party so the kids can receive presents from their moms." Juliet set a pile of folded capes on the fireplace hearth.

"Wow, that *is* a worthy cause," Kelly said, letting the seductive fabric slide from her fingers at last. "I know Megan plans to buy one of your capes."

"Oh, that reminds me, dear. Megan gave me a message for you," Lizzie said, placing the last cape atop the others. "She said don't forget to bake cookies. The bazaar is next weekend, and she's in charge of cookie collection."

Kelly had already forgotten. "Uhhhh, thanks, Lizzie. I confess the cookies had slipped off my radar screen. I finished my first Hat for the Homeless. So I guess I can only remember one charity obligation at a time."

"Excuse me, ladies, but I have to continue my deliveries. I'll see you both at the bazaar, right?" Juliet said as she turned to go.

"Yes, indeed," Lizzie said with a conspiratorial smile. "Meanwhile, I'll be waiting on pins and needles for your call tomorrow."

Juliet blushed and gave an embarrassed little wave before hurrying from the crowded front room.

Kelly couldn't resist following up on Lizzie's last comment. She sensed Lizzie was up to something. Or wanted to be. "What's happening with Juliet?"

Lizzie's eyes danced, and she beckoned Kelly farther from the customers milling about the room and standing in line. "It's so exciting! Jeremy called Juliet this morning and asked her if she would meet him for dinner tonight. He had something important to ask her." Lizzie glanced over her shoulder but the customers were totally absorbed in their fiber pursuits and purchasing. "Juliet told me Jeremy drew her aside at the library the other day and apologized for his recent 'preoccupation,' as he called it."

Preoccupation. It sounded like Jeremy's romance with the vivacious Merry Widow might be cooling. Jeremy's waning interest would be another blow to an already emotionally fragile Claudia. How would she handle the end of their romance? Kelly wondered.

"Do you think Jeremy is regretting his, uh . . . dalliance with Claudia?"

Lizzie's eyes went wide as she bent to whisper, even though no one nearby seemed to be paying attention to their conversation. "Perhaps so. I must admit I'm not surprised. Jeremy is a quiet soul with habits much more attuned to Juliet's simple life. They're both quite similar in personality—"

Lizzie never finished, because Claudia suddenly rushed up to them. Her face was flushed with excitement. "There you are. I was hoping I'd find someone to talk to. I'll simply burst if I don't share the good news," she gushed.

Kelly blinked at the transformation. Gone was frightened, panicked, beaten-down Claudia-the-Victim. Now Claudia glowed, clearly joyful about something. What could have happened to cause such a sudden transformation?

"Wow, Claudia, you really look happy. What's the good news?" Kelly asked.

"My Prince Charming is coming to the rescue. He called me on the phone," she declared rhapsodically, one hand at her breast. "I knew he would. Now I'll have a strong man in my life to protect me again. Like Mama said. I knew Jeremy would propose. I just *knew* it."

Kelly managed to hide her surprise. But Lizzie wasn't so successful. "Did . . . did Jeremy *propose* to you?"

"Not yet, but I know he will," Claudia declared, clasping her knitting bag to her bosom, face still radiating her happiness. "He wants me to meet him for lunch in Old Town this afternoon. He said he had something very important to tell me. Oooooooo, I'm so *excited*!" Claudia spun about in a circle like a delighted schoolgirl.

Suddenly she stopped, grabbed one of Juliet's Christmas capes, and held it up. "These must be the Christmas capes I've been hearing about. Oh, I simply must have one. This red is perfect for me, don't you think?" she asked of the roomful of shoppers.

Claudia's girlish laughter trilled as several customers oohed and aahed their admiration and encouragement.

Lizzie stared at Claudia's joyful display, clearly speechless, while Kelly wondered to herself, *What is Jeremy Cunningham up to?*

Seven

Kelly maneuvered the grocery cart around the supermarket produce aisle. Lemons. She needed lemons. Organic or regular? Kelly checked the list. Aunt Helen's recipe didn't say, so she figured regular ones should be fine. She chose three fat yellow lemons and dropped them into the empty cart. Now, off to the baking aisle for the flour and sugar and spices and all that other stuff on the list. With a little luck, she could finish this early morning grocery errand, then return to the client accounts beckoning from her home office.

Why she'd decided to attempt Aunt Helen's gingersnap cookies, Kelly didn't know. Maybe it was the twinge of nostalgia she'd felt when she found Helen's recipe book in the garage last night. She remembered that book. Helen used it all the time and especially for the holidays. Kelly swore she could still smell ginger as she turned the pages.

Then again, it might have been the challenge. Kelly found it hard to resist a challenge. After all, she was known as the Microwave Cook, and the Kitchen Klutz. It would be fun to surprise everyone with homemade cookies. Assuming she could translate Helen's recipe properly. Kelly still wasn't sure exactly how to do these different procedures the instructions called for.

Her cell phone rang as she rounded the corner of the baking aisle. "Kelly, I just got off the phone with my Florida friend," Burt said. "He knows a guy in the Sarasota police department and was able to check out the stolen car situation. Apparently there hasn't been an official report filed yet, so nothing has gone into the national database. The Sarasota cop told him that during their investigation at the retirement home, one elderly resident recalled Claudia telling her she was borrowing Mary Ann's car for a while. So the cops haven't decided how they're going to proceed. This woman appears credible, he said. That's why they haven't issued a warrant for Claudia's arrest."

Kelly pulled her cart to the side of the aisle beside the bags of sugar. She grabbed one. "That's fantastic news, Burt. It proves Claudia's telling the truth. She didn't steal the car."

"Well, not exactly. It simply shows there's another version of the story. After all, that resident had no way to know if Claudia was lying to her or telling the truth. Apparently, the family's convinced Claudia's lying."

"Hmmm, you're right," Kelly said, stepping aside so a

man could gather two large sacks of sugar and drop them atop an already full cart. "So what's going to happen now?"

"My friend said the Sarasota police have been interviewing more people at the home to see if they can figure out what happened. They're hoping to have some answers soon."

She selected a rectangular plastic bag of dark brown sugar and dropped it into the cart. "Well, I'm sure Claudia will be relieved to hear that. Maybe they'll find more corroboration of her story, and she'll be cleared." Kelly pushed her cart ahead to get out of the way of the holiday bakers pawing over the sugar. Parking near the sugar shelves obviously wasn't a good idea.

"I'll give her a call later. Right now, I've got a spinning class to teach."

"If you have time, Burt, why don't you give Sheila a call, too? Tell her what you've learned. Maybe that will be enough to convince her to tone down the accusations. Claudia may turn out to be innocent."

"I'll give it a try, Kelly. Mimi said she'd persuaded Sheila to take a crochet class, so she may show up today. Talk to you later." He clicked off.

Kelly shoved her phone into her jacket pocket and continued her pursuit of recipe items. Baking soda and baking powder. What's the difference? Kelly examined the small can and the small box before she tossed both into the cart, where they rattled between the lemons. Her cart was relatively empty compared to the ones some of these other shoppers were pushing around. Their carts were piled with flour, sugars of all kinds, spices, chocolate chips, baking chocolate, tins of cocoa. Obviously they were serious holiday bakers.

Kelly aimed for the shelves loaded with five-pound bags of flour only to be presented with a quandary. There were many kinds of flour. Regular white flour, self-rising flour, whole wheat flour, cake flour, and others too numerous to mention. She scowled at the multiple bags and back to the recipe. Aunt Helen had written "flour." That was all. No mention of type. *Oh, brother.* She knew her cooking inexperience would throw a wrench into things.

Noticing a middle-aged woman browsing the aisle beside her, Kelly smiled her brightest. "Excuse me, ma'am, but I'm trying to make my late aunt Helen's cookie recipe, and I'm not much of a cook. In fact, I don't cook at all, so I'm confused about this recipe. Could you help me decipher it, please?"

The woman returned Kelly's smile. She appeared to be in her fifties or so and had a round, friendly face. "Certainly, I'll be glad to help."

Kelly eagerly handed over the recipe. "Thank you so much. I don't want to poison anyone with my first cooking effort."

The woman laughed as she scanned the paper. "Oh, gingersnap cookies. They're some of my favorites. And this is a good recipe, too. Dark brown sugar, molasses, lots of ginger." She peered into Kelly's cart. "Looks like you've got some of the stuff already."

"I was doing fine until I got to the flour." Kelly pointed to the shelves. "I have no idea which kind my aunt used. Look at all these. Should I use cake flour since cookies are kind of like cake?"

The woman grinned at her. "Not really. Cake flour is

mostly used for cakes. You'll want to use regular white flour. A five-pound bag will be plenty. This is such a good recipe, you may want to make it again."

Cooking twice? What a concept, Kelly thought as she added a bag of flour to her cart. "Where would I find molasses?"

"That's right down here," the woman said, walking down the aisle. "Let's take a look. Let's see, you'll need unsulfured molasses, so this would be fine." She retrieved a bottle from the top shelf and handed it over.

Kelly stared at the thick black substance in the glass bottle. "This one is unsulfured. Does that mean the rest of these brands taste like sulfur?" She wrinkled her nose.

"No, not really," the woman said with a good-natured laugh, clearly enjoying the recipe guidance.

"See how confusing this stuff is for us noncooks," Kelly said as she pushed the cart behind the woman.

"Don't forget eggs," the woman continued. "Oh, and do you have a grater for the lemon? It calls for grated lemon rind."

Kelly shook her head. "Nope, afraid not. Boy, am I glad I met you. I would never have been able to make these cookies tonight."

"You remind me of my daughter. She's not too domestic, shall we say," the woman said as she retrieved little spice canisters of ground ginger and cinnamon.

"Ahhhh, that pretty much describes me. But I can microwave with the best of them."

"Well, I think you'll enjoy making this recipe. These cookies sound scrumptious." She grabbed a metal grater from a hanging rack beside the spices and dropped it into Kelly's cart. "You'll do fine."

"Thanks to you. You've been a sweetheart to help. Thanks so much again," Kelly said, turning the cart around. "I hope you and your family have a happy holiday. Oh, and if you want to support a worthy cause, come to the holiday bazaar at the community center this weekend. All proceeds go to charity. I'll be helping at the Lambspun booth. And hopefully, these cookies will be on sale."

"I may do that," the woman promised with a grin. "But aren't you forgetting something? Eggs are that way." She pointed to the dairy section behind her.

Kelly gave a sheepish grin and turned the cart around.

The bell atop Lambspun's front door tinkled as it closed behind Kelly. She freed up one hand to squeeze a tempting ball of red and white yarn as she paused at the bins in the front room. New holiday yarns were always a distraction. However, she couldn't afford to be distracted right now. She wanted to make headway on Steve's scarf this afternoon. Tonight she was making cookies.

"Hey, Kelly," Burt said as he approached from the adjoining yarn room. He beckoned her over to the corner, away from the noise of loud voices drifting from the main room.

"Sounds like you have a full house in there," Kelly said, fondling more candy-striped yarn. How did Mimi expect them to finish projects when she kept putting tempting new yarns on display?

"I wanted to tell you that I had a chance to speak with

Sheila right before her class, and I told her that police interviews at the retirement home had turned up a resident who could corroborate Claudia's claim that she didn't steal the car."

"How'd Sheila take it?" Kelly asked, lowering her voice.

Burt shrugged. "Well, she acted surprised by the news but didn't flare up or anything. In fact, she didn't say a word. She just went into the class. So maybe Mimi's magic is working." He pointed toward the doorway. "She's around the table right now, crocheting."

Kelly grinned. "Fantastic. I can't think of anyone who needs high-powered mothering more than Sheila. She is wound tighter than a seven-day clock, as Aunt Helen used to say."

"I haven't heard that old expression in years," Burt said with a chuckle. "Talk to you later, Kelly. Gotta take inventory downstairs in the basement."

Kelly fondled a few more yarns then forced herself away and headed toward the main room, which was crowded with knitters, crocheters, and stitchers of all kinds. There were even spinners in the corners. She spotted Hilda, Lizzie, and several of the regular fiber folk. But there were newcomers around the table as well. Sheila was beside them, crocheting away. Kelly pulled out an empty chair and squeezed in beside Lizzie.

"Ah, Kelly, I'm so glad you dropped by," Hilda said from her usual spot. "You'll be delighted to hear the good news. Our little brown wren is officially engaged. She showed us the ring this morning. Jeremy proposed last night. Isn't that wonderful?"

Kelly tried to hide her surprise as she pulled the alpaca wool scarf from her knitting bag. "That *is* wonderful news. Lizzie and I saw Juliet yesterday when she brought her Christmas capes to the shop."

"That reminds me, I want one of those capes," a knitter beside Hilda said.

"Me, too," another chimed in. "They're gorgeous."

"Well, you'd better hurry and grab one. There aren't many left," said a spinner in the corner.

"I think Mimi sold four of them yesterday. I saw Claudia with one of them before she left. It was stunning."

"How ironic," Hilda announced, her deep voice taking on an unmistakable tinge of sarcasm. "The Little Brown Wren has run off with Prince Charming, and left the Merry Widow with only the cape. It's fitting. Does Claudia even know that she's been competing with Juliet for Jeremy's affections these last few weeks?"

"Probably not," said the knitter at Hilda's elbow. "Claudia's too self-absorbed."

"Oh, don't be so harsh," the woman crocheting beside Lizzie replied. "Claudia's just full of herself and full of fun, that's all."

Kelly felt the atmosphere change around the table as talk turned to the Merry Widow and her behavior. Hilda held forth that Claudia was a gold digger and out to snare a rich husband, while some of the other fiber folk came to Claudia's defense. Gone was the mood of holiday cheer. Dissension crackled and snapped like a live electric wire.

"Sleeping with Jeremy didn't get Claudia a ring, did it?" Snide laughter followed.

"Sounds like Juliet's keeping Jeremy warm at night now."
More laughter.

"You're mistaken," Hilda said in a disapproving tone.
"Juliet is a modest woman and not about to sully her reputa-
tion. She's an old-fashioned girl with old-fashioned morals.
She does not spend the night with her fiancé—"

"How do *you* know?" someone jibed.

Hilda lifted her long nose. "Because she *told* me so. These
past few months when she's been dating Jeremy, she walks
home every night after they've dined together. Jeremy's a
gourmet cook, so he insists on making dinner."

Light laughter sounded again.

"She walks? In the winter?" a crocheter asked in a shocked
voice.

"Old-fashioned girl," a knitter replied.

"She only lives a few blocks away," Hilda continued. "Besides, Juliet is an environmentalist of the first order. She
barely uses her car unless she has to drive to Denver."

"Walking is good exercise," a spinner offered.

"I can't imagine Claudia walking home from Jeremy's at
night." More snickers.

"Neither can I."

"Oh, for heaven's sake. Give it a rest. Leave Claudia
alone."

"Attention, everyone!" Mimi's voice suddenly sounded
from the doorway. Louder than usual. "I'm giving a free
demonstration of felting techniques if any of you are interested. If so, please join me in the classroom." Mimi eyed
everyone around the table before she disappeared into the
adjoining classroom.

Evidently, Mimi had overheard some of the rancorous discussion and decided to put a stop to it in her own special way. Mimi's felting techniques were second to none and usually available only in workshops. The knitting table cleared immediately as fiber folk flocked into the classroom, leaving Lizzie, Hilda, Sheila, and Kelly behind.

Kelly knitted two rows quietly while she tried to find a way to ask the question that was dancing in her head. Juliet must be ecstatic, but how was Claudia taking this rejection? Especially since she'd been so convinced that Jeremy would ride to her rescue and save her from the scary things that threatened in her future. Finally Kelly just jumped in, in her usual forthright manner.

"I'll bet Juliet is floating on air." She deliberately caught Lizzie's gaze.

"Oh, she is, she is," Hilda replied instead. "And the diamond ring is beautiful. Apparently Jeremy is making a celebratory dinner tonight."

Kelly tried again. "You know, I can't help worrying about Claudia—"

"*Ha!*" Hilda's triumphant cackle resounded.

"She'd set her heart on a proposal, too," Kelly continued.

"Serves her right," Sheila interjected in a harsh tone. "You reap what you sow, as my father always said."

Kelly persevered, despite the comments. "Lizzie, you know Claudia better than anyone. How is she taking this? Have you spoken with her?"

Lizzie lifted her chin, her cheeks flushed with an uncharacteristic anger. "Yes, I have, and she's devastated, simply devastated. And if anyone's taking satisfaction from this poor woman's heartbreak, I think you should be *ashamed* of yourselves!"

Both Hilda and Sheila stared intently at their yarns, not speaking.

"Well, I for one feel sorry for Claudia," Kelly announced for what it was worth. "It sounds to me like Jeremy may have been stringing her along."

Lizzie released a huge sigh, her tensed shoulders drooping. "Maybe you're right, Kelly. But I don't care a fig about Jeremy Cunningham's motives right now. I'm concerned about Claudia. She's in an awful state. She was crying so much when I called this morning, I could barely understand her. Apparently she retreated to the motel in tears after meeting with Jeremy. This morning, she sounded hysterical on the phone. I was so worried I went over to see her immediately." Lizzie wagged her head as her needles continued their busy pace. A pair of forest green mittens dangled.

"I'm sorry to hear that," Kelly said. "Is there anything I can do?"

"I don't think so, Kelly, but it's kind of you to be concerned," Lizzie said pointedly. "Poor Claudia's in no shape to have visitors, I'm afraid. She was crying and sobbing and walking about wringing her hands. I confess, Kelly, I'm worried about her. It was all I could do this afternoon to keep her from throwing her clothes into a suitcase. She kept saying 'I have to leave, I have to leave.' "

Sheila's head came up at that. "Well, she'd better not drive off in that stolen car."

Kelly bit back her first response to Sheila's comment. Obviously Sheila wasn't concerned about Claudia's fragile mental state. "I don't think you have to worry about that, Sheila," Kelly said in a low voice. "Claudia told me she no longer uses the car. She takes taxicabs everywhere now."

"Hmph," Sheila replied, not looking up from the pale blue blanket she was creating.

Kelly figured she should leave the unpleasant discussion before she said something she regretted, so she gathered Steve's alpaca scarf and rose. "Excuse me, but I think I'll listen in on Mimi's class while I knit."

Lizzie sprang from the chair beside her, more sprightly than usual. "I'll join you. Don't hold dinner, Hilda. I'm not coming home until I've checked on Claudia."

She joined Kelly, who was already halfway to the door.

"Whoa, wait a minute," Steve called out from the cottage doorway. "I must be in the wrong house. Kelly, is that you in the kitchen? It looks like you're *cooking*, but that can't be."

Kelly stopped stirring the floury mixture in the huge glass mixing bowl she'd found in the garage. She scowled over her shoulder at Steve, who was leaning in the doorway, grinning at her. "Yes, I'm cooking. So don't bother me, or you'll break my concentration."

"I can't believe this," Steve said as he sauntered into the kitchen. "You're actually cooking something. Is it edible? I mean, can we eat it for dinner? I'm starving."

"Then you'd better grab a pizza from the freezer. This is not for dinner. I'm making Helen's gingersnap cookies for the holiday bazaar."

"Whoa! You're kidding me! I remember her cookies.

They were delicious." He leaned over the bowl, watching Kelly stir the last of the flour into the dark mixture. Aromas of spices drifted up from the bowl. "Are you sure that's the right recipe? What's that brown stuff? It looks weird."

Kelly swatted him away. "It's molasses. Now stop asking questions. I don't want to lose track. Let's see . . . what's left?" She peered at the recipe taped on the wall behind the counter. "Hand me that saucer over there, will you?"

Steve scanned the counter, which was totally filled with used dishes and bowls of every size. "Which saucer? You've got the entire dish cabinet out here."

"The little one beside the toaster." She pointed between stirring. "And don't drop it."

"What's this?" Steve asked, handing her the saucer. "Smells like lemon."

"It's grated lemon rind. I swear I must have cut myself three times grating those lemons. Nobody told me cooking was hazardous."

Steve laughed softly. "You've got flour on your nose. Wait a minute, I've gotta take a picture. This is too cute." He headed for the dining room.

"Steve, are you deliberately trying to annoy me?" Kelly complained as she tried to mix the lemon rind throughout the sticky mixture. "I told you I don't want to make a mistake."

"Hold it right there. I want to immortalize the moment."

Kelly fought the urge to stick out her tongue while he aimed the digital camera. "Satisfied?" she said when it flashed.

"I won't be satisfied until I taste this dough," he said, scooping a finger full right under Kelly's nose.

"Hey, stop that! Megan wants a gazillion cookies." She swatted him again. "Be good, or I'll put you outside like Carl. He got in my way and look where he is now." Kelly pointed to Carl, staring mournfully through the patio door.

"I'm trickier than Carl. You can't lure me outside with kibbles." He snitched another finger full of dough, then neatly dodged Kelly's swipe of the wooden spoon, laughing all the while.

"Go away, I'm almost finished." She scanned the recipe again.

"Mmmm, I taste cinnamon and something else," he said, leaning against the counter as he licked his finger.

"Ground ginger. Lots of ginger. Okay, I think that's it. At last." She plunked the heavy bowl on the counter. "Brother, I've been at this for over an hour. These cookies better taste good."

"Got any plans for that spoon?"

Kelly handed it over. "Here. I've gotta wrap this big mound of dough into a huge ball and put it in the fridge."

"How long before you can bake them?" he asked between licks.

She pulled out a sheet of plastic wrap, then plopped the dough in the middle. "After the dough chills, I can roll it into little balls and then in sugar, then bake them. If you promise not to eat all the dough, you can help me. In fact, I'm gonna need help. That's a big hunk of dough."

"Be glad to help, but no promises about the dough," Steve said as he dropped the spoon into the soapy dishwater in the sink then sidled up behind Kelly and slipped his arms around her waist. "Mmmm, you smell like cinnamon, too."

"Not surprised. I thumped the bowl of flour and spices and a huge cloud floated up." She settled into Steve's warm embrace.

Steve sniffed the bare skin of her neck. "Do you smell like this all over?"

Kelly just laughed as she finished wrapping the huge ball of dough.

"Uhhh, how long does that have to chill?" he asked as she opened the fridge.

"About fifteen minutes or so, the recipe says."

"I have an idea. Why don't we warm up while the dough is cooling off?"

"I take it we're having cookies and milk for dinner."

"Beats dry kibbles. Just ask Carl."

Eight

Kelly leaned over the café counter and dangled her mug at the waitress. "Hey, Julie, could you fill 'er up, please? I've got to drive to Bellevue Canyon."

"Sure thing," Julie said as she poured a steaming dark ribbon of coffee into the mug. "You taking a break this morning?"

"Nope, I'm going up to see a client." Kelly unzipped her ski jacket. The café's warmth made it unnecessary.

She'd need the jacket's warmth later in the canyon. Jayleen's ranch was midway to the top, approximately seventy-five hundred feet high. Definitely colder than Fort Connor's altitude of five thousand feet. Temperatures in town now floated between the fifties and sixties. Still warm for December. Add to that, no precipitation in any form. No rain, let alone snow. At this rate, Kelly figured Christmas dinner would be a barbeque in Curt Stackhouse's backyard.

"What's in the box?" Julie pointed.

Kelly patted the cardboard box on the counter. "Gingersnap cookies. I'd give you one, but they're all wrapped in plastic and foil. I'm trying to keep them safe for the holiday bazaar this weekend. I swear, Steve and I must have eaten over two dozen last night."

"They sound delicious. Maybe I'll drop by the bazaar and buy some," Julie said as she headed for the tables, coffeepot in hand.

Kelly screwed the top of her mug and took a deep drink. It tasted so good, she took another. Then another. Savoring Eduardo's brew, she glanced toward the folded newspaper a customer had left on the counter. Her gaze skimmed the headlines quickly. She hadn't taken the time to check the newspaper this morning. One headline caught her attention.

Woman Killed in Late-Night Hit and Run, it read. No name, no details. Body was found last night. No witnesses, police report. Kelly thought the area where the accident occurred was in one of the older sections of town, not far from the university.

"Hey, you coming in for a break?" Lisa's voice sounded from behind her. "I've got a few minutes before my next physical therapy appointment, so I thought I'd drop by."

"Can't right now. I've gotta go up into the canyon to see Jayleen. We're going over her financial statements." Kelly dropped the newspaper and retrieved the giant cookie box with one hand. "Is Mimi here? I thought these cookies would be safe with her."

"Those are all cookies?" Lisa exclaimed. "Good Lord! How many did you make?"

"I doubled Aunt Helen's recipe. There were supposed to be six dozen, but Steve and I gorged on them last night for dinner. So I think there're only four dozen now."

Lisa grinned. "So you really did make Helen's ginger-snaps. Good for you, Kelly. I'm proud of you."

"Yeah, yeah, yeah." Kelly deflected the praise as they wound their way toward the knitting shop. "I was going to hand them over to Megan, but then I remembered Marty. Those cookies wouldn't survive to the weekend if Marty was in the vicinity."

"You got that right. Hey, there's Burt. He's trustworthy," Lisa said, pointing across the adjacent yarn room.

"Who, me?" Burt teased as he approached, a plastic bag in his hand. A white wool fleece peeked from the top. "What've you got there, Kelly?"

"Cookies for the bazaar this weekend, and I need a safe place to hide them. They can't stay at home, because Steve and I can't be trusted. We went nuts last night."

"She made Helen's gingersnaps," Lisa explained know-ingly.

Burt's eyebrows shot up. "You did! Wow, Kelly, I'm im-pressed. I thought you didn't cook."

"I don't, so you can imagine what a sacrifice this effort entailed." She handed the box to Burt. "I figured you and

Mimi could be trusted better than Megan. Marty would sniff out anything she tried to hide."

"It'll be safe with us, Kelly," Burt assured her. "We won't even snitch. Until the bazaar, that is." He winked.

"That's okay. My job was to deliver them, and I've fulfilled my culinary obligation." Kelly held her hand over the box. "May they rest in peace. Or pieces. Whatever. See you later, guys. I've gotta drive up into the canyon."

"All hail, Cookie Chef," Lisa called out as Kelly headed for the door.

Kelly stared at the snow-capped peaks in the distance. They were calling for more snow in the High Country this weekend. It would be great if she and Steve could take a weekday off and head for the ski slopes. Maybe Lisa and Greg could join them.

"Boy, it would be nice to escape one weekday and go skiing," Kelly said as she and Jayleen walked down the wooden ranch house steps into the open barnyard. "But there's no way I can swing it before the holiday. Too much work. And neither can Steve, not since he started another Old Town project. If we're lucky, our schedules should both lighten around Christmas."

Jayleen hooked her fingers through the belt loops of her jeans as they walked. "Funny, isn't it? The more successful you get, the busier you get. You'd think you would have more time to enjoy it, but you don't. You're too busy working."

"I know what you mean. Now that those Wyoming gas wells are producing, I've had to brush up on the rules and regulations of royalty accounting. That's the problem with being your own CPA. You can't hand the work over to someone else." Kelly stopped and took in the stunning view of the Rockies. "I've always loved this view. It's so gorgeous."

"Yeah, it is," Jayleen said with a sigh. "Every time I get a little anxious about the future, I come out here and stare at those mountains. They calm me down."

"I still feel a little twinge, knowing I almost had a place up here."

Jayleen glanced her way. "You'll find a place someday, Kelly. That ranch wasn't for you. Bad juju, remember?"

"I remember," Kelly said with a chuckle as she and Jayleen strolled past the barn. "Listen, Jayleen, you have no reason to be anxious. Your accounts are in good order. Your alpaca business is growing, and I might add, prospering." She gave her friend a pat on the back.

Jayleen scuffed her boots through the barnyard dirt. "You know, that still sounds so funny. The idea of my being prosperous. Lord a'mighty, I never envisioned it."

"Well, you've worked hard, Jayleen, and you were willing to take some risks to succeed. Calculated risks. And they're paying off."

"Thank God," Jayleen said as they approached the corral. Several alpaca milled about the corral, watching them. The brave ones came right up to the fence. A big smoke gray male pushed his face over the fence at Kelly.

"Hey, Zuni, how're you doing, big boy?" Kelly said,

stroking the alpaca's neck and rubbing his nose at the same time. Zuni responded by pushing his face up closer.

"He wants a kiss," Jayleen teased.

Kelly nuzzled Zuni. "You saved my life, didn't you, Zuni? If not for you, I wouldn't be alive." She patted him again. "He looks great, Jayleen. His coat is full already."

"Just about. It's been so warm lately, the animals don't know what to make of it."

"If it keeps up like this, we may be celebrating Christmas dinner outside with a barbeque at Curt's ranch."

Jayleen laughed, then gazed out at the mountains for a full minute before speaking. "He wants to give me a horse."

Kelly stroked Zuni's neck, not sure what Jayleen was talking about. "Who wants to give you a horse?"

"Curt."

"Really? That's cool. I'll bet it's Seeker. That's your favorite, right? You were riding him the last time Steve and I came out to ride with you and Curt."

Jayleen scuffed the dirt in the barnyard again, staring at her boots. "Yeah. Seeker's a good horse. He's a pleasure to ride. Curt says he wants to scale down his livestock. You know, cut back a little."

Kelly did a mental check of Curt's stables. "That makes sense. Curt will have six horses left. That's plenty for his family and grandkids."

"Yeah." She scuffed the dirt again.

Kelly stared at her friend. Something was obviously bothering Jayleen. Normally the plain-talking, straight-shooting Jayleen had no trouble speaking her mind. But for some reason she was hesitating. What on earth . . . ?

Out of the corner of Kelly's mind, a little idea wiggled. *Well, well, well. It's finally happened.* Colorado Rancher Curt had started to court rough-around-the-edges Jayleen. At last.

Kelly decided to test the waters, but she also knew her friend. She'd have to circle around Jayleen and hope she'd start talking.

"It sounds like you don't want to accept the gift, Jayleen. I know how you feel about paying your own way all the time, and that's a great rule. For strangers. But it's okay to accept gifts from friends."

Jayleen glanced at Kelly then stared out at the mountains again. "You're right, Kelly. It's just that . . ."

"What?" Kelly gently prodded.

Jayleen expelled a huge breath. "It's just that I know what it means. What it *really* means."

"It means he's giving you a horse. You'll have to feed it, stable it."

Jayleen shot her an impatient look. "You know what I mean, Kelly. When a man starts giving a woman gifts, well, then, it usually leads to something. And . . . and I don't think I can go there."

"Where?" Kelly tried to hold a straight face until Jayleen shot her another "look." Then, Kelly broke into laughter. "Sorry, Jayleen. I couldn't help it."

Jayleen tossed her graying blonde curls over her shoulder. "You can laugh, but it's not funny. When a man starts paying attention to a woman, that means he's serious. And I cannot get serious about any man."

"Why not?" Kelly figured the best thing she could do would be to keep playing devil's advocate and provide a sounding board for Jayleen.

Jayleen rolled her eyes. "You know damn well why not! Face it, Kelly, I'm a two-time loser. And a drunk—"

"Alcoholic," Kelly corrected. "You've been sober ten years, you said."

"Eleven, actually. But this sort of thing could drive me to drink. I swear it could. I had to swear off men when I swore off booze."

Kelly blinked. "Really?"

"Yep, men have always been my weakness. I get messed up with all that stuff, and then I'm a goner."

"That was ten, uh, eleven years ago, Jayleen."

"Men are addictive. Just like liquor."

"I think you mean sex."

"Same thing." Jayleen shrugged. "Men and sex. That's why I'm always keeping an eye out for Jennifer." She shook her head. "That girl reminds me waaaay too much of me. I was out on the town all the time."

Kelly pondered what Jayleen said. At least Jennifer didn't drink that much. Well, too much. Usually. But the men . . . yeah . . . Jayleen had a point there. Jennifer was with a different guy every week.

"Jayleen, I worry about Jennifer, too. But we're not talking about her. We're talking about you and Curt here. If ever there was a man you could trust, it would be Curt."

"You're right," Jayleen said with a sigh, staring off. "It's just that I'm afraid to start down that path again."

Kelly had to smile. Colorado Cowgirl Jayleen was skittish. Kelly could understand that. She'd been skittish herself about getting into a serious relationship with Steve. Her friends had teased her mercilessly for months about moving so slowly. But old baggage from Kelly's past kept getting in the way. She'd found the "right guy" once before, years ago. Or so she thought. Turned out, she was wrong. All Kelly knew for sure was that relationships were risky, and they often ended in loss.

But last winter, all of Kelly's hesitation was swept away one snowy February afternoon. Nearly losing her life in a car crash had brought everything into clear focus. Steve had won her heart and her trust months ago. They belonged together.

"Why don't you just take it one step at a time, Jayleen? Curt's giving you a horse, not a diamond, for Pete's sake."

Jayleen snickered.

Emboldened, Kelly reverted once again to humor. "I mean, this is Curt we're talking about. Upstanding Colorado Rancher, stalwart, still good-looking—"

"A fine figger of a man," Jayleen joined in with a laugh.

"Face it, Jayleen, the most Curt might do is invite you to his place for a bowl of chili."

Jayleen hooted with laughter. "Don't be too sure of that, Kelly girl. Curt's got that look. I can always tell."

"Okay, okay." Kelly went along. "I'll make you a promise. If Curt invites you over for dinner some evening, give me a call, and Steve and I will come along."

Jayleen snickered again. "As chaperones? Damn, girl, Curt and I are too old for that."

She caught Jayleen's eye. "In that case, just give me a sign, and we'll be out the door in a flash."

The sound of both women's laughter rang throughout the barnyard, startling the alpaca away from the fence and two ravens from a cottonwood tree. The large birds squawked as they flew off, their ebony wings flashing in the Colorado sunshine.

Kelly leaned over her computer keyboard and grabbed her ringing cell phone.

Mimi's voice came, breathless. "Kelly, where have you been? I couldn't get through to you on your phone earlier."

"I was up in the canyon with Jayleen, then my cell phone ran out of juice. Why, what's up?"

"Did you read the paper this morning? Did you see the article about the hit-and-run last night?" Mimi's voice went up higher.

"Yes, I did. What's the matter, Mimi? Was it someone you knew?"

"Yes, yes, it was. It was someone we both knew. It was Juliet Renfrow. You and Jennifer helped her at the church knitting class, remember? Juliet brings those beautiful capes every holiday. She . . . she was run over by a car and killed last night."

"*What!* Are you sure it was Juliet?"

"Yes, it was her. I had a call from a friend who worked with Juliet at the library. Police found her last night lying there on the pavement . . . dead. That's so awful I can't bear to think about it." Mimi started sniffling.

"My God . . ." was all Kelly could think of to say. She sat and stared at the computer screen but saw nothing. All she could see was Juliet—the little brown wren—standing proudly in the middle of the knitting shop in her beautiful Christmas cape.

Nine

Kelly looked up from her knitting. Steve's alpaca wool scarf was heading into the home stretch. "Have the cops learned anything new?" she asked as Burt pulled out a chair beside Mimi at the knitting table.

"No, not yet. They've interviewed the nearby neighbors, but no one reported hearing any disturbance outside. They were probably asleep or watching television. Plus, the houses are set back farther from the street in that older section of town. And most residents have tall shrubbery and hedges designed to keep out noise. Lots of college students live in those old sections now, so there's always a problem with loud parties and noise."

"Tragic, simply tragic," Hilda said in a mournful tone as

a bright blue hat came to life on her needles. "Our little brown wren cut down after the happiest day of her life."

"Please, Hilda, no more," Lizzie begged softly as her fingers worked the green mittens. "I cannot bear to think about it. It's too awful."

Kelly kept silent, unwilling to add any more sad comments this morning. She and Mimi, Hilda, and Lizzie had spent the last hour sharing their shock at Juliet's sudden death and their sorrow for her loss. Kelly hadn't known Juliet very long, but she'd liked the dedicated librarian and talented fiber artist. Juliet clearly loved creating gorgeous fiber art and sharing it with children. It was such a shame that she had fallen victim to a senseless, tragic accident.

"Any hope the cops will catch the driver?"

"I sure hope so, Kelly, but with no eyewitness, police have no idea what kind of car was involved, let alone the license number. Without that, they won't know who was driving. They are interviewing some students, though. There was one of those huge mob scene parties that night only three blocks from Juliet's street. Apparently there was a hit-and-run over there, too. An elderly man stepped out from between two parked cars, and a carful of students ran right into him, breaking his leg." Burt shook his head. "Crazed students racing to the next party."

"Maybe that's what happened to poor Juliet," Mimi suggested. "It's gotten really bad in those older sections. I know several friends who've had to sell their homes to escape the wild parties and the noise. And drunken students pounding on their doors at night."

"Unfortunately, that's all too common for a college town,"

Burt said as he shifted into the corner chair and pulled out his spinning wheel. "Mimi, could you give me that bag of fleece behind you, please?"

Mimi handed Burt the large plastic bag, which spilled over with fluffy white fleece. "I'm going to get some more tea—does anyone else need something?"

"I'm good, Mimi, thanks," Kelly said as the others demurred.

Burt took a hunk of fleece and started pulling the fibers apart, creating roving or batten, as spinners call it. "The department also put a notice in the newspaper asking anyone who was driving or walking in that vicinity of town to call the police. Someone may have seen something and not paid attention at the time. One clue can be all they need to track down the driver."

"How could anyone be so heartless as to hit a woman and leave her lying in a pool of her own blood—"

"Hilda, *please!*" Lizzie protested, obviously upset by the gruesome image.

Undaunted, Hilda continued, "Lying alone on the pavement, dying—"

"Merciful heavens, stop!"

Kelly chimed in, hoping to squelch Hilda's morbid depiction. "Hilda, you should stop now. You're upsetting Lizzie."

"Only a coward would do such a thing," Hilda mumbled, staring at her knitting.

"Is there anything else the police can do, Burt?" Kelly said, steering the conversation in another direction.

"Yes, the department always checks auto repair and body shops to see if someone has come in with suspicious-looking damage to their car. You'd be surprised how many people are caught that way."

"How is Jeremy taking it, I wonder." Kelly concentrated on her stitches. Only ten inches or so to go, and she could bind off. Then Steve's Christmas scarf would be done. Of course, it had started out as an autumn scarf, then a Thanksgiving scarf, changing with the calendar. Kelly was simply glad that the weather was cooperating. Thanks to the warmer spell, Steve was still going to his building sites with denim shirts and jacket. No wintry winds so far and none in sight, according to the weatherman.

"I have no idea," Hilda volunteered. "I imagine he's in a state of shock."

"Well, I for one don't care—" Lizzie began.

"I don't *believe* it!" Hilda exclaimed, staring into the central yarn room. "How can that woman have the gall to show up here today? After Juliet's death."

Kelly turned to see the object of Hilda's consternation. There was Claudia, in one of her two well-worn designer suits, talking with Mimi beside the yarn bins.

"Good for her, I'm glad to see Claudia's come out of hiding," Burt said, glancing up.

"Goodness, yes. I'm so glad she took my advice," Lizzie said, giving a little wave. "I told her she could not hide from the world in her motel. She had to get out and see friends again. It will make her feel so much better."

"Hummph! What friends?" Hilda fumed.

"Hush, Hilda!" Lizzie shushed.

"I have a feeling Claudia doesn't even know about Juliet's death," Burt said from the corner, fingers working the roving as it fed onto the wheel. "She probably never knew Jeremy was seeing someone else."

"Self-absorbed, of course."

Lizzie simply rolled her eyes and didn't respond.

But Kelly did. "Keep it to yourself, Hilda. They're coming this way, and Mimi will *not* be pleased at your barbed comments," she warned.

"Amen," Burt said over the hum of the wheel.

Hilda darted a look at Claudia and Mimi as they approached. "Archangel Michael, give me strength."

"Why don't you take a seat over there next to Burt?" Mimi suggested as she led Claudia into the room. "I'll have the café bring us some tea and chocolate."

Claudia darted a quick glance around the table. "Good morning," she said in an uncharacteristically hesitant voice. Clearly, Claudia's confidence had taken a beating during the last few days.

"Good morning, Claudia," Kelly said, sending her a bright smile. "It's so good to have you back. We've missed you."

"And all the saints!" Hilda declared.

Claudia gave a little start, then glanced at Hilda before scurrying around the table to a chair beside Burt. Refuge.

"I'm so glad you came, Claudia. The shop isn't the same without you." Lizzie beamed, her rosy cheeks dimpling.

Hilda gave a snort, but said nothing.

Mimi gave Claudia a dazzling smile. "I think we all need some hot chocolate. To celebrate the holidays, right? After all, it's the season of good cheer." She clamped her hand firmly on Hilda's shoulder, causing the elderly knitter to glance up. "I'll be sure to make yours extra sweet, Hilda. It sounds like you need it." With that, Mimi spun around and stalked out of the room.

Burt bent his head, ostensibly to focus on his spinning, but Kelly spotted the unmistakable signs of laughter.

"I'd like some hot chocolate. How about you, Claudia?" Kelly gave her a smile.

Claudia sent a small smile in return and withdrew the nearly finished magenta shawl. "That would be nice." Then she glanced up, and what color had come to Claudia's face drained away in an instant. She stared toward the central yarn room, blue eyes huge.

Kelly turned to see what on earth had caused such a change and saw two Fort Connor police officers walking through the yarn room, heading their way.

"Burt, I think we have visitors," she said in a quiet voice.

Burt glanced up, spotted the approaching officers, and rose from his place at the wheel. "Can we help you, Officers?" he offered as he walked around the table.

Kelly darted a look at Claudia. She was staring open-mouthed at the officers, who now stood in the archway between the two rooms. With their broad shoulders, police paraphernalia, and weapons on their hips, they seemed to fill the opening. The officers looked completely out of place amid the soft, warm, and fuzzies of Lambspun.

"Are you the owner of this shop?" the blond officer asked Burt when he drew nearer.

"No, Officer. The owner and manager is in another room right now, but I can get her for you," Burt replied. "Is there a problem?"

"Not with the shop, no, sir," the dark-haired officer said. "We just want to ask some questions, that's all. We're looking for a woman who is reported to be a regular customer here."

Burt paused. "Do you have a name?"

The blond officer consulted a notepad. "Yes, sir, we do. We're looking for Claudia Miller. Are you acquainted with anyone by that name?"

A gasp escaped from Lizzie, and she clamped her hand over her mouth. Kelly let her knitting drop to her lap, and glanced over at Claudia again. Claudia was shaking like an aspen leaf in fall.

Burt addressed Claudia in a gentle voice. "Claudia, these officers want to ask you some questions. Would you like for us to leave the room or would you like us to stay here with you?"

Claudia opened her mouth, but nothing came out at first. She licked her pale lips and tried again. "Stay . . . please," she said in a tiny voice.

Burt turned to the officers again. "I'm sure you officers don't mind if Mrs. Miller has her friends around her while you're asking questions." More a statement than a question.

Both the young officers looked at each other. The darker-haired one replied. "Actually, we'll need to take Mrs. Miller down to the department, sir. You see, we're following up on a stolen automobile report from the Sarasota, Florida, police department." He glanced at his notepad again. "Mrs. Miller is charged with stealing a 1999 Ford Taurus, green in color, license number 233234, on or about the date of October tenth of this year. Charges were filed yesterday by the family of the vehicle's owner, one Mary Ann Howard, who is now deceased."

A strangled cry came from Claudia, and she clapped both hands to her mouth, her whole body shaking. Burt stepped beside her and placed his hand on Claudia's shoulder.

"Do you have a warrant for Mrs. Miller's arrest, Officers?" he asked quietly.

"Yes, sir, we do." The blond officer pulled a paper from his shirt. "We've also located the vehicle in question, parked at the Happy Traveler Inn on East Mulberry Street, near the interstate. It has been impounded and is being taken to the police garage at this time."

"I believe you're presently residing at that motel, Mrs. Miller, is that correct?" the other officer asked.

Claudia didn't answer. She just nodded her head, her hands still at her mouth. She was white as a sheet.

Burt pulled out the chair beside Claudia and took both her hands. He held them between his as he spoke in a gentle tone. "Claudia, these gentlemen need to take you downtown to the police department. I'll be glad to come with you if you'd like."

Claudia turned a terrified gaze to his. "Y-y-yes, please, please . . . don't leave me alone," she begged.

Burt patted her hands and rose. "Don't worry, Claudia. I'll be right there beside you. Do you have a jacket?"

Claudia stared blankly. "Uh, no . . . no."

Burt reached over and helped Claudia to stand. It took a second try. The first time, her legs seemed to give way beneath her. "Officers, would you be so good as to contact my old partner, Detective Dan Patterson, and tell him I'll be accompanying Mrs. Miller?"

Kelly had held her tongue throughout the entire shocking episode but could no longer. "Burt, do you want me to call Marty? Claudia will need a lawyer."

"You're right, Kelly. Give Marty my cell number," Burt said as he half-escorted, half-pulled Claudia around the table toward the officers of the law waiting for her.

"Here we go, everyone, hot chocolate," Mimi cheerfully announced as she rounded the corner, carafe in hand. She came to an abrupt stop and—like Claudia—went white as a sheet. "Burt . . . what's the matter? Is Claudia sick?"

"No, I'm just accompanying her to the police department. These officers have a few questions. I'll call you as soon as I can," Burt said as he and Claudia reached the archway. The two officers had already retreated into the central yarn room, heading for the front door.

The café waitress following behind Mimi nearly crashed into her with the tray she was holding. Her eyes popped wide at the sight of Claudia and Burt leaving with the police.

"What . . . what was that all about?" Mimi surveyed the shocked faces around the table. Tears already trickled down Lizzie's pale cheeks. Even Hilda looked shocked, either that or appalled.

"The Florida police filed an arrest warrant. They've charged Claudia with auto theft, just like Burt said they would," Kelly explained. "Now the Fort Connor police are taking her in. Burt's going with her because she's scared senseless, as you can see."

"Oh, no . . ." Mimi breathed, quickly setting the carafe upon the table.

Kelly shoved the alpaca scarf back into the knitting bag and dug out her cell phone as she rose from the table. "I'm calling Marty. Claudia needs a good lawyer, and she needs one right now."

Checking the directory for Marty's number, Kelly punched it in as she headed into the central yarn room. She was startled into a stop when she saw someone in the corner.

Sheila. Standing in the corner out of sight, clearly watching and listening to the entire incident.

She glanced at Kelly briefly before turning her back and walking toward the front of the shop. It was a quick look, but it was long enough for Kelly to glimpse Sheila's expression. The light of triumph shone in her eyes.

Ten

Kelly pushed away her half-finished breakfast. She didn't have her usual appetite this morning. Even Eduardo's huevos rancheros couldn't tempt her today. Leaning both arms on the café table, she looked across at her friends. "Thanks, Marty, for coming to Claudia's rescue yesterday. Talk about short notice. I'm glad I caught you in your office."

Marty draped his arm across the back of Megan's chair. All decked out in lawyerly dark gray suit and burgundy silk tie, there was no hint of the impish court jester who lurked within the conservative exterior.

"I'm glad I was able to help, Kelly. If ever there was someone who needs legal counsel, it's Claudia Miller. That's quite a list of charges waiting for her in Florida. Auto theft,

theft of an electronic device, and credit card fraud." He shook his head, his usual smile missing. "She nearly fainted listening to the judge read the list of charges at her hearing. Burt had to hold her up."

Megan toyed with a teaspoon, stirring her cup of tea. "Poor Claudia. I feel so sorry for her."

Marty sipped his coffee. "At least Burt was able to arrange her bond so she didn't have to go to jail."

"That was sweet of him to do that," Megan said, leaning back in her chair. "But then, Burt's a sweetheart."

"Yeah, he is," Kelly added. "And make sure you send me your bill, Marty, okay? I don't want you to—"

Marty interrupted her with a wave of his hand. "No charge, Kelly. I was glad to do it. I haven't felt so needed in years. Ever since I had to stop taking pro bono clients."

Megan grinned at her boyfriend. "Well, you could always tell those corporate clients that you'd rather work with the poor. If you really want to feel needed, that is."

"Maybe in a few years. The corporate cases pay really well, so it becomes addictive. But you've got a point. I have thought about it," he said, suddenly earnest.

"Marty, I was only teasing you." Megan placed her hand on his arm.

"Yeah, I know," he said, good-natured grin returning. "But it's something I miss. So it's always been in the back of my mind."

"What will happen to Claudia once she's turned over to the Florida police? Were you able to find someone to represent her down there?" Kelly asked.

"Yeah, I was able to contact my buddy in Florida, and his firm has an office in Sarasota. He said they've got some younger associates on staff that do pro bono work, so one of them will represent Claudia when she returns."

"Where will she stay?" Megan asked, clearly concerned. "I mean, she gave up her apartment in the retirement home. And Sheila certainly won't let her stay in her former house."

Kelly gave a wry laugh. "Hardly. I saw Sheila lurking around the corner yesterday when the officers were here. She was obviously eavesdropping." She scowled at the memory. "I swear, that is one bitter woman. She had this triumphant look on her face."

"Well, I hope she's satisfied now that Claudia's been dragged away by the police." Megan's pretty face frowned. "I bet she was the one who told the police where to find Claudia."

"Oh, for sure," Kelly agreed. "Sheila admitted she was calling the Sarasota cops every day to check on the progress of the stolen vehicle charges. She was waiting to see if a report had been filed in the national database yet."

Marty nearly choked on his coffee. "You're kidding!"

"Nope. You can ask Burt." Kelly leaned back in her chair, realizing her shoulders were tensed. "She even admitted that she tracked Claudia to Fort Connor with credit card receipts."

"No way," Marty countered.

"Yeah, way," both Kelly and Megan chimed together.

"We were there in the shop when she marched in and confronted Claudia." Megan shook her head. "So, Sheila should be satisfied. She's won. And Claudia will be dragged to jail in defeat."

"Wow, she's one heck of an investigator," Marty said.

"I have to admit, as a part-time sleuth myself, Sheila's pretty impressive," Kelly said.

Megan arched a brow. "Part-time sleuth? Are you thinking about sniffing around for clues again, Sherlock?"

"Naaaah. This case is already solved, right, Marty? I mean, Claudia's caught red-handed with the stolen car and credit card in her possession and no proof she didn't steal it. I have to agree. It doesn't look good."

"You know, you never answered my question, Marty," Megan continued. "Where will Claudia stay once she gets to Florida?"

Marty drained his cup of coffee. "Actually, Claudia will be a guest of the state of Florida while she's there."

Megan brightened. "Oh, really? Why, that's wonderful. Will they put her up in a hotel, you think?"

Marty gave her a big grin. "I love you." He leaned over and kissed her.

Megan looked surprised at Marty's response, but Kelly immediately picked up on Marty's train of thought. "I think Marty means Claudia will be in jail."

"Oh, no!" Megan said, shocked.

"I'm afraid so," Marty said as he rose from the table. "Gotta get to the office. See you tonight, hon." Pointing to Kelly he added, "Aren't we meeting you guys on the court tonight?"

Kelly had almost forgotten. "Oh, yeah. You're right. Maybe we'll beat you. One game at least."

"You're getting too close for comfort," Marty said with a wave as he headed for the café door.

Megan met Kelly's gaze. "Good Lord. I cannot imagine Claudia in jail."

"Neither can I," Kelly commiserated. "When Burt and I talked to Claudia the other day, he mentioned she'd be taken to the jail for booking, and Claudia flipped out. She was nearly hysterical just thinking about it."

"Where is she now?"

"Burt said Lizzie's staying with her at the motel. Bless her heart. Lizzie's a lot tougher than she looks. We've gotta give her credit." Kelly looked up and saw Mimi approaching. "Here comes Mimi. Do you have time to bring her up to speed on what Marty said? I really need to get back to my client accounts."

Megan nodded. "Sure, my consulting has already slowed down for the holidays. Corporate IT always does. I'm going to catch up on e-mail here at the shop today. Sit and knit and catch up."

Kelly pushed back her chair. "You mean, sit and knit and gossip about Claudia, right?"

"Was that Marty I saw leaving? What's happening with Claudia?" Mimi asked as she approached, pointing to the door.

"Megan will update you, Mimi. I've gotta get some work done now, so I can drop in this afternoon and finish Steve's scarf. See you guys later." She gave them both a wave as she headed for the café doorway.

At the rate that gossip and news spread via the Lamb-spun network and around the knitting table, Kelly had no doubt that the table would be crowded this afternoon with knitters and gossipers alike.

Kelly could hear the sound of voices coming from Lambspun's main room the moment she stepped into the foyer. Too loud to be a buzz. It was a cacophony of sound. Voices rising and falling. Excited voices. Angry voices. Kelly peered around the corner into the room.

Whoa. The knitting table was beyond crowded. People were wedged into the room so tightly it looked like they'd need a shoehorn to dislodge them. Chairs were shoved everywhere around the table, in the corners, and spilling over into the doorway to the classroom. Any more bodies, and it would be declared a fire hazard.

She hesitated in the archway leading between rooms and surveyed the scene. No sign of Mimi or Burt. They were probably preparing for the bazaar. Boxing up inventory or whatever. Or, maybe they were steering clear of the heated discussions taking place.

Kelly scanned the faces around the room. There wasn't a calm expression visible anywhere. The passion of strongly held opinions was evident on every face. Everyone seemed to be arguing. Loudly arguing, too. The topic of discussion, of course, was the now-disgraced Merry Widow, Claudia Miller.

Claudia was a self-absorbed, conceited, arrogant, man-hungry gold digger. Claudia was a funny, fun-loving social butterfly. Claudia was a thief. Claudia was innocent. It was calculated and deliberate. It was all a misunderstanding.

Kelly noticed the room appeared to have divided into two camps around either end of the knitting table. Hilda held forth from her favorite spot at one end of the table. Sheila sat beside her, and around her were several of Mimi's new spinning and crochet students. Clearly all wound up, and not with yarn. Two of Lambspun's regular knitters held down the opposite end of the table as well as the opposing argument with the help of some of the other shop regulars.

Kelly hesitated, not sure she wanted to enter the maelstrom of dissent. All she wanted was a few quiet minutes of relaxed knitting so she could finish Steve's scarf. But with all those arguments swirling around her, she might get swept up in the intense emotions and drop stitches or mess up the bind-off.

That wouldn't do. Kelly wanted to make sure the scarf edges were smooth and even, particularly since she wasn't using fringe. Steve wasn't a fringe kind of guy.

She was about to retreat to the café when she scanned the faces again. Was that Megan? And Lisa right beside her? They were facing opposite directions. They looked angry, too. Were they angrily debating Claudia's motives or just angry to be stuck in the middle of it?

Kelly couldn't believe her eyes. *What is happening here?* Lambspun was normally a haven of solitude and peace and tranquility. Now, it fairly bubbled with an incendiary witches' brew. It was the holiday season, for Pete's sake!

Mimi's voice sounded behind her. "I cannot bear it a minute longer, Kelly. This dissension is spoiling the holidays for me. All this rancor and arguing . . . I can't stand it."

Kelly eyed her friend. The warm, motherly Mimi was

gone. Nowhere to be seen. A new Mimi stood beside her. This Mimi was mad.

"I agree with you, Mimi, but what can we do to stop it? Short of throwing everyone out of the shop, I mean," Kelly joked, hoping to elicit a smile.

Instead of a smile, Mimi's eyes lit up. "That's a wonderful idea! Let's do it. Right now!"

Kelly's jaw dropped. "Mimi, I was kidding. You can't throw your customers out of the shop. It's . . . it's the holiday season. They're making their gifts. . . ."

"No, they're not. They're arguing with each other. Forming ugly cliques." Her hand shot out in aggravation. "Customers can't even reach the yarns. Assuming they're brave enough to venture close to that quagmire of dissent. I've *had* it! I'm putting my foot down right now!"

Mad Mimi swooped down on the knitting table like a Valkyrie, minus the sword. This Mimi didn't need one. She fairly radiated Righteous Zeal.

"Attention, everyone!" she announced in a loud voice. Kelly hadn't known Mimi could talk that loud. "As the owner of this shop, I have the right to operate Lambspun as I see fit. As of this moment, there is a No Arguments Allowed policy at the knitting table." She surveyed the cowed participants, who stared at her, openmouthed. "This room and the knitting table are officially off-limits to anyone who insists upon arguing or discussing volatile subjects while they work on their holiday projects. If you cannot knit or crochet or spin or stitch without verbal dissent, then you'll have to go elsewhere. Lambspun is off-limits to arguing, loud voices, or heated discussions. Period."

The knitting table went quiet. Not a peep was heard. Not only dissent, but all conversation ceased. Until Megan's voice piped up loudly. Kelly recognized Megan's on-the-field game voice.

"Good for you, Mimi," Megan declared as she quickly rose from her chair. "I don't think I could take this arguing another minute. It's giving me a headache."

Lisa sprang to her feet as well, shoving her knitting into its bag. "I second that, Megan. This is the holidays, people! Get it together!"

Megan and Lisa's support seemed to embolden Mimi even more. "From now on, the girls here will be my eyes and ears and will keep order." She pointed to Kelly, Megan, and Lisa. "I warn you, they're athletes, so I wouldn't give them any trouble if I were you."

Kelly had to look away to hide her smile. Clearly, she and her friends were going to be the "muscle" to enforce Mimi's Peace Policy. What were they supposed to do? Escort angry knitters outside to cool off?

Most of the fiber folk around the table were either looking embarrassed or hiding their own smiles of self-recognition. Mother Mimi's kindergarten message had clearly gotten through. *Either play nice, or you can't play at all.*

Jennifer sidled up beside Kelly, coffee cup in hand. "Boy, I'm glad I left the office early. I wouldn't have missed this for the world. Mimi is really hot."

"Oh, yeah. She was about to throw them out a minute ago, but I think she's changed her mind."

"So, right now, I need this table cleared," Mimi announced. "There's a weaving class tonight, and I've decided to teach it here." She clapped her hands, sounding every bit like a kindergarten teacher.

"Then again, maybe not," Kelly observed as Jennifer laughed softly beside her. Meanwhile, chagrined and embarrassed knitters and needleworkers gathered their things and skulked from the table.

"**So** you and Megan are gonna be Mimi's enforcers, right?" Marty said as he bounced the chartreuse tennis ball on his racket. "I love it."

Kelly stretched one leg out behind her as she leaned against the net post. "Yeah, Steve nearly busted a gut laughing when I told him."

Marty grinned. "Good. I'll remind him when he's about to serve."

"Mimi's enforcers, that's us. And Lisa, of course." Megan bent her arm behind her back, still holding her racket, stretching. "If you're real quiet, you can hear Greg laughing from here."

"Hey, Mimi's Muscle, grab your racket and start hitting," Steve said as he walked up, two tennis balls in hand. "Someone else has signed up for this court after us."

"You're kidding," Kelly said, looking around the indoor tennis facility at the waiting players. "Not fair. We always have it until nine o'clock."

"You wanna go beat 'em up?" Steve said with a laugh. "Good practice for Mimi's Peace Police."

"You guys are having way too much fun with this." Kelly

grabbed her racket and swung it up, over, and around her head, while Steve cackled in reply.

Marty pointed to the waiting twosome as he sprinted backwards to the baseline. "They look kind of puny. Kelly and Megan can take 'em easy." He dropped the ball and sent a solid forehand over the net.

Kelly watched Steve race to the ball. Mimi's Peace Police. They would never live that down.

Eleven

"**Run,** Carl, run," Kelly called to her dog as he raced to the fence.

Saucy Squirrel, of course, was way ahead of him, sprinting nimbly along the top rail of the chain-link fence surrounding the cottage backyard. Carl charged the fence anyway, barking furiously, little white puffs of frozen dog breath forming into clouds.

This morning had arrived surprisingly chilly, much to Kelly's delight. She'd actually needed a warmer jacket when she went for her regular run along the river trail. Until today, the temperatures had hovered around the fifties, sixties, and seventies for two weeks, dipping into the forties and low thirties only at night. Today there was a hint of the inevitable Colorado Winter yet to come.

But where the heck is it? Kelly wondered. It was the middle of December, for Pete's sake. Nearly two weeks to Christmas and it didn't feel like the holidays at all.

She slid the glass patio door closed as she heard her cell phone jangle. Grabbing her coffee mug, she settled at her computer desk and flipped open the phone. Burt calling.

"Hey, Burt, how're you doing? Still setting up the bazaar?"

"That's why I'm calling, Kelly," Burt said, his voice sounding tired. "Can you round up the others and head to the bazaar to help Mimi? I'm going to be tied up all day and Mimi will need people to set up those booths. We've got everything out there, but we need helping hands."

Kelly mentally checked her work schedule. "Sure, Burt. I'll give the others a call. Megan already said her workload was slowing down for the holidays, and mine will be, too. I'm already signed up to work tomorrow, but I can work today as well. Maybe it'll put me in a holiday mood. The weather sure isn't doing it."

"Thanks, Kelly. I knew I could count on you folks," he said, sounding relieved. "I may be here all day."

"What are you up to, Burt? Did Mimi send you on errands?"

"I wish. No, I'm over here at the department. Marty's here, too." He let out a tired sigh. "Claudia's been brought in for more questioning."

Kelly sat bolt upright. "What kind of questions?"

"She's under suspicion for vehicular homicide in connection with the hit-and-run that killed Juliet Renfrow the other night. When they brought in Claudia's car the other day, investigators noticed damage to the front end of the car.

133

They checked it out and found fibers caught on the grill. Crime lab matched them to Juliet's cape. They also found blood splatters on the hood and are checking those now."

Kelly stared ahead, unseeing. "Oh . . . my . . . God," she breathed at last. "Are you saying Claudia killed Juliet? Burt, I can't believe that."

"I have a hard time believing it, too, Kelly. But that kind of evidence doesn't lie. Listen, Dan's here now, and I want to talk to him. I'll call you later. Or Marty will. Talk to you later." He clicked off.

Kelly flipped her phone closed and stared out the patio door at Carl galumphing about the backyard. *Good Lord.* Claudia had auto theft charges filed on her in Florida, and now she was under suspicion in Colorado for vehicular homicide. *What is happening here?*

Kelly grabbed her empty mug and headed for the coffeepot on the kitchen counter. Had the ill-tempered Sheila been right about Claudia all along?

Kelly glanced down the crowded aisles of the holiday bazaar. It was late afternoon and people still clustered around the colorful booths that overflowed with gift items. Handmade candles, felted wall hangings, quilts, wreaths of evergreen and pinecones, and stuffed animals of every description covered the tables.

Other booths beckoned with homemade candies and cookies, sweet breads and ciders, jellies and jams. Kelly had already succumbed to homemade blackberry jam, her favorite. Heavenly.

Then, of course, there were the usual craft bazaar food booths selling pizza, cotton candy, hot dogs, chili, tacos, burritos. You could walk through the aisles and gain weight.

Kelly spotted Greg meandering through the aisle nearby. She waved to catch his attention. "Only a dozen gingersnap cookies left," she called, pointing to the foil-wrapped package nestled amid the colorful balls of yarn on the booth's front table.

"Save 'em for me," Greg said as he approached, munching a slice of pizza. "Boy, this place is cookie central. Every other booth is full of Christmas sweets. I'm in heaven."

"That's pizza you're eating."

Greg grinned. "I've gotta clear my palate of all that sugar, right?"

"Is Lisa here yet? She's supposed to take over for me at four." Kelly checked her watch. "I've gotta get more shopping done. I'm way behind. Even Steve is ahead of me."

"Lisa's over at the fiber craft booth talking to a friend. You and Steve want to meet for dinner later tonight? Bazaar closes at eight, so Lisa'll be finished by then."

"It all depends on how many presents I can find." Noticing another familiar face heading toward the booth, she waved. "Hey, Marty. I was hoping you'd come by. I've got a lot of questions."

Marty strolled up, dark overcoat over his arm. "Hey, where'd you find the pizza?"

"Two booths down." Greg pointed. "Why're you still suited up? Lawyers don't work Saturdays."

Marty smiled. "Today I've got a client who needs a lot of help."

Greg nodded, suddenly serious. "Sounds like the woman Lisa was talking about."

Kelly leaned over the front table. "Burt said the cops found Juliet's cape fibers on the grill of Claudia's car."

"Whoa, not good," Greg said.

"Have they found anything else?"

Marty loosened his tie. "Yeah, they also confirmed Juliet's blood is splattered on the hood. The police think Juliet was knocked on top of the car when she was first hit, then thrown onto the street when the car braked."

"That is so awful," Kelly said softly.

"Yeah, I know," Marty said. "And to make it even worse, police found tire skid marks on the street that indicate the car was parked, then took off fast. The driver gunned the engine."

Kelly flinched. "Oh, no . . . that means it was deliberate, right?"

"I'm afraid so," Marty said with a sigh.

"Man, it sounds like that woman is guilty of murder," Greg said. "What's going to happen now?"

"Well, Claudia maintains she's innocent," Marty replied. "Says she never even met Juliet Renfrow and didn't know her at all. And she swears she was in her motel room all night. She didn't go out. Of course, she has no witnesses to back her up. Lizzie was there earlier in the afternoon, but left before eight o'clock."

"How's Claudia taking this?"

"Not well. It was all Burt could do to keep her from breaking down when the police made the allegations and read the list of possible charges. She was nearly hysterical."

"You know, Marty, I find it hard to believe that Claudia

would deliberately kill Juliet Renfrow. I mean, Lizzie said Claudia didn't even know Juliet. Besides, Claudia was in hysterics all day at her motel, according to Lizzie."

"Maybe Claudia's lying," Greg suggested. "Maybe those hysterics are all an act. Maybe she's a good actress and is playing helpless to get sympathy."

Kelly pondered what Greg said. "That's possible, Greg. I've met convincing liars before. And they all seem to be good actors. Or actresses."

"I guess we'll find out," Marty said with a sigh. "Regardless, Claudia's my client and I'll do my best to keep her out of jail." He glanced down the aisle. "Man, I'm starving."

"When aren't you?"

"Pot calling the kettle black?" Kelly teased.

"Where's that pizza again?"

"Two booths down on the right." Greg pointed. "Kelly, let me pay you for those cookies now."

"Hel-*lo*! Did I hear cookies?" Marty made a quick about-face. "Where and what kind?"

"Dude, they're mine, so back off," Greg warned, reaching for the package.

Kelly got there first. She snatched the package and held it over her head. "Hey, how about an auction? Cookies go to the highest bidder."

"No fair! You promised them to me," Greg protested.

Marty was already reaching for his wallet. "Ten dollars."

"Homemade gingersnaps," Kelly tempted. "Made with my own hands. Aunt Helen's famous recipe."

"All right, all right. Fifteen dollars," Greg countered, reaching into his back jeans pocket.

"Twenty." Marty offered, removing a bill.

Greg pulled out his wallet. "Man, this is so unfair."

"Stop whining. It's for a worthy cause. Christmas presents for kids of incarcerated moms," Kelly said.

"In that case, thirty." Marty opened his billfold again.

Greg leaned closer to Marty. "Nice wallet. Italian?"

Marty nodded, then grinned. "Yep. A screaming deal, too. Lemme have the cookies, and I'll give you the website."

"Naaaah. I'll find it on my own." He flourished two twenty-dollar bills. "Forty. And that's all I've got, Kelly. In the name of all the baseball greats, gimme the cookies."

"Too bad for you," Marty countered. "I can pay more. You shouldn't have bought the pizza."

"You take credit cards?" Greg fished through his wallet.

Kelly laughed, giving Lisa a wave as she approached. "Okay, okay, I'll make you guys a deal. I'll divide up the cookies for twenty bucks each, okay?"

"Fair enough," Marty said, handing over a twenty. "Worthy cause."

"Yeah, I guess," Greg agreed, dropping a bill on the table as Kelly unwrapped the package. "You don't mind if I watch. Marty might grab one."

"Are you guys fighting about food again?" Lisa asked as she joined them.

"Who, us?" Marty looked astonished.

"Hey, Kelly, I just had a call from Lizzie. She's going over to Claudia's place again. Keeping her company tonight like she has been."

"Has Lizzie heard the news about Claudia?" Kelly asked as she rewrapped the divided cookies.

"Yeah, Mimi told her. But Lizzie's still convinced Claudia's innocent."

"See, that's one person," Marty said, accepting the cookies. "Now all I have to do is convince a jury."

Lisa shook her head, blue and green scarf dangling around her neck. "I don't know, guys. It's hard to know what to think."

Kelly handed Greg his package and glanced at her friends. "That makes two of us, Lisa."

Twelve

Kelly glanced around the exterior surroundings of Claudia's motel as she knocked on the door. Sheila was right. Seedy was a good description of the Happy Traveler Inn. Cars were parked in a cluster across the broken concrete from the rooms themselves. A scrubby excuse for a hedge ran the length of the walkway beside the motel. Obviously a previous owner had made an attempt to muffle the noise of the interstate highway nearby.

The door opened a fraction and Lizzie peeked through the opening. "Oh, Kelly, come in! Come in! Claudia will be so glad to see you," she said, holding the door wide.

"I thought you ladies might like some hot cinnamon rolls for Sunday morning breakfast. I even brought coffee,"

Kelly said as she entered the small room. She spotted Claudia sitting in a straight-backed chair beside the television set in the corner.

"Oh, that's lovely. How thoughtful of you, Kelly. Isn't it, Claudia?"

A pale Claudia answered in a soft voice from across the room. "Yes, thank you."

No designer suit this morning. Today Claudia wore a dark blue tailored shirt over navy pants. Kelly had never seen her look so somber. Claudia barely resembled her former vivacious self. She sat slumped in a chair, unsmiling, and barely made eye contact. She also appeared to be wearing no makeup, which was unheard of for a woman like Claudia, who prided herself on her appearance.

Kelly deliberately sought Claudia's gaze and gave her an encouraging smile. "I thought I'd give you ladies an update on the holiday bazaar. Lisa, Megan, and I took turns manning the booth Saturday, and we're going back today. Mimi has her hands full supplying both the Lambspun booth and the fiber crafts booth. I swear, we must have sold over eighty sets of hats, gloves, and mittens yesterday."

She handed one of the warm pastries to Claudia and placed a carryout cup of coffee on the table beside her. Claudia glanced up, and Kelly saw her struggle to produce a little smile.

"Thanks, Kelly. That's . . . that's sweet of you."

Kelly pulled out a chair for Lizzie and settled herself on the edge of the bed. "You'll both be pleased to know that your knitted hats and mittens were some of the first purchases. Superior quality, no doubt."

Lizzie smiled obediently as she toyed with her coffee cup. Claudia had touched neither pastry nor coffee. Kelly took a deep drink of her own coffee, searching for the right words to say what she wanted to say. Finally, she simply blurted out her feelings.

"Claudia, I can't tell you how sorry I am about your, uh, your legal situation. I wish there was something I could do to help, but . . ." Her voice trailed off.

Claudia looked up and stared directly into Kelly's eyes. "You've already helped, Kelly. You found wonderful young Marty to represent me. He's an excellent lawyer and smart as a whip, too. He'll save me. I know he will." Claudia nodded with fervor, her eyes alight.

Kelly felt her heart squeeze. No matter how smart or how fine a lawyer Marty was, he couldn't change the facts in the case. Claudia looked guilty as hell. And Lawyer Marty couldn't "save" her from the facts.

Since Claudia had already opened that door, Kelly decided to walk right through it. "Marty said you told him you never left the motel that night."

"I didn't, Kelly. Please believe me!" Claudia swore earnestly as she leaned forward. "I never left the motel. Besides, I don't even know that woman, Juliet Renfrow. I've never even met her."

"When did you leave that evening, Lizzie?"

Lizzie stared at her cup. "I left around eight o'clock or so. It was getting close to my bedtime, I'm afraid." She glanced up with a contrite expression. "Oh, how I wish I'd stayed later. Then Claudia would have an . . . an alibi, isn't that what they call it?"

Kelly had to smile. "That's okay, Lizzie. You can't worry about such things." Turning to Claudia again, she said, "Think back, Claudia. Was there anything you did that might prove you were in your room? Did you order food? Anything at all?"

Claudia frowned for a moment. "No, I didn't. Lizzie was kind enough to bring me something from the restaurant down the street before she left." She shook her head. "No one came to the door. I stayed in and tried to watch television. Then my daughter called, and I talked to her for quite a while."

"Hey, that's something," Kelly said, feeling a little rush of excitement.

The excitement of discovery. The discovery of clues. Kelly hadn't poked around in any crimes since last winter. "Sleuthing," as her friends called it. She'd forgotten how addictive it could be. And how dangerous.

"When did your daughter call? Can you remember?"

"Uhhhh, it was later that evening. I can't remember exactly."

Later in the evening. Juliet Renfrow was hit and killed later in the evening, when she walked back to her home from Jeremy's house. "Claudia, did you tell Marty about your daughter's call?"

Claudia looked away. "I . . . I can't remember. Everything about yesterday is just a blur. Maybe I didn't tell him."

Lizzie reached over and placed her hand on Claudia's arm. "You must call him, dear. Right now. Your daughter's phone call could prove that you were here in the motel that night."

"Yes . . . you're right. I'll call him . . . right away," Claudia said, glancing about the room. "Have you seen my cell phone?"

That was Kelly's next question, and Claudia just answered it. Claudia had a cell phone. Cell phones were portable. If Claudia's daughter did indeed call her mother in late evening, the fact that Claudia's call came in on a cell phone would prove nothing. As far as the police were concerned, Claudia could have been parked in her car on the street, talking with her daughter while she waited for Juliet Renfrow to appear.

"That's a good idea," Kelly encouraged anyway. "Marty can contact your daughter and obtain her phone records as well as yours."

"Oh, that's wonderful news!" Lizzie exclaimed. "It will prove Claudia's innocent!"

Kelly couldn't let them build up false hope. It would be unkind. "Well, not exactly, Lizzie. Since Claudia has a cell phone, which is portable, the police won't consider it proof that Claudia was in her motel room."

Lizzie's happiness deflated in an instant, like a child's popped birthday balloon. She bit her lip.

Claudia appeared crestfallen. "You're right, Kelly," she murmured. "But . . . but what about a call here in the room? My daughter had to call me twice, because my cell phone battery was low. And she called me the second time here in the motel room."

Kelly stared back into Claudia's eyes. Her gaze was clear and open. Honest and sincere. She appeared to be telling the truth. Why then was there a little niggling doubt in the back of Kelly's mind?

Why hadn't Claudia remembered that crucial information before? If there were phone records, they would show the motel phone number. Maybe that could help prove Claudia's whereabouts. Why then hadn't she remembered it until now, after Kelly told her the cell phone wouldn't prove anything?

"Claudia, you need to call Marty right away and tell him all of this. It's important," Kelly said as she stood up. "I've got to leave for the bazaar, but I'll be in touch."

"Thank you, Kelly," Claudia said as she dug in her purse. "I'll call Marty right now. You're a lifesaver."

Kelly didn't reply. She simply walked to the door, Lizzie accompanying her. "Give me a call later, will you, Lizzie?"

"Oh, yes, dear, I certainly will." Lizzie's excited coloring had returned.

"Has anyone come to relieve you? Have you gotten to church?" Heaven help that the churchgoing Lizzie would miss Sunday Mass.

"Actually, I've convinced Claudia to come with me. We're going to the twelve noon service." Lizzie glanced over her shoulder at Claudia, who was already engaged in a phone conversation. "Claudia needs to get out of this room and back with people, but she's afraid that no one will speak to her. She's convinced everyone in town is gossiping about her.

Even so, I'm going to do my very best to take her out. Even if I have to force her."

Kelly saw the determination on the elderly knitter's face. "That's a good idea, Lizzie. And a church service is a good place to start," she said as she opened the door. "Better say a prayer for Claudia."

Kelly leaned against the knitting booth's front table. It was nearly empty. The last of the Hats for the Homeless had flown off the tables as if they had wings. Lambspun sweaters, scarves, crocheted shawls, felted purses, everything fiber-related went like veritable hotcakes. Clearly, the throngs that clogged the bazaar aisles were doing their Christmas shopping.

Now all Kelly had to do was finish hers. She'd only gotten four presents yesterday. Lisa, Megan, Jennifer, and Mimi. She was seriously behind on shopping. Once Megan came to relieve her, Kelly could join the holiday hordes once again.

A middle-aged woman walked up to the booth beside Kelly's. Quickly shedding her winter coat, she set about arranging the stacks of fliers and brochures that littered the front table. They all advertised an antique shop on the southern edge of Fort Connor.

"I was wondering if someone would show up at your booth today," Kelly said. "There were several people working yesterday."

The woman glanced up with a smile. "Those were mostly family members. I had to man the shop all day."

Kelly remembered a comment Mimi made at Thanksgiving. "So, you're the antique shop owner. I think we have a mutual friend, Mimi Shafer."

"Oh, yes. Mimi and I go way back," the woman said as she approached. "From the days when we were first young professors' wives here in town. Getting used to the university life and Fort Connor. Of course, Fort Connor was much smaller then."

Kelly extended her hand. "I'm Kelly Flynn, and I think Mimi must have mentioned me. I sold an older farmhouse in Wyoming last summer, and it was filled with antiques. My cousin Martha had quite a collection."

The woman's eyes lit up. "Ohhhh, yes! I remember Mimi telling me about that. Apparently she'd seen them, too. She said you had some lovely pieces. She also mentioned you might be interested in selling some."

Kelly shrugged good-naturedly. "Not yet, I'm afraid. I want to wait and see if I find a house I like. Nothing has struck my fancy yet. Meanwhile, they're all in storage."

"Well, if you change your mind, please give me a call." She handed Kelly a business card. Then, glancing to the side, she said, "Sheila, you didn't have to come in again today. My daughter said you worked last night."

Sheila Miller approached, dark blue winter jacket dangling over her arm. "It's the holiday season, and I wanted to be useful," she said, darting a look at Kelly.

Kelly decided to stifle any annoyance or dislike she might feel toward Sheila and be friendly. In the spirit of the holidays. "Hey, Sheila. Looks like you're doing double duty like me. Didn't I see you the other night at Saint Mark's helping with the children's knitting projects?"

Clearly surprised at Kelly's pleasant observation, Sheila managed to return Kelly's smile. "Yes, I've been trying to help them every night for a couple of weeks now, so the kids could finish on time. Besides, there's so much to do at the church, getting ready for the holidays." Her smile widened, and Kelly watched Sheila's normally stern expression melt away.

"Good for you. Jennifer and I have only been able to manage a few nights. But Hilda and Lizzie have been working every night, especially since . . ." She left the rest of the sentence dangling to avoid any mention of Juliet Renfrow's death.

Sheila's expression sobered anyway. "Yes, they're organizing everything at Saint Mark's, it seems. I heard they're even in charge of the Nativity portion of the Christmas Eve family service. Now that's a job I wouldn't want. Teenagers are nothing but trouble, from what I've seen."

Kelly had to laugh. Sheila Miller actually had a sense of humor. Who would have thought? Turning her attention back to the browsing bazaar shoppers strolling past, Kelly called out, "Holiday hats and mittens! Only a few left."

Three women approached the antique booth, and Kelly recognized them as some of Mimi's new crochet students. They were also the same ones who had clustered near Hilda and Sheila at the knitting table the other day. They were the Anti-Claudia group and had been asked to leave with all the rest of the arguing fiber folk.

"Sheila, have you heard?" one of the women said as she raced up, the others close behind.

"Claudia Miller *killed* Juliet Renfrow!" another interrupted as they clustered about the front table.

"I told you she was desperate, didn't I?" another barbed, jabbing her friend's shoulder.

Sheila caught Kelly's gaze briefly then turned her attention back to the hovering gossipers. "Yes, yes, I've heard. It's simply awful, isn't it? Claudia's behavior has shocked even me, and I thought I'd seen everything."

Kelly started rearranging the assortment of yarns left for sale, while she stayed attuned to the conversation nearby.

"I heard the police want to put her in *jail!*" the first woman announced.

"How awful!" another declared.

"Serves her right. She's a *murderer.*" The third emphasized the word.

Kelly had to bite her tongue to keep from responding to the vicious gossip. Claudia wasn't imagining things. The news of Claudia's implication in Juliet's death was spreading faster than a Colorado wildfire.

"**Away** in a manger . . ." the recorded choir sang overhead. Kelly shuffled her grip on her packages so she could grasp the Cinnamon Spiced Latte the young barista handed over the counter.

"Thanks," Kelly said before weaving her way through the crush of holiday shoppers who'd decided to take a sugar break the same time she did. Maneuvering around them, Kelly escaped the popular mall coffee shop and headed toward the central plaza. She vowed to keep shopping until she'd found at least one more present for Steve.

Since Megan had relieved her at the bazaar booth, Kelly had been shopping all afternoon. She'd been to three outdoor shopping centers and several niche brand-name shops. All in the hunt for the "perfect" gift for Steve. So far, she hadn't found it.

Tools? He had everything.

Cologne? The one he used was her favorite.

Music? She'd already created a mix of his favorites. Ready for Steve to download onto his music player.

She'd also bought him new tennis warm-ups. And found the latest novel from his favorite mystery author.

But she needed another gift.

In desperation, Kelly fell back on the tried-and-true holiday present that women everywhere—be they wives, mothers, girlfriends, or daughters—fall back on when they can't think of anything else to buy for the men in their lives.

The Holiday Sweater.

She'd already searched through all the trendy brandname shops and found several sweaters she knew he'd like. They were all soft and lush with deep forest colors. Steve would love any of them.

Kelly looked down the length of the mall to the department store anchoring one end. Big-Name Department Store. It beckoned, too. It would be awash in men's sweaters and women pawing through them. Good, solid, Establishment sweaters.

Hmmmm. Establishment sweater or Trendy Brand-Name sweater. Decisions, decisions.

She took a sip of the sugary coffee. It almost made her teeth ache. Pausing near the central plaza, Kelly looked up at the huge Christmas tree dominating the center of the mall. Oversized decorations of every description hung from the branches as lights twinkled.

She wanted something else for Steve. Something different and unique. A sweater just wasn't unique. What else could she find?

Sipping the sweet drink, Kelly watched Santa's elves guide waiting children into line for their Santa visits. The younger children wiggled and danced about, barely able to contain their excitement. Older children bided their time, watching the model train circle around the Christmas tree, its track rising onto three levels.

Kelly sipped and watched the little locomotive choo-choo its way around the evergreen branches. Train whistle blowing that sharp tinny sound. Around and around . . .

A train. *Why not?* She'd had a train when she was a kid. Maybe Steve had, too. Kelly remembered how much fun she and her dad had had setting it up every year. Trains were fun. Sure, it would be a frivolous gift, but it was definitely unique. Would Steve like it?

She pondered that for a moment as the little engine pulled its colorful cars around the multilevel track again and again.

Okay . . . how about a sweater *and* the train set? Traditional and unique. Now, *that* felt right.

Kelly drained the sugary coffee and looked for a trash can. Time to go back on the Hunt. Face the crowds again. Somehow, she'd found a whole new enthusiasm for shopping.

Thirteen

Kelly pushed open the front door of Lambspun with her back, as she maneuvered a large cardboard box through the doorway and into the foyer. She spotted Hilda sorting through a yarn bin.

"Hey, Hilda, I didn't see you at the bazaar," she greeted the elderly knitter. "How's your holiday knitting coming along?"

"I'm starting my last baby blanket today," Hilda said, comparing yarns. "That is, if I can decide between pink rose and lilac lavender. Is that the balance of the bazaar items? I saw Burt and Mimi outside unloading their cars."

"Yeah, I thought I'd give them a hand. But I should have worn my jacket. It's chillier now than when I ran earlier this morning." She headed for the main room and plopped the box on the library table.

"If there are any hats, gloves, or mittens left, I can always take them to the homeless shelter for their giveaway box," Hilda said as she followed after Kelly.

"They're all gone," Kelly announced as she opened the box. "Also the felted purses and crocheted afghans and knitted chenille washcloths sold out. In fact, everything fiber-related was sold. Even the yarn is gone. Lisa closed up the booth last night, and she must have had a going-out-of-business sale. This box is full of stickers and credit card vouchers and odds and ends. Oh, and a snow globe Mimi bought at the last minute."

Kelly gave the small glass-encased wintry scene a shake, sending miniature snowflakes swirling as she set it on the table.

Hilda smiled. Kelly remarked to herself that it was the first time she'd seen Hilda smile for quite a while. She seemed subdued, somehow. Kelly surmised that Lizzie's frequent absences to babysit Claudia had been difficult for Hilda. She'd been alone more than usual. Kelly also guessed that the rift that had occurred between the two sisters weighed heavily on both their minds. They'd been lifetime companions and good company for each other.

"I'm so glad the sale was successful. And I'm sure it was all due to you and the others. Your youthful enthusiasm is contagious." Hilda settled at the end of the table in her usual spot.

Kelly started unloading office supplies and other items from the box. "How are you doing, Hilda? You seem quieter than usual."

Hilda picked up a knitting needle and started casting on with the lavender yarn. "Well, I must confess, I've been a bit overwhelmed lately. What with all the extra activities at church, I've barely had time to knit. That's why I'm so late in finishing my Christmas gifts."

"I can imagine you're overwhelmed. I heard that you and Lizzie stepped in to take over most of Saint Mark's holiday preparations after Juliet died. You need to take care of yourself, Hilda. You're not as young as Juliet."

"Mind your tongue, miss," Hilda said, arching a brow, a hint of her old self peeking out.

Kelly smiled. "Let me rephrase. You're not as young as you *used* to be, okay? You shouldn't wear yourself out. Is there anything Jennifer and I can do to help? We worked with the kids' knitting group several times."

Hilda's busy needles stilled, and she looked up. "Well, now that you mention it, Kelly. There is one holiday event that is not going very well, and Lizzie and I are at a loss as to how to proceed. Perhaps you and Jennifer could bring your youthful eyes and enthusiasm to the task."

"Jennifer and I would be glad to help. Which holiday event is it?"

"It's a rather important part of the Christmas Eve family service. We're doing a reenactment of the Nativity, complete with the Holy Family, shepherds, angel, and Wise Men."

The Christmas Eve family service? *Whoa.* That was a biggie. Kelly hadn't even seen a family service for years. She usually went to the peaceful midnight Christmas service. What had she gotten into? Jennifer would kill her.

"Wow, the family service is pretty important. How could Jennifer and I help?"

Hilda exhaled a huge breath. "You could take over completely. Lizzie and I are unable to communicate with those children. We've met with them twice and tried to go over the service with them, so they'll know what to do. But they just sit there and stare blankly at us with those . . . those things in their ears." She looked at Kelly dolefully. "Only the narrator seems to pay attention, and he's still stumbling over the reading. Lizzie and I are at our wits' end, Kelly. The Christmas Eve family service is too important to mess up. And these children don't seem to care."

Kelly began to understand. "How old are these, uh . . . children, Hilda?"

"They're eighth-graders, so most are thirteen—"

"Going on thirty, right?" Kelly had to laugh.

Hilda looked up. "Yes! How did you know?"

"Steve and I coached youth baseball and softball teams last summer. We had tons of junior high kids." She wagged her head sympathetically. "They must have given you fits, Hilda."

"Mercy, yes," she sighed again. "Lizzie and I just cannot seem to get through to them."

Kelly could picture it now, Hilda and Lizzie, veteran schoolteachers that they were, trying to hold forth in front of a bunch of bored, surly teenagers already wired into their iPods or sending text messages to friends on their cell phones.

"I think Jennifer and I can help you out with that one, Hilda. When's the next rehearsal scheduled?"

"Tomorrow night at seven in the sanctuary at Saint Mark's."

Kelly pushed off the table and dug her empty coffee mug from her knitting bag. "Tell you what, Hilda. You have the church secretary print up copies of the script. Lots of them. I'll drop by the church and pick them up this afternoon. Odds are, most of the kids have already lost or misplaced theirs."

Hilda's knitting dropped to her lap, and she gazed at Kelly. "Oh, my dear, I cannot thank you enough. I will call the secretary right away. Meanwhile, Lizzie and I will meet you at the church tomorrow evening."

"Glad to be of help, Hilda. We'll see you tomorrow." Kelly gave a wave and headed for the café and coffee. Now all she needed to do was make sure Jennifer didn't have a hot date for tomorrow night.

Kelly wove her way around the midmorning customers that filled the shop. Only a week and a half before Christmas, and gift panic was starting to settle in. She could tell by the expressions on some of the faces. Frantic. Would they finish their project on time or be knitting-spinning-crocheting-weaving after midnight Christmas Eve?

The Lambspun Elves had been busy, refilling yarn bins and shelves and chests so that they spilled over with colorful candy-colored yarns. Wools. Mohair. Silk. Cotton. Wound in tidy bundles and soft balls, twisted into fat skeins, and wrapped in luscious coils. Bunches of gossamer froth were draped along cabinets and walls. All of it waiting for customers and their imaginations.

Kelly spied one of Lambspun's trusty elves waving at her

from the front counter, where a line had already formed at the register. "Kelly, are you going to be here for a while?" she called as Kelly approached.

"Yeah, I'm helping Mimi with the bazaar cleanup. What do you need, Rosa?"

Rosa waved a pink sticky note. "If you see Sheila, would you give her this note, please? I can't take time away from the front counter. I swear, that woman must think we're her personal secretaries or something. This is the second time she's gotten a call here at the shop."

Kelly took the sticky note and read the name and phone number. "Ginger Bessum, 941-555-5555. Who's that?"

Rosa shrugged. "I don't know. She says she works for some retirement home."

Kelly's little buzzer went off inside. Retirement home. Was that Claudia's retirement facility? Sheila said she had an informant on the staff. Was Sheila still asking questions about Claudia? Why?

"Sheila has a cell phone. I've seen her use it. Wonder why this Ginger Bessum called her here."

"Beats me, but it's getting old. We're in the crazy Christmas crunch now. None of us has time to deliver messages," Rosa said, clearly impatient.

Kelly headed for the café once again, scrutinizing the number. She didn't recognize a Florida area code on sight, but she'd bet this was one. As she rounded a corner into the café, she spied Sheila at the counter, ordering coffee. Glancing at the phone number once more, Kelly committed it to memory. That was one of the benefits of being an accountant. She memorized numbers easily.

"Hey, Sheila, Rosa gave me this note. She said a woman called asking for you."

Sheila turned quickly, her look of surprise quickly turning to irritation. She reached for the note and frowned at the number. "I've told that woman not to call me again. She's been trying to get me to join her legal firm, and she simply won't take no for an answer. I've told her I'm perfectly happy with my present position."

"Some people are hard to discourage," Kelly answered, wondering who was telling the truth. Ginger Bessum had told Rosa she worked in a retirement home.

"You're right," Sheila said, pulling out her cell phone as she took her coffee and walked down the hallway leading toward the restrooms.

Kelly continued to the counter and dangled her mug for a refill as she flipped out her phone. Curious as to who was leaving messages for Sheila, Kelly punched in the number she'd memorized, while a waitress filled her mug.

"Evergreen Retirement Facility," a woman's voice answered after a couple of rings.

"I'm trying to reach a Ginger Bessum. Does she work at your facility?" Kelly asked.

"Yes, she does," the woman replied. "She's on another line right now. Would you like to leave a message?"

"No, that's okay. Thanks," Kelly said and clicked off.

She'd bet anything that Sheila was talking to Ginger Bessum right now. Why would Sheila lie about something as innocuous as a phone call? Perhaps she didn't want people to know that she'd been checking on Claudia. Maybe.

Kelly started down the hallway, about to enter the central

yarn room, when the sound of Sheila's angry voice stopped her. It came from the corner near the restrooms.

"I have told you before, Ginger, stop calling me. Do you hear? I've paid you already. You are *not* getting another dollar."

Sheila's voice was tight with anger. Kelly edged around a corner out of sight, unable to stop listening.

"Is that a threat? Don't try that with me, Ginger. I work with lawyers, do you hear? I can make your life miserable."

Kelly held still, not breathing. She didn't want to miss a word. What was this all about?

"I'm hanging up now. And don't try to call the shop again, because I'm telling them you're a stalker, and I'm alerting the police. Don't push me, Ginger, I'm warning you."

Quickly, Kelly darted into the yarn room ahead and sank one hand into a bin, hoping to look like she was browsing in case Sheila suddenly entered. Instead, she heard Sheila talking with Hilda in the main room nearby. After fondling the green and red candy-striped yarn a few seconds longer, Kelly headed for the front door.

Maybe Burt was still outside. She wanted to run Sheila's conversation past him and get his take on it. Clearly, Sheila was being threatened by this Ginger Bessum in Florida. *Why?* Was Ginger the spy she'd used to watch Claudia as well as the police investigation into the missing green Taurus?

Mimi stepped into the foyer then and gave a shiver. "Brrrr, I believe we're finally getting our winter temperatures."

"Mimi, is Burt still outside? I wanted to ask him something."

"Yes, he is, but he's probably still on the phone," Mimi said, beckoning Kelly into the tiny alcove near the front door where sale items were displayed. "Burt just heard from Dan at the department, and it's . . . it's not good news." Her face clouded.

"What's happened? Did they take Claudia in for questioning again?"

Mimi sighed. "No, but they went to her motel room with a search warrant looking for evidence. Apparently the police had an answer to their newspaper notice asking people to call in if they were in that area the night of the hit-and-run. A college student reported he had driven down the street that evening and had seen a dark car stopped on the side of the road. He couldn't remember what kind of car it was, but he remembered seeing the driver. Apparently a woman was kneeling by the side of the road. He called out his window and asked if she had a flat tire and needed help. But she said no, so he drove away. He never saw Juliet lying there."

Kelly held her breath. "Did he get a good look at the woman? Was it Claudia?"

Mimi shook her head. "He said he couldn't really see her face that well in the dark, but he did remember she was wearing a hooded cape. A *red* hooded cape." Mimi emphasized the words. "That's why police got the search warrant. They've confiscated Claudia's cape."

"Oh, no," Kelly whispered, remembering Claudia proudly displaying the bright red cape on the day she purchased it. One of Juliet's Christmas capes. Was she kneeling beside Juliet? Was she checking if Juliet was dead?

"I know, Kelly, it's awful. Burt said he wanted you and

me to know, but he emphasized that we absolutely, positively cannot tell anyone else. The police aren't releasing that information. I swore to him I wouldn't breathe a word, and I knew you wouldn't, either."

"It's hard to believe Claudia would deliberately kill Juliet like that," Kelly said. "But every time the police discover something, it makes her look guilty. Yet she swears she didn't do it."

"Kelly, I'm fond of Claudia, too, but now I don't know what to think. Has she been lying to us all this time? Was she so devastated at Jeremy Cunningham's rejection that she went off the deep end or something?"

"I don't know, Mimi. We've all been giving Claudia the benefit of the doubt. But now, I don't know if we should."

Mimi frowned. "Maybe she's a little bit off or something. If so, then she needs help. Medical help." Mimi shook her head again, clearly worried. "And if that's true, then I don't think Lizzie should be staying over there at night."

"I agree, Mimi, but it'll be hard on Lizzie. She's really become Claudia's strongest supporter."

"This is so awful, and to be happening around the holidays, too. That makes it feel worse. Holidays are supposed to be happy and joyous."

"Well, real life intrudes, even in the holidays, Mimi. Let me know if you need any help, will you?"

Mimi found her smile, and she reached out to pat Kelly's arm. "I will, dear. Why don't you go back to your own work. You've helped enough today."

"Good idea, Mimi. I'll see you later," Kelly said as she pushed through the front door and outside.

The cold air cut right through her sweater and wool pants. Indian summer had left for good. December weather had finally come, and it was staying. Now, if it would only snow.

Spying Burt beside the open trunk of his car, Kelly headed his way. There was not much client work in her in-box this morning. The holiday slowdown had started.

"Hey, Burt, Mimi told me the bad news," she said as she approached. "I hate to say it, but it's looking more and more like Claudia really did kill Juliet Renfrow."

Burt shoved both hands into the pockets of his beige suede coat. "Yeah, it does, Kelly. I mean, how many people who bought one of those capes held a grudge against Juliet Renfrow?" He shook his head. "Marty would have to be a magician to clear Claudia with all these facts stacked against her. In fact, I'm not sure even fast-talking Marty could pull that off."

"Yeah, you're right," Kelly said, rubbing her arms.

"You ought to go in, Kelly. You're shivering."

She turned to leave then suddenly remembered her earlier thought. "Hey, Burt, would you do me a favor?"

"Sure, Kelly. What do you need?"

"I overheard a conversation earlier this morning and it's got my curiosity up. I wondered if you could talk to your friend in Florida again. You know, the one who checked into the stolen car situation at Claudia's retirement home."

"I guess I could. Why? What's up?"

"A little while ago, Rosa gave me a note for Sheila. Apparently a woman in Florida has called the shop twice and left messages for Sheila. Rosa's not too happy about it, either."

"At the shop? That's weird. Doesn't Sheila have a phone?"

Kelly nodded. "She sure does. In fact, I gave her the message, and Sheila said it was some woman in Florida who wanted to hire her for a law firm. But Rosa claimed that the caller said she worked for a retirement home." Kelly paused for emphasis.

Burt's brows arched in what Kelly recognized as his skeptical expression. "Oh, really? Is it the same retirement home where Claudia lived? Why would they be calling Sheila?"

"That's what I wondered. In fact, I dialed the number myself and reached the Evergreen Retirement Facility. And the woman who left the message for Sheila works there, too. Her name's Ginger Bessum. Why would Sheila lie about that?"

"I don't know, Kelly. It makes you wonder."

"Yeah, it does. But what really made me curious was the phone conversation I overheard when I walked past the hallway. Sheila must have been talking to that woman because she called her Ginger. And she sounded mad."

Kelly repeated the overheard conversation for Burt in its entirety, then waited for his response.

Burt's brows shot up again. "Really?"

"Yeah, really. It sounds to me like Ginger Bessum is trying to blackmail Sheila into paying her more money for something. Do you think it's for spying on Claudia? I mean, Sheila admitted that much already. What do you think, Burt?"

Burt glanced away. "I don't know, Kelly, but I'd like to find out. Let me see if I can actually speak to the guy in Sarasota my buddy contacted. That way I can get more information. I'll keep you posted. Now, why don't you get inside before you freeze." He pointed to her cottage across the driveway.

"Thanks, Burt," Kelly said as she took off at a run.

Fourteen

Kelly grabbed her shoulder bag and hastened across the driveway, her ski jacket flapping open with the chill breeze. Client work had only taken a couple of hours this morning. If she was lucky, she could sneak in an afternoon of holiday shopping to finish off her gift list. All she needed was a quick fill-up of Eduardo's brew, and she would be on her way.

As she neared the stone pathway leading to Lambspun's front patio, Kelly spied Lizzie's car heading down the driveway. Pausing on the path, Kelly waited for Lizzie to join her. Shopping could wait a few minutes.

"How're you doing?" she asked as Lizzie approached.

Lizzie was decked out in her holiday season festive red and green, with a red bow in her hair. A holiday corsage of angels and bells adorned her lapel. She greeted Kelly with a smile that held only a fraction of her usual good cheer. "I'm doing pretty well, dear, considering all the horrible things that are happening right now."

Kelly paused in the stone entry. "Lizzie, both Mimi and I think you shouldn't spend the nights with Claudia anymore. She's a grown woman and will have to learn how to get through all of this without someone holding her hand."

Lizzie looked up in surprise. "But she's so fragile, Kelly. She really is. Why, she bursts into tears just thinking about everything. Having me there helps her."

"If she's really that emotionally fragile, then she may need professional help. We know you mean the best, Lizzie, and your efforts are well intentioned. But you may not be the help that Claudia needs. I'll ask Marty what he thinks."

Lizzie's paper-thin cheeks puckered with concern. "But I can't just *abandon* her like that—"

"You don't have to abandon Claudia, simply visit her during the daytime. Take her out to the senior center and bring her here for knitting. That will be good for her. It'll keep her mind off . . . well, everything else."

"I was planning on picking her up today after I'd done my morning errands. I wanted to bring Claudia to the shop for the afternoon gathering."

"That sounds like a good plan," Kelly said as she opened the wooden door.

Following the plump little knitter into the shop, Kelly spied Burt in the doorway to the adjacent room. He beckoned Kelly over. Holiday shopping was obviously going to wait some more, she figured as she headed his way.

"What's up, Burt?"

"Let's go have some coffee, Kelly," he suggested, walking toward the hallway leading to the café. "I heard from that Sarasota detective who's investigating the missing Taurus."

"Great. Does he remember Sheila Miller?"

"Ohhhh, yeah. According to this Dick Watson, Sheila is a royal pain in the butt." Burt pulled out a chair for Kelly and one for himself. "Apparently Sheila was obsessed with Claudia to the point of stalking her. And she did have someone in the retirement home spying on her. I guess that was this Ginger."

"And the Sarasota cop knew all about that?"

"Oh, yeah. Several months ago, Sheila gave him a printed report of all the facts concerning Claudia's previous two husbands and their deaths. She really did travel to those states and interview people." Burt shook his head. "Anyway, when she returned, she presented Detective Watson with the report and insisted that an investigation be opened into her father's death. She swore Claudia had killed him. Of course, Watson told Sheila that there was nothing in her so-called report that would cause them to question her father's death. Apparently Sheila didn't take that too well. Afterwards, she started trying to get newspapers to print her accusations."

"Whoa, Burt. Couldn't he do anything to stop her? That sounds like harassment to me."

"Me, too, but Claudia never responded. She never filed a complaint. She never reported any of Sheila's activities to the police. And she never contacted a lawyer to file a civil suit alleging harassment. Nothing."

Kelly remembered Claudia's words. She "just wanted to crawl in a hole and die."

"But then it really got interesting in October when

Claudia left the retirement home. Apparently Mary Ann Howard's family didn't realize their mother's car was missing at first. They were too busy handling funeral and burial arrangements following her death. They didn't even check the parking garage for almost two weeks. But when they discovered the car was gone, they started asking questions. Sheila's spy must have alerted her to the situation, because Sheila put it all together. Watson said he heard from Sheila that a car was missing from the retirement facility, and she claimed Claudia stole it."

"Did he believe her?"

Burt shook his head. "Nope. Watson blew her off. But he did inquire at the retirement home about a missing car, just in case. The facility director told him the family didn't know if their mother had lent the car to her church or a charity. So they were still asking friends and acquaintances. They weren't sure if it was a theft or not. Then, the credit charges arrived on the next month's bill. They revealed a trail of gas, restaurants, and hotels from Florida heading west. That got on Watson's radar. And it also convinced the family the car was actually stolen. Of course, Claudia's spy kept track of everything the family learned and reported it to Sheila."

"So that's how she found out where Claudia was."

"Yeah, but it was the phone bill that really nailed the location. When that came in, there was a collect phone call from Claudia's motel in Fort Connor to Mary Ann Howard right before she died. Apparently that's when Sheila headed to Colorado, hot on Claudia's trail."

"Gotta hand it to her, Sheila's a helluva sleuth."

"Yeah, if you like obsessive and you don't mind bribing

people to spy on others." Burt signaled the café waitress. "Watson said Sheila called a couple of weeks ago, informing him that she had located Claudia and the missing car in Fort Connor, Colorado. Then she asked when he was going to charge Claudia with auto theft. He told Sheila that police were investigating the vehicle's disappearance, but no charges were filed yet. They were still interviewing residents of the retirement home because questions had arisen as to whether the car was stolen or simply borrowed."

The waitress appeared, coffeepot in hand. Kelly presented her king-sized mug. "Fill 'er up, Julie. I've got to face holiday shoppers again."

Burt poured a stream of milk into his coffee. "Watson said that another resident at the retirement home remembered Claudia telling her that Mary Ann let Claudia 'borrow' her car." He took a sip. "Watson said that statement made them take another look. After all, Claudia did call Mary Ann Howard when she arrived in Fort Connor. Police wondered if Mary Ann really had lent Claudia her car as the elderly resident said. Of course, the family was convinced Claudia had tricked their aging mother. They figured Claudia had taken advantage of their mother's trusting nature to steal both her car and the credit card. Anyway, the police kept asking questions. And when the family finally learned that particular resident had memory problems, they didn't waste time. They officially reported the vehicle as stolen, and the rest we got to witness ourselves."

Kelly screwed the top of her mug tightly. "I have to agree with you, Burt, Sheila has been all over that situation from the start. And it wasn't from concern about the Howard family. It appears all Sheila was interested in was pinning a crime on Claudia."

"It sure looks that way, Kelly. After the police told her they weren't going to investigate her father's death, that's when Sheila started tracking Claudia at the retirement home. Almost like she was hoping to find something." Burt took a sip of coffee. "Watson told me that Sheila called him last Monday and actually asked what kind of sentence would be given if Claudia was convicted of auto theft. Can you believe that? And she was furious when he said it depended on the judge. After all, Claudia had no arrest record, and there had been questions as to whether she borrowed the car or stole it. So the judge might be lenient. Claudia might serve jail time, then again, maybe not. She might serve on a work release program instead. It was up to the judge."

"Whoa, I bet Sheila didn't take that very well."

Burt gave her a crooked smile. "Apparently not. He said Sheila lost it and started swearing and yelling over the phone, so he had to hang up."

"No wonder Sheila's angry. Well, she ought to be satisfied now that Claudia is implicated in something really serious." Kelly rose from her chair. "So what do you make of the call yesterday? Is Sheila's spy hitting her up for more money?"

"Sounds like it, Kelly. That's the trouble when you start twisting the law, like Sheila's been doing. You usually wind up entangling yourself."

Kelly breathed in the scent of evergreen as she and Jennifer walked up the aisle of Saint Mark's Catholic Church. There were even more decorations in the church now than before. Two spruce trees flanked the altar steps, decorated with crimson red bows and holly sprigs, candles nestling in the branches. Ropes of greenery draped along the walls. The Yuletide season was upon them.

Another aroma teased her nostrils, stirring memories from the back of Kelly's brain. Incense. That was it. She remembered that scent, pungent and spicy. The priest walking up and down the aisles, swinging the ornate metal censer, while a cloud of fragrance wafted over the bowed heads in the pews.

"Most of those kids have already tuned out Hilda," Jennifer observed as she paused in the aisle. "Check it out."

Kelly peered at a teenage boy perched on the steps to the left of the altar and spotted ear buds connected to a popular miniature music player. She also spied two other boys sprawled on the steps above, their hand movements a dead giveaway to where their attention was—text messaging.

Close by was the traditional Nativity scene, with delicately painted figures of Mary and Joseph, shepherds, the Wise Men, and a beatific angel standing over all.

Now, if only the group of teenagers she saw scattered across the altar steps could come close to the original tableau, this project might work. But the bored expressions she spied on several faces didn't bode well. Two girls and four boys. Surely, that couldn't be all. Where were the rest of them?

"Let's hang back till Hilda finishes. I don't want to cramp her style."

"Boy, does this bring back memories," Jennifer said, crossing her arms as she grinned at the bored teens. "Of course,

Hilda and Lizzie don't come close to Sisters Robertia and Mary Agnes. You didn't dare look bored around those gals. They'd break a ruler across your head. Or butt. Sometimes both."

"I sense you took a toll on their supply of rulers."

"Every chance I could. I'd go out of my way to give Sister Mary Agnes a hard time. She loved me anyway. Never could understand why. That's probably why she kept casting me as Mary."

Kelly did her best to look incredulous. "You portrayed the Virgin Mary?"

"Don't look so shocked. I had my innocent moments. But Sister Mary Agnes had my number, all right. Maybe she was hoping that virginity would be contagious."

A laugh started, but Kelly stifled it, because Hilda had turned their way, beckoning them forward. "Now, boys and girls, let me introduce the young women who'll be in charge from now on. Kelly Flynn and Jennifer Stroud."

Kelly and Jennifer stepped beside Hilda. Lizzie was already at the doorway leading to the basement classrooms below. Another busy night at Saint Mark's.

Kelly gave the kids a friendly smile. "Hey, guys, how're you doing?" Then she turned to Hilda. "Thanks, Hilda. Jennifer and I will take it from here." Hilda didn't waste a moment in leaving, as she hastened toward the doorway. Kelly scanned the teenagers' faces. "Jennifer and I are going to take over for these overworked ladies and help you guys do a great job. I brought extra scripts with instructions if you've lost yours." Watching Hilda close the door behind her, Kelly turned to Jennifer.

Jennifer was already in sync. She checked over both shoulders. "All clear. No clergy in sight."

"Okaaaay," Kelly said, strolling to the edge of the steps. "Let's talk. Jennifer and I are here because those sweet little old ladies told us you guys weren't paying attention. So, now the sweet old gals are gone, and you've got us. And, believe me, we're not sweet." She gave them her Disappointed Coach stare. "We're here to make sure you guys don't make fools of yourselves or embarrass your parents next week when you're up in front of the entire congregation."

"So, pay attention, and we'll have you prepped and outta here in an hour, okay?" Jennifer promised.

Kelly observed the distracted gazes mixed with a couple of attentive looks that met her announcement. Time to take action. Handing the scripts to Jennifer, Kelly slid her hands into her back jeans pockets and withdrew her music player and her cell phone.

"*Okay, listen up!*" she yelled in her On-the-Field Coach voice. The teenagers' heads jerked up like puppets. Holding her electronic devices in the air, she ordered, "Unplug *now*! Cell phones, iPods, BlackBerries, off and in your pockets. I wanta see 'em. And either pop the ear buds, or I do it for you."

She eyeballed the boy who sat at the foot of the steps. He gave her a sheepish look and shoved his electronic gear into his pockets. Advancing up the steps, she watched the two sprawling teens try to hide their cell phones. "Too late, guys, you're busted. Hand over the phones. You can text when we're finished." She stretched out her hand.

"Awwww, man," one of them replied, giving her the Aggrieved Teenager look. Utter disgust, disbelief, and disrespect all rolled into one. He glanced up at Kelly and saw that she was unfazed. *"Awwww, man!"* he whined again and handed over the phone.

"Hey, I'm not your mom, so I don't care if you're pissed."

Kelly heard a snicker beside her. The other boy clicked off and handed her his phone.

Jennifer stepped forward then, hands on hips. "All right, now that we've got your attention, how many of you don't have a clue what you're supposed to do during the service?"

All but two hands shot up to the sound of snickers. The blonde girl sitting beside one of the now-phoneless guys spoke up. "Well, I'm the angel, and I already *know* my part," she announced proudly.

The boy beside her rolled his eyes. "Oh, yeah, Britney-Beyoncé. Is your mom making your costume?"

She scowled at him. "Shut *up!*"

Kelly exchanged a knowing glance with Jennifer. Ahhhh, junior high school years. Memories best forgotten.

Jennifer pointed to the blonde girl. "Theater group, right?"

"Yeah! I was the lead in our school musical this fall."

The boy beside her rolled his eyes again.

"Fantastic," Jennifer continued, glancing around the rest of the group. "Now, we've got Angel, who else have we got here?" She pointed to the guys beside the drama queen. "Let me guess, shepherds, right?" They both nodded.

The boy sitting beside the lectern spoke up. "I'm the Narrator."

"And you've got all the lines. Have you learned them yet?"

He shrugged with a good-natured smile. "I'm working on it."

Maggie Sefton

Kelly caught the eye of the quieter boy at the foot of the steps. "Who're you?"

"I'm supposed to be Joseph."

Kelly glanced around the empty sanctuary. "We're still missing people. Aren't we supposed to have Wise Men?"

Jennifer approached the girl who leaned on a middle step, still looking bored. "Well, we've got Angel so you must be Mary. They're only two girls' parts."

"Whatever," the girl said, barely glancing at Jennifer.

"I know how you feel. Sister Mary Agnes made me play Mary three years in a row."

The girl deigned to give Jennifer a fleeting glance. "My *mother* is making me do this." Her voice dripped disgust. Oh, the horror.

"Just be glad you don't have Sister Mary Agnes. At least you can complain to your mom and make her feel guilty. Sister Mary Agnes would just whomp you upside the head."

The shepherds snickered again.

Kelly couldn't resist. "Boy, I'm glad I didn't go to your school." More smiles appeared.

"Okay, I'm gonna make it easy and call each of you by your part," Jennifer announced, pointing to the teenagers. "Angel, Shep One, Shep Two, Narrator, Joseph, and Mary." She started handing out scripts. "Here are extra scripts. Don't lose these. I'll be directing you guys in this production, so listen up. Kelly coaches baseball, so she's in charge of keeping you guys in line. Don't mess with her. She's even tougher than Sister Mary Agnes."

"How come you get to be director?" Kelly played along, taking a script.

176

"Because I went to parochial school. All you did was show up for Sunday Mass."

Kelly threw up her hands in surrender mode and didn't say a word, enjoying the sound of youthful laughter rippling through the group. Thanks to Jennifer, maybe they could whip this bunch into shape.

Then came the sound of doors opening at the back of the sanctuary, followed by young male voices. Changing voices. Cracking high, dropping low. Kelly turned to see three teenage boys stroll up the aisle. The missing Wise Men, at last. The sandy brown–haired one in front looked familiar.

"Coach Flynn?" he called as he and his companions drew near. "What are you doing here?"

"*O'Leary?*" Kelly exclaimed, recognizing her favorite baseman, best hitter, and all-around troublemaker from last summer's baseball leagues.

"In the flesh, Coach," he said as he and Kelly clasped hands in a jock handshake. "You runnin' this show now?"

"Let me guess, you and your friends are the Wise Men, right?"

"That's us, Coach." O'Leary and his buddies wrapped arms around each other's shoulders and mugged with cheesy smiles. "Three Wise Men. We got the goods."

The shepherds groaned. So did Narrator.

Kelly grinned. "Goods or not, guys, if you're late again, I'll kick your butts."

"Whoa!"

"Hey, she can hit it outta the park, so shut up," O'Leary said.

"Awesome!" the third boy exclaimed.

"Hey, Coach Flynn, when are you gonna have tryouts for next year? O'Leary said you straightened out his swing."

O'Leary made a dramatic swing with an invisible bat. "*Home run!* Outta the park!"

This time the entire cast on the steps groaned.

Kelly just laughed. "They any good?" She nodded to O'Leary.

"Oh, yeah. Not as good as me, of course," he said with a swagger.

"Gonna hurl," Narrator warned.

Kelly laughed out loud, as did Jennifer. *Okay, now we're getting somewhere.* Humor always worked.

"Tell you what, guys. Do a stand-up job with this Nativity scene, and I'll watch for you in the tryouts. I'll even put in a good word with Coach Townsend."

"Whoa!"

"Awesome!"

"Totally!"

Jennifer handed them scripts. "Three Wise Guys is more like it."

"Hey, that's good," O'Leary said, incapable of insult. "Which of us is which? You know, Bal-something or another."

"Melchior, Caspar, and Balthazar," Jennifer announced, then pointed. "O'Leary, you're Melchior. You bring the gold."

"Got that right."

Jennifer just shook her head and pointed to the other two boys. "Caspar, you're bringing frankincense. It's used in perfumes, so it's really valuable. And you're Balthazar. You bring myrrh, most precious of all. Couldn't bury people without it."

Balthazar raised his fist, threatening. "See? I'll bury you guys next summer!"

"Now I'm gonna hurl," O'Leary threatened.

"Get on up there," Kelly ordered, pointing toward the steps. "No more mouthing off. O'Leary, that means you. And keep your buds in line."

"Got it, Coach."

"Do we have to wear those stupid bathrobes?" Caspar complained as he followed O'Leary.

"Yeah, they're *so* lame," Balthazar said, screwing up his face as he sank on the steps beside Mary. She gave him an Annoyed Teenage Girl stare, only used when trying to ignore annoying teenage boys.

"Well, if you guys have a costume or something that looks like a robe, go ahead and use it," Kelly suggested.

"My mother is making my costume," Angel announced, tossing her blonde curls over her shoulder. Stardom was waiting. "She's even making wings."

As if on cue, O'Leary and his buddies grabbed their stomachs and heaved. Loudly. Sheps One and Two convulsed on the steps. Even Mary smiled.

"Shut *up*, you guys!"

"Use whatever you can that fits the setting," Jennifer said when the laughter died down. Then, glancing at Mary, she added, "You have beautiful reddish brown hair. Why don't you wear it loose around your shoulders, okay? I've got a shawl that would look great on you. I'll bring it that night."

Mary looked up, obviously surprised, and gave Jennifer a little nod. "Okay."

"Oh, and one more thing. I'm fairly certain the Blessed Mother didn't wear a nose ring, so lose it for the service, all right?"

Mary rolled her eyes. "Whatever."

Fifteen

Kelly stared at the menu board hanging on the wall. She couldn't decide between the Holiday Spiced Latte or the Mint Chocolate Hot Chocolate. Decisions, decisions. Feeling the press of customers behind her awaiting their sugar rush, she handed a bill to the barista. "Holiday Spiced Latte to go, please."

Stepping aside, Kelly surveyed her favorite specialty coffee shop in Old Town Fort Connor. Over a century old, the building's high ceiling was still the original beaten tin imprinted with designs. The aromas of coffee, spices, and chocolate hung in the air, making Kelly hungry. She deliberately turned away from the glass case containing to-die-for desserts. The shop was jammed with holiday shoppers doing exactly the same thing she was—taking a caffeine and sugar break before facing the crowds again.

The barista handed over the latte, and Kelly inhaled the sweet aromas she always associated with the holidays—cinnamon, cloves, allspice, nutmeg. All mixed into something sweet with caffeine. Now, if she could just finish her shopping before the sugar put her to sleep. All she had left to buy was wrapping paper and gift tags. Tomorrow night would be the perfect time to wrap Steve's gifts while he was out at a local builders' meeting. Tonight was another tennis match with Megan and Marty.

Kelly took a sip and savored the drink while she wove her way around the customers and tables. Late morning sun highlighted the colors of the mural of Van Gogh's *Starry Night* that was painted on the wall. As she neared the doorway, she recognized a young woman entering the shop. Her dark hair was pushed up under a knit cloche hat and a fabric baby carrier hung around her neck and shoulders. Inside the carrier was a sleeping baby.

"Lucy! I haven't seen you for weeks. How're you doing?"

"Hey, Kelly, I'm doing great. It's good to see you. By the way, I've finally spun the last bag of your Wyoming wool. I'll get it to you next week if you like."

Kelly gave a dismissive wave. "Naw, wait till after Christmas. I'm keeping that one for myself." She leaned over and checked the snoozing babe. "Wow, he's gotten so much bigger."

"Yeah, he's gonna be a big boy, aren't you, David?" Lucy said, stroking the front of his snowsuit.

"Are you coming to the Lambspun Christmas party?"

"I wouldn't miss it for the world. You know Lambspun is like my family. Thanks to you guys, my spinning business is doing really well." Her pretty face spread with a smile.

"Everyone will be there, so you'll get a chance to catch up. It's on Christmas Eve this year, because some of us are helping at the Saint Mark's family service that afternoon." She held up crossed fingers. "Jennifer and I took over Hilda and Lizzie's teenagers last night. They're doing the Nativity story, and believe me, it's a challenge."

Lucy laughed. "Hilda and Lizzie told me all about it. I'll be at the service, so I'll keep my fingers crossed for you and Jennifer."

Kelly could remember when Lucy didn't have much to laugh about. A year ago Lucy was pregnant and abandoned by her cheating lover—and the prime suspect in his murder.

"Thanks, Lucy. Jennifer and I will need all the good wishes we can get." Her cell phone jangled then, and Kelly dug in her pocket. A business client's number flashed on the screen. "See you next week, Lucy. Take care," she said, waving goodbye.

Kelly flipped her phone open as she pushed through the doorway and out into the crisp air and sunshine. Sunny, bright, and cold. Colorado cold.

The trunk top of Kelly's sporty red car popped open, and she lifted a huge bag of dog food from inside. Carl's favorite kibbles. Carl started his yipping I-see-food bark as he danced beside the backyard fence. Late afternoon sunshine slanted over the foothills, ready to disappear. Sunset came early now.

"Yes, it's all for you, Carl," Kelly said as she carried the bag to her front door. Digging for her keys, Kelly heard her name.

"Hey, Kelly," Rosa yelled across the driveway. "I need to ask you something."

"Sure thing," Kelly called over her shoulder as she pushed the cottage door open. Hefting the bag into the kitchen, she plopped it onto the floor. She could off-load it into the plastic storage bin later.

Rosa rushed into the cottage. "Kelly, did you buy one of those Christmas capes?"

"No, I'm not really the cape type. Why?"

"Darn," Rosa said, deflated. "One of our best out-of-state customers called this morning, and she wants a cape, really bad. And we're sold out, of course."

"Did she see a picture or something on your website?"

"No, apparently a friend sent her a photo of hers, and now this woman is hot to have one for herself. She buys a ton of yarns regularly, so we're trying to help her find a cape. She's hoping to buy someone else's, and she's willing to pay double."

"Wow, she really does want one badly."

Rosa nodded and tucked a fallen strand of dark hair behind her ear. "Juliet only brought us seven capes. We could have sold twice that many."

"How are you going to track the buyers? Credit card receipts?" Kelly asked as she checked her coffeepot. Empty. *Rats.*

"Yep. Six customers paid with a check or credit card. Megan, Claudia, Sheila, one newcomer to the shop, and two online customers. I've checked with each, and they all want to keep their capes."

"Sheila bought one?" Kelly asked, surprised. Sheila didn't look like a cape type, either. And she certainly hadn't demonstrated a flair for fashion. "Somehow, I can't picture Sheila wearing it."

"I think she said it was a present for her niece."

"How about the last buyer? Do you have any kind of record like a receipt or something?"

"Only one customer bought with cash, and I sold it to him. I remember his saying he was visiting Fort Connor on business, and he just happened to see our shop. Of course we have no record of his name, just the receipt." She sighed. "That's why I'm asking everyone I can think of. We'd really like to keep this lady from Michigan happy, if you know what I mean." Rosa headed for the door. "I'd better get back to the shop."

Kelly followed her outside. "I'll keep my ears open and ask around, Rosa. See you later."

A familiar red truck lumbered down the driveway. Steve. Kelly reached for the tennis rackets in her trunk before closing it. Was there still pizza in the freezer? she wondered. If not, maybe she and Steve could make a run through a fast-food place before they headed to the courts.

"Better leave those rackets," Steve said as he stepped down from his monster truck. Serious trucks roamed Colorado roads, scaring away the smaller ones. "Marty called and said he and Megan can't make it tonight. So what do you say we go out to dinner?"

"I take it you've already checked, and we're out of pizza," Kelly said, smiling as he approached. "We could steal some of Carl's kibbles. I just bought a big bag."

"And risk losing an arm? I don't think so. Carl would break through the glass door if he saw us eating his food. How about the Jazz Bistro? We haven't been for a month."

"Works for me," she said, watching Megan suddenly drive up and pull to a stop in front of the cottage.

"Hey, how come you two can't play tonight? Turning chicken?" Kelly made cowardly chicken squawks as Megan leaned out the car window.

"You wish," Megan taunted with a grin. "Naw, I've gotta drag Marty out shopping tonight. He's barely bought a thing and Christmas is next week. I had to bribe him to give up tennis tonight."

"With what?"

"Food, what else? I promised him a blueberry pie. And that reminds me. Can I ask you a big favor?"

"You can ask," Kelly teased. "What do you need?"

"I told Mimi I'd be in charge of organizing food for the Lambspun Christmas party. Mimi and the others are simply swamped with taking care of customers. And I wondered if you would make some more of Helen's gingersnap cookies for the party. Please, pretty please."

"Wow, I'm not used to someone asking me to cook anything. Let me think—"

"Hey, we'll be glad to make gingersnaps," Steve interrupted. "I saw more of that stuff left in the cabinet. You know, molasses, brown sugar, and ginger. All that stuff."

Kelly turned and saw the devilish grin on Steve's face. "What's this 'we' business? You just want to eat the cookie dough like last time. We pigged out. I thought we were going to the Jazz Bistro tonight."

"Hey, don't change your plans for me, guys. . . ."

"No, that's okay, Megan. The jazz can wait. Mimi needs our help, right? And Kelly and I are both busy every night this week. So, why don't we stay home and make cookies tonight? You know, like we did last time." He wiggled his eyebrows.

Kelly laughed deep in her throat as she caught his meaning. She remembered the last time they made cookies. "Sure, we can stay at home tonight and . . . make cookies."

"Thanks, guys. I really appreciate it."

"Our pleasure, Megan, believe me," Steve said.

Sixteen

"**Carl,** sit!" Kelly ordered as she walked her dog across the driveway.

Carl hesitated just a fraction, then sat on the gravel.

"*Good* dog, good sit," Kelly said, rubbing his smooth black head. "Now, *down.*" She gave the hand signal to lie down. Once again, Carl hesitated a couple of seconds before complying. "*Good* dog!" Kelly enthused again. "Now, *stay,*" she ordered, hand up, signaling the command.

She dropped the leash and backed away slowly. Carl stayed put. Until a black truck turned into the driveway and headed their way. Carl sat up quickly.

"Okay, Carl, we'll continue our training inside the shop," Kelly said, snatching the leash from the gravel as the truck pulled into a space in front of Lambspun.

REYNOLDS SHEEP BREEDERS read the white block lettering on the side of the truck.

A tall woman in jeans and denim jacket hopped out of the truck. "Hi, there," she called to Kelly. "Do you know if Mimi Shafer is in the shop? I'm looking for her."

Kelly paused on Lambspun's front patio. When she stopped, Carl sat obediently on her left. "Good dog," she said, patting his head before answering the woman. "Sorry, I don't. I haven't been inside the shop this morning." She scanned the cars parked outside. "I don't see her car, so I don't think Mimi's arrived yet."

"That's okay. We can wait out here," the woman said.

We? Kelly wondered.

The woman walked to the back of her truck, opened it up, and lifted out a fuzzy white bundle. An armful of fuzzy white. A small lamb rested comfortably in her arms as if used to being there.

"Whoa, what a cute lamb," Kelly said as the woman approached. The lamb bleated but didn't make a move.

Carl, however, immediately broke his sit and stood up. *"Woof?"*

It was more a questioning what-the-heck-is-that bark than a declarative stay-away-from-my-house bark.

"Carl, sit," Kelly ordered, giving a little reminder tug on his collar to make sure he complied. "Don't worry," she reassured the woman. "Carl obeys pretty well, but I don't think he's ever seen a lamb this close. So it's pretty darn tempting to go check it out. He's pretty curious."

"That's okay. Annie's real used to dogs. We've got three sheepdogs at the ranch." The woman leaned over and held Annie's hooves close enough for Carl to sniff.

Carl sniffed each hoof thoroughly while Annie gave an occasional bleat.

"Whoa, she's so tame," Kelly said, unable to resist stroking Annie's fuzzy white side. Soft white wool. Very familiar to the touch. A little rough in its natural state, still on the sheep.

"She should be. We raised her from birth after her mother died. We had to bottle-feed her by hand."

"You're kidding!"

"No, I'm not," the woman said with a laugh. "Round the clock, too. My husband and I took the night shifts."

"Whoa, no wonder she's so docile." Kelly stroked again, while Annie hung in her owner's arms contentedly. She looked up at Kelly with jet black eyes.

"Baaaah!"

"She is *so* cute," Kelly said, rubbing Annie's little head, her little round nose. She could feel Carl scowling at her, so she reached over to pat his head. "You're cute, too, Carl, even if you're not little and cuddly."

"Yeah, my kids just fell in love with her from the start. After a few days of hand-feeding this wee little fuzz ball, I looked at my husband and said, 'This one is definitely not going to auction.' By the way, I'm Shelly Reynolds." She reached a hand out beneath Annie.

Kelly shook her hand. "Nice to meet you, Shelly. I'm Kelly Flynn. And I think you made a good call. Does she live in the barn now that she's bigger?"

"Oh, no." Shelly shook her head. "She's in the house with us. She's even housebroken, believe it or not."

Kelly rolled her eyes. "Oh, my gosh. Don't tell me how easy she was, or you'll give Carl a complex. He's peeved enough as it is."

"I hear you. We have to give the dogs enough time as well." She set Annie on the ground beside them. Annie bleated twice and set about exploring the stone steps of the patio. "Animals truly rule around our place, I guess."

"Your ranch is near Wellesley?" Kelly pointed toward the sign on the truck.

"Yeah, on County Road 17, near the intersection with County Road 68. It's been in my husband's family for generations."

"You know, my aunt and uncle raised sheep. They owned all this land once upon a time," Kelly said, gesturing toward the stretch of golf course, which extended all the way to the river that cut diagonally through Fort Connor. "I can still remember coming here as a little girl and seeing Uncle Jim out in the pastures." She watched Annie sniff the shrubbery bordering the stone patio. "They kept it going as long as they could make a profit, then times got bad and they had to sell the sheep. Uncle Jim started working for the state land service after that. They boarded horses, too."

"You know, I remember Helen and Jim coming to visit my father-in-law years ago. I grew up here, too, so I remember them. You must be their niece from the East. Mimi said you'd moved back to town."

Kelly nodded. "Yep. Helen's cottage is mine now. Complete with mortgage."

Shelly laughed a throaty laugh. "Isn't that the truth."

A familiar car pulled into the driveway then. "There's Mimi now," Kelly said, getting an idea. "Are you and Annie here for a visit? Because Mimi and the others could sure use a stress reliever right now. Annie is just the ticket. Fuzzy and cute."

"Actually, Mimi and I met at the community bazaar last weekend. We brought some sheep and goats for the petting zoo. And Annie posed for pictures. Ever since a story appeared in the newspaper about her, we've had schools and church groups ask for her to come for kids' events and such."

"Really? Hey, you're a celebrity, Annie."

Annie couldn't be bothered to reply. She was much too interested in sniffing and sampling dried plants beneath the shrubbery.

"Hey, Mimi, you should let us take your picture with Annie, here. She's a celeb. You can use it in your holiday ad," Kelly said as Mimi walked toward them.

"That's a cute idea, Kelly. Maybe I will." Mimi reached down and stroked Annie, who glanced up and bleated once, then returned to nibbling plants.

Meanwhile, Carl sulked beside Kelly, head on his outstretched paws. "You-Know-Who is jealous, so you'd best pay some attention to him," Kelly added.

"Oh, of course," Mimi said, coming over to stroke Carl's head. "We'll make sure to take a photo of Carl, too. He's such a handsome dog, aren't you, Carl?"

Carl lifted his head regally. Noblesse oblige. It was about time someone paid heed.

"I'll make sure Carl's ready for his photo op." She patted her left leg in the signal to *heel* and quickly headed down the stone pathway that wound around the shop to the back, Carl falling into step beside Kelly. Pete's café and caffeine awaited.

"Good job, Carl," Shelly called after them.

Annie watched Carl trot away and bleated once, then returned to nibbling dead grass.

"I'm afraid doggies aren't allowed in the café, Carl," Kelly said as she approached the back door. "So you'll have to wait outside." Draping Carl's leash around a banister, she gave him the *down* and *stay* commands before racing up the steps.

Jennifer greeted Kelly as she came through the door. "I saw you coming, so I figured I'd save you the time." She poured a large mug of coffee and handed it to Kelly. "No need to keep Carl waiting. I'll be over on break in a few minutes."

"Wow, now that's what I call service," Kelly said, accepting the mug. "Is anyone else at the table?"

"Oh, yeah, and they can use your help, too. So it's a good thing you've finished Steve's scarf," Jennifer said as she returned to her customers.

Help with what? Kelly wondered as she took a sip of the black brew and hastened outside. Carl was dutifully waiting.

"Good dog, *Carl!*" she praised him, giving another head rub before patting her left leg. Carl immediately rose to walk beside her all the way to the shop.

Kelly couldn't believe it. She was knitting another hat. A hat for the shop, too. For sale, yet. Kelly still couldn't grasp the concept that someone, anyone, would actually pay money for her knitting. *Imagine that!*

But according to Mimi, some poor unsuspecting person was going to buy her hat, wrap it up, and present it to another unsuspecting person as a gift. *Her* knitted hat. Who would have thought?

Lambspun needed hats quickly. They'd sold out last weekend, and customers were still coming in asking for the "special" knitted hats. Special because of the colorful yarns Mimi created when dying the fibers. Mimi's answer was to recruit every Lambspun regular to knit hats—as many hats as they could between now and Christmas. And knit them fast. She would supply the yarns for the last-minute knitting sessions. She'd even brought pizza.

Kelly looked around the library table, crowded with knitters like herself who'd answered Mimi's call. All of them knitting hats. Kids' hats. Baby hats. Ski hats. Hats with pom-poms. Hats with tassels. Striped, solid, patterned. All kinds of hats. Kelly had chosen one of Mimi's gorgeous variegated yarns—bubblegum pink, deep rose, and fuchsia. So far, the knitted cloche was turning out exactly the way it should. Thanks to the circular needles, all Kelly had to do was the knit stitch and stockinette magically formed.

"You need more coffee, Kelly?" Jennifer asked as she gathered empty dishes off the table.

"When don't I need more coffee?" Kelly joked. "How come you're still waitressing? Aren't you going to the real estate office this afternoon?"

"No need. Everyone has gone into holiday mode. Clients aren't calling, either, so I thought I'd help out Pete. The café is in holiday crush like the shop." She looked around the table. "Anyone else need something?"

Various knitters called out to Jennifer. Even Claudia asked for something, Kelly noticed. Surrounded by two of Lambspun's friendliest regulars, Claudia seemed almost like her old self—talking with the others, smiling occasionally. Talk around the table concentrated on the holidays and all things related. Safe territory. Kelly was glad to see Claudia included once again. Everyone was in a jovial holiday mood.

Everyone except Lizzie, that is. Kelly noticed Lizzie was not her usual bubbly, talkative self this afternoon. She joined in occasionally but mostly sat and knitted quietly. Kelly sensed there was something bothering Lizzie, but there was no way she could ask at the crowded table. Everyone else would be privy to the conversation.

Carl let out a loud sigh as he lay at her feet. Another loud sigh. He'd been sulking and sighing for nearly two hours while Kelly knitted with the others. He'd been the picture of obedience. Staying in his *down*, despite the constant provocation that continued to trot around the shop, sniffing yarns, nibbling at loose fibers, causing all manner of oohs and aahs and "Isn't she cute?" and other adoring comments. All to the rhythm of regular bleats and "baas." *Annie, the Celebrity Lamb.*

Kelly reached down and stroked her dog's shiny black head. Annie was, once again, holding court in the central yarn room, posing for pictures with customers. "Good dog, Carl. You're a sweet boy, yes, you are," Kelly crooned. "And so patient, too. You're a saint. Saint Carl."

Carl collapsed his head on the floor between his paws again with an even louder sigh.

Suddenly a familiar laugh sounded from the foyer, floating over all the hubbub. Jayleen.

"Lord a'mighty! Has Mimi turned Lambspun into a petting zoo? Hey, Shelly, I take it this little rascal is one of yours."

Kelly waved and watched Jayleen chat with Annie's owner for a minute before approaching the knitting table. "Hey, Jayleen. Wanta knit a hat? Lambspun needs hats. They're all out."

Jayleen chuckled as she grabbed a chair beside Kelly and straddled it backwards in her usual style. "No, thanks, Kelly. I knitted a bunch for the homeless shelter earlier this month. I'm knitted out right now. I've got my hands full just getting ready for the holidays."

"Don't tell me you volunteered to run another kids' party."

"No, someone else has the pleasure this year. I'm heading out to the shops to buy presents. I've been so busy, I haven't bought a thing."

"That sounds like Marty. Megan had to take him shopping last night."

Claudia's head turned swiftly at the sound of her attorney's name. "Are you talking about my Marty?"

Kelly gestured. "Claudia, meet Jayleen. Like Marty, she's been too busy to do her Christmas shopping until today. Megan took Marty out for the first time last night."

Claudia gave a little smile as she returned to her knitting. "That's because Marty's working so hard to help me. He's so smart, and he's taking such good care of me."

Jayleen shot Kelly a look and lowered her voice. "That's the gal, huh? Mimi told me she's facing a passel of trouble. Damn shame. She looks like a nice gal."

Kelly waited until the conversation rose in volume before leaning closer to Jayleen. "Yeah, she is, and things aren't looking too good right now. But Claudia is still convinced that Marty's going to 'save' her." Kelly shook her head.

Jayleen arched a brow. "Damn. At her age, she oughta know better than that. The only person who can save you is *you*."

Kelly gave her a rueful smile. "I guess Claudia hasn't discovered that yet. Apparently she's always depended on her husbands or other men to take care of her. This must be the first time she's ever had to stand alone. And she's not doing too well. We're all afraid she's going to break down completely if she ever has to go to jail."

Jayleen stared across the table. "That's too bad."

Suddenly, Annie trotted right up beside Jayleen and bleated.

"Well, hey there, you little cutie," Jayleen said, stroking Annie's head.

Unfortunately, Annie's butt was right in Carl's face. Insult to injury. It was clearly more than he could bear. Carl rose to his feet and shoved his face beside Jayleen's free hand.

"Whoa . . . hey, Carl. How're you doing?" Jayleen said, chuckling as she rubbed both animals' heads. Annie continued to bleat while Carl glared.

"Does anyone have a camera?" Kelly called around the table. "This is too cute."

"I do," one of the knitters said, pulling it from her bag.

"This is a precious shot." She scrambled around the table and clicked away.

"Good boy, Carl. I think that's about all you can tolerate for today, right? Come on, I'll take you home," Kelly said as she gathered his leash. "Jayleen, make sure you and Curt come to the shop party next week."

"Wouldn't miss it for the world."

"Oh, and if you want a double dose of Yuletide spirit, drop by Saint Mark's and see if Jennifer and I were able to corral those teenagers into line for the Christmas family service." Turning to leave, she added, "Save my seat, Lizzie, I'll be right back. Carl, *heel*."

Lizzie quickly rose from her chair and followed after her. "It'll be safe, dear. I'll walk with you to the door."

Kelly figured her instincts were correct. Lizzie had something on her mind and didn't want to share it in public. Kelly headed for the front door and outside, Lizzie right behind her. They paused in the driveway, where no one was around.

"What's up, Lizzie? I can tell something's on your mind."

Lizzie glanced toward the golf course for a few seconds before speaking. "I've been worrying ever since this morning, Kelly, and I need to tell someone. But I'm not sure who to tell."

"What is it, Lizzie? What's the matter? Did something happen to you?" Kelly peered at the elderly knitter with concern.

Lizzie shook her head. "No, not to me. It's . . . it's Claudia. I . . . I heard something this morning at the senior center which has turned everything upside down. I . . . I don't know what to think anymore."

"What did you hear?"

Lizzie stared at the ground for a few seconds then spoke in a soft voice. "I was talking with one of my friends, Marjorie. We've known each other for years. Well, I was sharing with her how upset I was that everyone was treating Claudia differently. Like she'd caused Juliet's death. Well, Marjorie looked at me strangely and said that she believed Claudia was guilty, too. That surprised me, so I rushed to Claudia's defense again, saying she didn't even know Juliet Renfrow."

She looked up into Kelly's eyes. "That's when Marjorie told me that Claudia had asked her about Jeremy's librarian girlfriend over a month ago. Marjorie said she told Claudia all about Juliet. How Jeremy and Juliet had been dating for several months. And Marjorie even pointed Juliet out to Claudia one day at the senior center when Juliet came to pick up library books."

Kelly stared back at Lizzie and saw the shock and betrayal in her pale blue eyes. *Claudia had lied.* She did know who Juliet Renfrow was. She'd lied to Lizzie. She'd lied to Marty and to the police. She'd lied to them all.

Had Claudia been deliberately misleading them all this time? Were her "emotional breakdowns" simply good acting? Had the Merry Widow played them all for fools, trying to gain sympathy so everyone would feel sorry for her? Manipulated them into helping her?

"I'm so sorry to hear that, Lizzie," Kelly said, reaching out to give Lizzie's arm a squeeze. "That's a shock to hear, for all of us. We really like Claudia, but . . . but this does change things, and you know it."

"Oh, my, yes." Lizzie gave a big sigh.

"You're going to have to tell Burt. Do you want to come over to my cottage for some privacy? I'll see if I can snatch Burt away from the shop for a few minutes."

"Thank you, Kelly, that would be better. I . . . I just don't feel like going back to the shop just yet."

"And don't worry about taking Claudia to her motel tonight," Kelly said as she signaled Carl to heel again. "I have a feeling Marty will want to speak with Claudia."

Seventeen

Kelly sipped her coffee as she leaned over the café table. "Did Marty call you after he spoke with Claudia last night?"

Burt shook his head as he traced an invisible pattern on the oak tabletop. "No, he called this morning. He sounded down in the dumps, too. Understandably. The police will now be able to show that Claudia lied to everyone about not knowing Juliet."

"That definitely makes it look like Claudia killed her on purpose, doesn't it?"

"I'm afraid so."

"This is so sad," Kelly said, running her finger over the edge of her mug. "Claudia is such a great gal, and she had so much going for her. Why did she kill Juliet Renfrow? Did she just flip out? Go over the edge, you think?"

"Yeah, Kelly, I think that's exactly what happened with Claudia. I've spent a lot of time with her, and she is always a hair trigger between being okay and losing it. I mean, she was usually hanging on to my arm, sobbing, or just about passing out. I swear, I had to hold her up every time she was at the department. She kept collapsing." He shook his head again.

"Do you think that was all an act, Burt? I mean, it's a really effective way to gain everyone's sympathy and help. It worked with us. All of us. Maybe Claudia was manipulating us all the time."

"I don't know, Kelly. It makes me sad to think that, but maybe Claudia was convinced she could manipulate us into believing her and ignoring the evidence."

Kelly sank back into her chair. "You know, there's still a part of me that finds this whole situation hard to believe, Burt. Claudia kills Juliet to get her out of the way. Did she think Jeremy would come back to her or something? It just doesn't make sense."

Burt gave her a crooked smile. "It doesn't make sense to you, Kelly, because you've got a logical mind. But Claudia, well, logical isn't the word I'd use to describe her. She is the most emotional woman I've ever met. I have yet to see Claudia sit and think about her situation. All I've ever seen her do is react emotionally. She reacts, she doesn't think. At least not when I've been around."

Kelly pondered Burt's comment. He seemed to have nailed Claudia's behavior perfectly. At least her behavior around men.

Mimi hurried through the café doorway, heading toward the counter, apparently not noticing Burt and Kelly.

"Hey, Mimi, slow down," Kelly said. "You've still got several days till Christmas."

Mimi turned quickly and broke into a smile as she approached their table. "Hey, you two, I didn't see you there."

"You sure look happier than when I saw you a few minutes ago," Burt said, giving her hand a squeeze. "Did you convince someone to sell a cape?"

"As a matter of fact, yes. Sheila said she'll sell her cape to our Michigan customer. Yesterday, she told Rosa she didn't want to sell, but this morning she called and told me she'd changed her mind. Wasn't that nice of her?"

"It sure was. I'll have to thank Sheila when I see her," Burt said, before draining his coffee.

"Well, she'll have to get her niece another present now. Wonder if she'd like a nice Lambspun hat?" Kelly joked.

"Who's that?" Mimi asked.

"Sheila told Rosa she was giving the cape to her niece for Christmas. So why don't you sell her a Lambspun hat instead?" Kelly said as she pushed back her chair.

"That's funny. I could have sworn Sheila said she was an only child," Mimi said as she accepted a coffee mug from Eduardo. "I guess I was mistaken. Oh, Burt, can you help me bring up some dyed fleeces? Rosa can't leave the register."

"Will do. See you later, Kelly."

Kelly swung her knitting bag over her shoulder and was about to follow Mimi and Burt into the shop, when something kept her in her chair. She wanted to get up, go into the shop, and finish her Lambspun hat. It was nearly done. Still, Kelly found herself sitting where she was.

What is it? Something about Mimi's last comment kept nibbling at the back of her brain. What was Mimi talking about? Dyed fleeces, Christmas capes, Sheila's niece . . .

The little buzzer inside Kelly's head went off. She remembered something. Mimi was right. Sheila did imply she was an only child. Kelly remembered it, too. "It was just my father and me," she'd told them around the knitting table.

Why then would Sheila tell Rosa she'd bought the cape for her niece? Was that another instance of Sheila lying? Why would she lie about something so innocuous? Just like she'd lied about the phone message from the Sarasota retirement home. Why would Sheila lie about such trivial things?

Kelly signaled the café waitress for more coffee as she pulled out her knitting. She could just as easily finish her Lambspun hat here in the café where it was quiet. There was something else buzzing around the back of her brain. *What is it?*

Picking up the knit stitch where she left off, Kelly watched the neat stockinette pattern form on her circular needles. Meanwhile, the annoying little thought kept buzzing. Not close enough to come into her awareness, staying just out of reach. Something about Sheila's present for her niece. Was she an adopted niece? Childless people often called their friends' children "nieces" or "nephews."

Kelly reminded herself there was a simple way to find out. Claudia would know. After all, Claudia had married Sheila's father. She'd know if there were stray relatives in the family.

The irony of calling Claudia to verify something registered on Kelly as she punched in the number. Claudia had
been proven to be a liar, too. *Good Lord.* Claudia lied. Sheila
lied. How was Kelly ever to find out the truth?

Claudia's voice came on the line after a couple of rings.

"Hey, Claudia, this is Kelly. How're you doing?"

Claudia's voice immediately started quavering. "Oh, Kelly,
I'm not doing very well at all," she said, sniffling. "I'm afraid
to leave my motel room ever since Marty told me about that
awful woman at the senior center. Oh, why would she lie
about me like that? It's just terrible! Now everyone thinks
I'm guilty. . . ." Tears saturated her voice now as it turned
into a wail.

Kelly decided to hold her tongue and let Claudia cry,
hoping she'd stop in a moment. She didn't. Finally Kelly
decided a firmer hand was needed.

"Claudia, you have to stop that crying, because I can't
hear a word you're saying."

Amazingly, the wailing stopped. Sniffles came over the
phone now. "I . . . I'll try, Kelly."

"Good girl," Kelly found herself saying, almost as if
Claudia had executed a Carl-like *sit.* "I wanted to ask you a
question about your late husband's family. Did he have any
other children besides Sheila?"

There was a pause, then Claudia's voice came clearly. No
sniffles to be heard. "Why, no. Sheila was his only child."

"So, he didn't have any other children from a former marriage either?"

"Heavens, no. Nathan and his wife Frances were married
over forty years."

"Did Sheila have anyone she referred to as a niece? Maybe a friend's child or something like that?"

"No, I never heard Sheila refer to anyone that way. Sheila was a solitary person. She didn't really have many friends that I knew of. Why do you ask?"

Kelly was amazed by the change in Claudia's voice. Now it was a normal conversational tone. No wailing, no quavering. Clearly Claudia could turn those emotional tirades on and off in an instant. Like a light switch.

"Oh, someone said that she'd heard Sheila had a niece. I guess the woman was mistaken," Kelly lied quickly, surprised how easily it had come. Now she was lying like Claudia and Sheila. Not good. "By the way, don't be afraid to return to the shop, Claudia. It was good to see you around the table yesterday. Like you used to be. After all, it's the holidays."

"Well, if you think so." Her voice softened again.

"Absolutely. Take care, Claudia."

Kelly clicked off before the tears started. Flip of a switch.

"Hi, Kelly, how's that Lambspun hat going? It looks almost finished," a familiar voice said nearby.

"It's getting there, Connie," Kelly said to the middle-aged woman who stood in the doorway, arms laden with Christmas yarns. "I haven't seen you here at the shop much lately. Are you cutting back your work hours for the holidays?"

Connie shrugged. "Yeah, a little. I've been having lots of family visiting this month. It's really getting hectic."

"Hectic holidays, you got that right," she said, gathering her knitting bag and following Connie into the shop. "I'm amazed you're able to work and shop and still entertain relatives."

"Well, they really entertain themselves," Connie said as she refilled yarn bins along the wall that opened into the shop. "They're in the mountains now, skiing. They'll spend several days up there. Then they'll spend time in Denver, poking around before they return to Fort Connor and start exploring Old Town."

Kelly fingered a skein of variegated blue alpaca wool before Connie tucked it into a bin with the others. "Steve and I are hoping to find some time after the holidays to go skiing. After all the hectic has slowed down to normal."

"Ummmm," was all Connie said in reply.

Glancing at her, Kelly noticed Connie was staring into the central yarn room, which was crowded with holiday shoppers. Only the very confident fast knitters or the most optimistic knitters were attempting new projects this close to Christmas.

"Excuse me, Kelly, I'm going to keep an eye on someone. I've seen her before, and I don't trust her."

Kelly reached out to stop Connie. "Have you seen someone stealing?"

Connie nodded. "A couple of weeks ago. I haven't told Mimi, because she wasn't stealing yarns. But I want to keep an eye on her anyway. She may start slipping stuff into her coat pockets."

"Which woman?" Kelly peered into the room.

"See the woman with the black slacks and green sweater? That's the one."

Kelly scanned the room and found the woman Connie

mentioned, and she did a double take. *Sheila.* "Are you sure that's the same woman?"

"Positive. I don't think she knew I worked for the shop, so she didn't pay attention to me at first. But I got a good look at her."

"What the heck was she stealing?"

Connie glanced around at the customers who were browsing closer and beckoned Kelly into the hallway. She bent her head closer to Kelly's. "I was sitting on a stool near the bookshelves, changing the magazines one day, and I watched her rifle through Claudia's knitting bag."

"Did she take anything?"

"Yeah, I saw her take Claudia's car keys. I recognized them, because there's a red pom-pom on the key chain."

Kelly stared back at Connie. "What did she do with them? Put them in her pocket?"

Connie nodded. "Yeah, and then she left. I watched through the window as she drove off. Then, the funny thing is, she came back in a little while and went through Claudia's purse again. This time, I deliberately turned around and started straightening stuff on the table. I saw her drop the keys back into the purse. She must have noticed me watching, because she mumbled something like she found them on the floor. Yeah, *right*," Connie said scornfully.

"Where was Claudia all this time?"

"Oh, she was prancing around the shop, showing off her Christmas cape. She'd just bought it." Connie frowned. "People leave their bags around the table all the time, and it's perfectly safe. That's why I want to keep an eye on that woman. I don't trust her."

Kelly stared back toward the yarn room, glimpsing Sheila in conversation with another knitter.

What in the world was Sheila doing with Claudia's keys? Why did she take them only to return them in a few minutes? Where could she go in a few minutes? Suddenly the image of the huge discount store in the shopping center across the street from Lambspun appeared in Kelly's mind. Big Box.

"Connie, do you remember when this happened? Think," she pressed.

Connie closed her eyes. "Uhhhh, when did I change all those magazines? It was early last week . . . oh, yeah, it was Sunday before last. I remember because it was the same day Juliet brought in all the capes, and I had to hang them on display up front."

Kelly counted back on her mental calendar. The day Juliet brought the capes was the same day Mimi and Burt joined Kelly for breakfast in the café. Then Claudia showed up and told Kelly and Burt her sad story. Sheila had confronted Claudia in the shop the day before. On Saturday.

"Listen, Connie, do me a favor and keep an eye on her, but don't tell Mimi just yet. She's got enough on her mind right now. Let me do some checking around first, okay?"

"Sure, Kelly. I haven't told anyone else, because I haven't seen her steal from us. But a thief's a thief, as far as I'm concerned. So, I'll keep an eye out and let you know what I see."

"Thanks, Connie. I'll talk to you later," Kelly said as she hastened back to the café. The knitting table would be noisy and filled with chattering, happy people preparing for the holidays. Kelly didn't want happy and chattering right now. She wanted peace and quiet so she could think.

Signaling for more coffee, Kelly settled back in her cozy corner chair in the alcove off the main café. "Julie, can you bring me one of those wicked cinnamon rolls with the coffee, please?" she asked the waitress as she pulled her Lambspun hat out of the bag again.

"Sugar for lunch, huh?" Julie said, laughing, as she refilled Kelly's mug.

Kelly picked up where she'd left off knitting. Only two more inches to go before she switched to the double-point needles to finish the top of the hat. The neat stockinette pattern formed around and around the circle. One row. Another row. Meanwhile, Kelly's thoughts raced in her head like bumper cars at a carnival. Banging and bumping into one another.

Sheila had made a copy of Claudia's car keys at Big Box. That had to be it. Why else would she pilfer the keys only to return them in a few minutes? Why would Sheila want Claudia's keys? Did she plan to "reclaim" the stolen car?

Her careening thoughts slowed down somewhat, no longer bumping into each other. Was Sheila worried that Claudia would leave Fort Connor? Did she copy the keys so she could drive the car somewhere else for safekeeping? No, that wasn't it. Claudia's car was still in the motel parking lot when police confiscated it later that week.

Something else was hiding in the back of her mind, teasing her. *What is it?*

Another neat row of stockinette formed, then another, and another. All the while, Kelly kept sorting through her thoughts now that they'd slowed down to cruising speed. That always happened when she knitted. The rhythm of the stitches was meditative and peaceful. She found her thoughts becoming more ordered, and new ideas appeared.

Keys. Keys. Claudia's keys. There was something else about those keys that Kelly wasn't seeing. *What was it?* Sheila had had Claudia's car keys copied. Why? What did she want them for? Maybe she just wanted to have them. But she didn't take the car. Keys, keys . . . what else could she do with Claudia's car . . . ?

Suddenly the elusive thought downshifted and cruised right to a stop in front of Kelly's eyes. Kelly stared at her stitches. *Oh-my-God.*

Did Sheila drive Claudia's car that night? Was Sheila the one waiting in the dark on the street, waiting for Juliet Renfrow? Did Sheila deliberately kill Juliet so Claudia would be blamed?

The warm cinnamon roll appeared on the table in front of Kelly, but she barely noticed. Thoughts careened through her mind again. Bumper cars no more. NASCAR zoomed through her head now. Triple speed.

Was that possible? Did Sheila hate Claudia so much she'd actually commit murder to implicate her? Clearly, Sheila was obsessed with Claudia. The Sarasota cop said so. Sheila was convinced Claudia had killed her father and was furious when police didn't believe her. They never investigated because there was no proof. After that, Sheila started shadowing Claudia's every move, as if she were looking for something to blame on her. But would she kill someone in order to frame Claudia?

Kelly took a bite of the cinnamon roll, tasted the rich brown sugar filling mixed with the tangy lemon cream cheese frosting. She sipped her coffee and continued knitting, watching the neat stockinette stitches form one after another. Neat and orderly. Soon her careening thoughts followed suit, slowing down, pausing long enough for Kelly to consider one at a time.

Slowly she ran through the events leading up to Juliet's death. Claudia dancing about the shop with her red cape, convinced Jeremy would propose to her that afternoon. Juliet's shyness when Lizzie teased her about her date with two-timing Jeremy later that night. The next day, Claudia collapses in her motel room in hysterics, devastated by Jeremy's rejection. Juliet's body found the following day.

One row, another row, stitching around the circle. Yarn slipping between stitches, connecting one stitch to the next. *What connects Sheila to all of this?* Kelly remembered Sheila always seemed to be at the shop, either at the table crocheting or gossiping with others or taking a class. Sheila was always around, so she could have easily learned about the melodrama going on between Claudia, Jeremy, and Juliet. Gossip spread easily, Kelly noticed.

But there was something else. Kelly could feel it at the edge of her mind. It just hadn't come into focus yet. Something the Sarasota cop had said about Sheila. *What was it?*

She continued knitting around the circle, another row of stitches. *What was it?* Why couldn't she remember?

Maybe she was rusty. She hadn't involved herself in any investigations—murder or otherwise—for nine months. No sleuthing of any kind. She'd promised her friends. Kelly figured she owed it to them. Especially after last winter when her sleuthing nearly got her killed.

She knitted another row. Okay, so she was rusty. *So what?* That didn't mean she shouldn't try. There was something about Burt's conversation with the Sarasota cop. What was it Detective Watson had said about Sheila? Something about the vehicle theft charges against Claudia. *What was it?*

Suddenly the memory came into focus. Sheila had called Detective Watson the week before and asked how much jail time Claudia would get on those auto theft charges. He told her it all depended on the judge. Claudia had a clean record and there had been questions as to whether the car was stolen or borrowed. She might get work release instead of going to jail. Sheila became incensed and started swearing and yelling over the phone.

Kelly paused her knitting and took a deep drink of coffee while the memory of that conversation danced in her head. What day did Burt talk with Detective Watson? *What day was that?* Scanning through her mind, Kelly started matching bits and pieces of memories together, piecing the timeline puzzle together.

She'd asked Burt to call his Florida friend again after she'd overheard Sheila's phone conversation. Burt said he'd try to speak with the Sarasota cop who was involved in the case. Burt called the day after the bazaar. And Detective Watson told him Sheila had called the Monday of the previous week.

Monday, Monday . . . Kelly sorted through memories in her mind. That was the same day she sat at the knitting table and everyone was gossiping about Juliet's engagement and Claudia's rejection. Juliet was dining with Jeremy that evening. Claudia was crying in her motel room. And Juliet Renfrow was killed later that night. *Monday night.*

Kelly took a big bite of the cinnamon roll. Something to absorb all the caffeine. She was getting way too excited piecing this puzzle together. She needed to calm down and sort through all this methodically. Neat and orderly, like the stitches.

Did Sheila even know what Juliet Renfrow looked like?

Kelly pondered that while she knitted. Then Sheila's comment at the bazaar surfaced. Sheila said she'd been helping Saint Mark's prepare for the holidays "for a couple of weeks." Juliet Renfrow was the volunteer in charge. Of course, Sheila would have met Juliet.

Another row formed around the needles.

Thanks to the gossip around the knitting table that Monday afternoon, Sheila also knew about Juliet's late-night rendezvous with Jeremy. Sheila knew Juliet's habits and her schedule, so she knew when to steal Claudia's car and wait in the dark on Juliet's street.

Kelly kept knitting. Everything she'd come up with so far was purely supposition. Nothing could be proven. There was no way to link Sheila to the crime. Kelly took another bite of the cinnamon roll in frustration. Let the sugar kick in and see what happened. She downed it with Eduardo's black brew.

Sheila was obsessed with Claudia. "So what."

Sheila met Juliet while working at Saint Mark's. "So what."

Sheila was seen taking Claudia's car keys. "So what."

There was no proof she had made copies, let alone stolen Claudia's car from the motel parking lot and driven to Juliet's street.

Kelly pondered that one. Maybe she could ask at the motel. See if anyone noticed someone switching cars that night. After all, Sheila would have to leave her car in the motel lot in order to drive Claudia's.

Sheila owned a red Christmas cape exactly like Claudia's. "So what."

The driver who saw a woman and her car along the street that night couldn't see the woman's face beneath the hooded cape. He couldn't identify her. It could have been Claudia beneath that cape or Sheila. No way to tell for sure.

Kelly pushed away the rest of the cinnamon roll and washed down the sugar with coffee. She still only had supposition. Nothing substantial. Nothing that linked Sheila to Juliet's hit-and-run.

She knitted another row. What with all these ponderings about Sheila, the knitted hat was almost finished. Or at least, almost to double-point needle stage. The neat stockinette pattern continued to form on the needles, while Kelly searched through the remaining puzzle pieces scattered throughout her mind.

There was one little piece that had been brushed aside when the big patterns started forming. Pushed aside when the fast cars were zooming through her head.

What was it? It was one of Kelly's first little niggling thoughts when she started wondering about Sheila. What was it? Something Mimi said. Something about Sheila's Christmas cape. Sheila had previously refused to sell it. Then

215

she agreed. She was bringing in the cape so Lambspun could make their Michigan customer very happy.

Kelly knitted another row, losing track. Lost in her conjuring. What was it about Sheila selling her cape that was bothersome?

Sheila had changed her mind. "So what."

But why *did she change her mind?* insisted Kelly's little voice. Was there a reason Sheila didn't want the cape anymore? What was it? It was a beautiful Christmas cape.

Suddenly the little annoying thought that had been buzzing in the back of her head came into focus at last.

Sheila wore the Christmas cape the night she killed Juliet Renfrow. She wore the cape when she knelt beside Juliet's body on the side of the road. That's when the passing motorist saw her. He didn't see Juliet's body, because Sheila's Christmas cape was probably blocking his view. The bright red cape that draped all around Sheila as she knelt on the ground. On the ground where Juliet lay bleeding and dying.

Blood. Juliet's blood. It had to have seeped into the cape. Sheila probably didn't notice at first. But when she did, she knew she had to get rid of the cape. And what better way than to send it to some stranger in another state far away from the crime scene?

Kelly stared at the multihued pink wool in her lap, no longer seeing the knitted hat. All she saw was Sheila in her Claudia look-alike Christmas cape, driving away in Claudia's car, leaving Juliet Renfrow to die alone in the dark.

Shoving the hat back into her knitting bag, Kelly dropped some money on the café table and headed for the door. She needed more answers. Glancing into the main room as she passed, Kelly searched for Lizzie but didn't see her.

She dug her cell phone from her pants pocket as she shouldered her way out the front door. A blast of very cold wind nearly pushed Kelly back inside the shop. *Whoa.* Winter was really here to stay.

Kelly punched in Lizzie's cell phone number as she raced across the gravel driveway to her cottage and her coat. Frigid gusts rattled the bare tree limbs above her head. Huge cottonwood branches, stark and bare, swayed in the wind.

A storm front had to be moving in. Every time the wind blew hard across the foothills, that meant the weather was about to change. Sometimes for the good. Oftentimes for the bad.

Lizzie's voice came as Kelly charged into her living room, dumping her knitting bag on the nearby black leather sofa.

"Hey, Lizzie, I've got some questions for you. Sheila said she was helping over at Saint Mark's every night for a couple of weeks. Do you recall if she ever missed a night or two?"

"Goodness, Kelly, let me think," Lizzie replied. "Sheila started helping right after she came to the shop. We saw her at Mass that Sunday, and Hilda asked her if she'd be interested in volunteering. Hmmmm, yes, I think there were a few nights she missed. Why do you ask?"

Kelly slipped on her ski jacket. "Just curious. Listen, Lizzie, do you recall Sheila being overly friendly with Juliet Renfrow while she was there?"

"Sheila?" Lizzie's voice sounded surprised. "I don't think I've seen Sheila being overly friendly with anyone. Of course, she knew Juliet because we all took our marching orders from her. But I never saw Sheila spend any extra time with her."

Kelly slid past the large Christmas tree that Steve had put up in the middle of their small living room. Now they had to wiggle around the tree every time they went from the living room to the dining room and kitchen. It was beautiful, but cramped.

"Thanks, Lizzie. That's all I wanted to know," Kelly said as she grabbed her car keys and raced out the door.

There were three hours left before Kelly was to meet Steve and her friends for dinner. Plenty of time to drive to Claudia's motel. Maybe she could learn who worked the night shift at the Happy Traveler Inn the evening of Juliet's death. Maybe the motel had cameras in its parking lot. Maybe someone saw a woman in a bright red Christmas cape switching cars that night.

Kelly jumped into her sporty red car, revved the engine, and pulled out of the driveway into holiday traffic. Flipping open her cell phone, she punched in Lambspun's number. She needed to tell Connie to make sure Sheila's Christmas cape stayed in the shop in a drawer—safe and sound. And out of the mail.

Eighteen

"**Brrrr!**" Kelly said loudly as she stomped into the shop.

"Cold enough for you?" Rosa teased.

Kelly tossed her knitting bag on the table and shrugged out of her ski jacket. She kept her warm alpaca scarf around her neck. "Why do people in Colorado ask that? It's always cold enough for me. Too cold, as a matter of fact."

Rosa arranged the remaining skeins of yarns in their almost empty bins. "This will be your second winter here. You should be used to it now."

"Yeah, I know. Hey, has Burt come in this morning, or is he out doing errands?"

"He was bringing up fleeces from the basement the last time I saw him."

Kelly spotted Burt in the next room heading for the foyer.

Maggie Sefton

"There he is now. Hey, Burt, can I talk with you for a minute?" She ran to intercept him before he could disappear.

"That's about all I've got, Kelly. What's up?"

"Burt, I know you and Mimi are swamped right now with stuff for the shop, but I really need to talk with you. Could you come over to the café for a few minutes, please? I promise it won't take long."

Burt peered at her. "Well, I'll be damned. You've got that old look in your eye. I haven't seen it for months. What're you up to, Kelly?"

Kelly had to smile. Burt could always tell when she was sleuthing. "I'm not sure, Burt. That's why I need to talk with you. You can tell me if I'm crazy or if I'm on to something."

"Well, you've got my curiosity going—"

Just then, Claudia swooshed into the foyer, followed by a gust of wind. Her holiday green and red scarf dangling, coat open, she rushed up to Kelly and Burt. Her face was flushed, eyes bright and dancing. She looked like her old self. The Claudia before police charges.

"We've just had the most wonderful news!" she gushed. "Marty called and said the motel's phone records came in, and my daughter's phone call is there! Right there in black and white! Proof that I was in my motel room that night. We talked for over two hours!" She paused to suck in wind. "Isn't it wonderful! That *proves* my innocence!"

Kelly stared into Claudia's blue eyes and forced a big smile. "That's wonderful news, Claudia."

"It sure is, Claudia," Burt said in a voice Kelly recognized. His kind voice. The voice Burt used when he wanted to spare someone the whole truth. "Mimi will be delighted with the news. I saw her up front a few minutes ago. Why don't you go tell her?"

"Oh, yes, oh, yes! I can't wait to tell *everyone*," Claudia said, almost dancing with excitement.

Kelly watched Claudia hurry toward the front room, then glanced to Burt. "I get the feeling that you don't think those phone records are going to help Claudia as much as she thinks they are."

Burt smiled ruefully. "Yeah, I didn't want to say anything. She was so happy. All those records will prove is that the phone in her room was busy for over two hours. It could have been off the hook."

"You think Claudia's daughter is lying about the call?"

Burt shrugged. "No, I think she probably did call Claudia a second time, but perhaps they only talked a little while. It wouldn't take Claudia long to drive over to Juliet's neighborhood from the motel."

Kelly paused, glancing over her shoulder at browsing customers in the next room. She lowered her voice. "Maybe Claudia isn't lying, Burt. Maybe she didn't kill Juliet."

Burt eyed her again. "What are you saying, Kelly?"

"Let's go find some coffee and privacy first," she said, leading the way toward the café.

Kelly chose a table in the corner of the alcove and signaled a waitress. Burt settled across from her and folded his hands together on the table between them. Kelly recognized his thinking pose.

"I can tell something's bothering you, Kelly. What's on your mind?"

Kelly paused, choosing her words. "I'm wondering if someone else killed Juliet Renfrow."

"Accidentally, you mean?"

"No. I think someone else killed Juliet and deliberately made it look like Claudia did it."

Burt screwed up his face. "*What?* Who on earth would do that?"

"Someone who hated Claudia enough to commit murder so Claudia would spend the rest of her life in jail."

Recognition flashed across Burt's face. "You're talking about Sheila, aren't you?"

Kelly nodded. "Yes, I am. I think she deliberately killed Juliet so she could frame Claudia."

"I hate to tell you, Kelly, but that sounds crazy."

"I know it does, Burt, but hear me out, okay? Let me tell you everything I've learned, and if you still think it sounds crazy, then I'll leave it alone."

The waitress appeared then and poured a dark stream of coffee into their empty mugs, then hustled away to other customers.

"Okay, then," Burt said, leaning back into the chair and folding his arms. Listening pose. "You've got my full attention and a cup of coffee. What've you got, Kelly?"

She took a deep breath and jumped in. "You remember when you called the Sarasota cop, Detective Watson, last Monday? He told you that Sheila was obsessed with Claudia. He also said that Sheila had called him on Monday of the week before and asked what kind of sentence Claudia would get on those auto theft charges. And she was incensed to learn that Claudia might not go to jail at all. She might get work release. It all depended on the judge. Apparently Sheila lost it on the phone then and started yelling and swearing at him."

"I remember."

Kelly leaned over the table, clasping her hands in her own pose. "Rosa sold a Christmas cape to Sheila that day, Monday. She's got the sales receipt. That Monday was also the same day we all sat around the knitting table and learned that Claudia was hysterical at her motel, following Jeremy's rejection. Juliet and Jeremy, however, were planning to meet that evening for a romantic engagement dinner. Juliet was killed later that night. Monday night."

She took a quick sip of coffee. "According to Lizzie, Sheila had met Juliet at Saint Mark's, where she'd been volunteering every night. And Sheila heard all about Juliet and Jeremy's romance around the table. Sheila knew Juliet, knew Juliet's habits and her schedule."

"You're forgetting the car, Kelly. Claudia's car had Juliet's blood on it as well as fibers from her clothing."

Kelly smiled. "I'm getting to that, Burt. Connie told me yesterday that she'd spotted Sheila stealing from Claudia's knitting bag the day after she arrived here. Connie saw Sheila take Claudia's car keys."

Burt's bushy gray eyebrows shot up. "Is Connie sure?"

"She's positive. She watched Sheila take the keys, leave the shop, and drive away. But get this. She returns in a few minutes and returns the car keys to Claudia's purse. Connie made it a point to let Sheila know she was watching. Sheila said she'd 'found them on the floor.'"

"And Connie is sure she saw car keys?" Burt asked again, eyes narrowing.

Kelly took a deep drink of coffee this time then nodded. "Connie recognized them from the red pom-pom on the key chain. I'm thinking a few minutes is all anyone would need to drive across the street to Big Box, have duplicate keys made, and drive back. What do you think?"

"That sounds about right, but that's still just supposition, Kelly. You know that."

"I know. Just hear me out. Sheila learns that Claudia might not go to jail on the car theft charges. She's furious. Then she hears that Claudia's locked herself in her motel, emotionally distraught at Jeremy's rejection. And Sheila gets an idea. Thanks to gossip around the knitting table, Sheila knows that Juliet will once again be at Jeremy's for dinner, then walking home later that night. She's already got Claudia's keys. So Sheila buys a cape exactly like Claudia's to conceal her identity and steals Claudia's car, then sits and waits in the dark for unsuspecting Juliet to come into view."

Burt stared at the table, clearly considering what she said. "I admit it's a thought-provoking theory, Kelly, but it's still just supposition. There's no way to prove Sheila drove Claudia's car, let alone killed Juliet."

"There would be if the crime lab could test Sheila's cape."

Burt's eyebrows shot up again, but he didn't say a word.

"The same cape that concealed Sheila's identity from the passing motorist could be the very thing that incriminates her. The guy saw Sheila kneeling beside the road. That's a big cape, Burt. Sheila had to be kneeling close to Juliet in order to obscure the man's sight. And when she knelt beside

Juliet's body, the cape would have gotten blood on it. The police said Juliet's blood was on the hood of the car, so she was probably bleeding even more when her body hit the pavement. I'm guessing there was blood on the ground."

"Most probably," Burt said, nodding slowly.

"Is there any way the police could check Sheila's cape, Burt?"

"Not without a search warrant."

"Darn. It's right here in the shop, too. I told Connie to lock it up in Mimi's drawer—"

"Sheila hasn't brought it in yet."

Kelly frowned in frustration. "Is there any way Dan might want to check into Sheila? What with her past history of stalking and harassing Claudia—"

"No charges were filed against Sheila in Florida, remember?" Burt took a sip of coffee. "Dan might be tempted to take a look if we had more to give him. But he's not going to do it because Sheila hates Claudia and bought a Christmas cape and stole Claudia's car keys. That's not enough. I admit, you've got me halfway believing Sheila could be involved, but you need something more before I could go to Dan with this."

"Well, I'm still working on it, Burt—"

"What?" Burt started laughing. "I can't believe it. You've got more?"

"Yesterday afternoon, I went to the hotel where Sheila is staying. It's one of those fancy residence hotels on the south side. I put on one of my CPA suits and went to speak to the manager. Told him I was the auditor for a tech company out of state and wanted to know what sort of security was in place in the parking garage. We were thinking of having a business conference there. Did they have cameras? Keyed entry only?"

"CPA suit, huh? I would have loved to see that."

"Trust me, I'm a force to be reckoned with when I'm suited up." Kelly grinned. "Anyway, the manager said the garage had both cameras and keyed entry that allowed only the residents access. And it recorded the date and time whenever they entered the garage and returned. Plus, all photo and data records are stored digitally for ninety days. So, I'm betting they'd have a record of exactly when Sheila returned to the garage the night of Juliet's murder, and I'm betting it was late."

"Still not enough, Kelly. You gotta give me more."

Kelly leaned her arms on the table. "I think there is more, but I'm going to need your help to get it."

Only one eyebrow shot up this time. "Exactly what do you need my help for?"

"Before I went to the hotel, I took a quick trip to the low-rent side of town to Claudia's motel. I was hoping maybe they had cameras in their parking lot or something that might have spotted Sheila switching cars that night. Face it, she'd have to leave her car in the motel parking lot in order to drive off in Claudia's car."

"I'm following you. Keep going."

"Well, they don't have cameras, but the manager said they do employ a security firm to patrol the parking lot regularly during the night. Since they're so close to the interstate, they've had some problems in the past. I told the guy

I was an antique dealer and often carried expensive loads in my van. So I needed a secure parking lot."

"I take it you weren't in your power suit."

Kelly just grinned. "The guy gave me the name and number of the security firm they use. Now I'm wondering how I should approach them. I mean, I need to ask some pretty specific questions, and—"

"What's the name of the firm? I know several of them in town because lots of cops start working security after they retire."

Kelly retrieved a piece of paper from her back jeans pocket. "Sunrise Security. He said a Manny Ramirez is the owner. Here's his number."

"Oh, yeah. Manny's hired lots of the guys when they leave the force. Sure, I'll help you on this, Kelly. Let me give him a call. See if we can pay him a visit." He reached for the paper.

"That'll be great, Burt. Do you think you could call him now? Maybe we could go over there this afternoon."

Burt chuckled. "I suppose we could, provided we could lasso one of the gang to take over these errands Mimi needs done. Why don't you see if you can find a volunteer?"

"I'm on it, Burt," Kelly said, digging out her cell phone.

"You know, Kelly, we still won't have anything definitive to give Dan. It's all just circumstantial. He may not buy it."

Kelly paused as she scanned her phone directory, searching for Megan's number. "Just like the evidence they have against Claudia. It's all circumstantial, right? I mean, Claudia's got phone records showing she may have been in her motel room that night. All the police really have is the evidence on Claudia's car. And what if Claudia wasn't driving the car that night? Think about it. Claudia's motivation to murder Juliet is pretty flimsy. Supposedly she went over the deep end and decided to win back Jeremy's affections by eliminating Juliet. That's quite a stretch. Meanwhile, Sheila's motivation to implicate Claudia in a serious crime can be shown by her actions in Florida and here. Hate is a powerful emotion." She fixed Burt with a direct stare.

"Not bad, Kelly."

Kelly acknowledged his praise with a modest nod as she punched in Megan's number.

"**We** really appreciate your taking time to visit with us, Manny," Burt said, as they shook hands.

"Hey, good to see you, Detective," Manny Ramirez said, beckoning Kelly and Burt into his office. "Please, have a seat, miss."

"Just call me Kelly," she said, shaking Manny's hand.

"Boy, it's been a while, Detective. You left the force a couple of years ago, right?" Manny asked as he sat in a green upholstered chair behind his desk.

Sunshine through the window behind him warmed the room. Winter sunshine was deceptive in Colorado. Warm inside, cold outside. Winter winds still held sway.

Burt pulled a chair up beside Kelly's. "Yeah, that's right. I left after my wife died. Heart attack, you know . . ."

Manny's face registered sadness. "Oh, yeah, I remember. Damn shame. Judy was a great gal. I'm sorry."

Burt nodded. "Well, it was rough for a while. But lots of good friends have helped me through. Like Kelly here. She's kind of like another daughter."

Kelly was surprised how good that felt to hear Burt say it. She already knew he thought of her as a daughter even though Burt had a daughter of his own. Burt had adopted all of her friends at the shop. But it still felt good to hear him say it, especially since her own father was gone.

"So, what can I do for you, Detective?"

"Please, Manny, call me Burt."

Manny shook his head, chuckling. "I'll try . . . so, what can I do for you, Burt?"

"Well, Kelly and I have been keeping track of some people who's staying at the Happy Traveler Inn over by the interstate. The manager there told us you were in charge of night security for the motel and parking lot."

"Yeah, they're one of our clients. Was there a problem with a guest? I don't recall Hank reporting any disturbances lately. The Happy Traveler is his beat."

"Nope, no disturbances," Burt said. "No problems at all, in fact. We were simply checking to see if your security guard noticed a car with a Florida license plate show up on the lot earlier this month. Would he keep records?"

"Yeah, our guards do make notes if they see anything suspicious or out of order. Let me check his files. We should still have the records for those weeks." Manny went over to the tall metal filing cabinets alongside the opposite wall. "Do you have a particular date you're looking at?"

"Matter of fact, we do," Burt said. "The night of Monday, December the eighth."

Manny pulled out a drawer and began thumbing through the folders. "Let's see, here's the Happy Traveler file. It looks like Hank was on duty that night. That would be the week of December seventh through thirteenth. Okay, here we go." He pulled out a folder, flipped it open, and returned to his desk as he read.

Kelly held her breath, hoping that the night guard had noticed a woman in a cape or switched cars or license plates or something. Something that would raise enough questions in Detective Dan's mind to make him investigate.

"Here we go . . . 'Monday, December eighth.'" Manny read out loud. " 'Checked lot at eight thirty-five p.m. and found motel guest's 1999 Taurus, Florida license 233234, gone from regular spot. Replaced by a 2005 Pontiac, Florida license 456457.'" Manny glanced up. "Is that what you're looking for?"

Kelly's heart was beating so loud, she was sure Manny could hear it. Meanwhile, Burt pulled out a small notepad from his shirt pocket and paged through it.

"Sure is. Sheila has a 2005 Pontiac, and that's her license plate. I checked it in the parking lot before we came." Burt glanced to Kelly with a twinkle in his eye. "You've still got it, Sherlock."

"Well, I'll be damned," Manny continued, reading the file. "Hank made another entry three hours later. 'Checked lot at eleven twenty-nine p.m., 1999 Taurus returned to regular parking slot, and 2005 Pontiac gone.' "

Kelly could barely keep her elation from showing. "Is that enough for Dan? What do you think, Burt?"

Burt smiled and flipped the notepad closed. "Oh, yeah,

Kelly. I definitely think Dan will be interested in what we've found. And in your conclusions. In fact, I'll go over there right now to tell him. Manny, can you make a copy of that file for me, please?"

"You betcha, Detective . . . uh, Burt."

Nineteen

Watching Carl gobble down his doggie-kibble breakfast, Kelly closed the glass patio door. The wind was picking up, blowing in over the mountains. That meant a storm front was heading their way.

"You going over to your folks' now?" Kelly asked as she watched Steve zip up his winter jacket.

"Yeah, I promised my dad I'd check out the stables with him, see what would be involved if he wanted to expand the stalls." He tossed his new alpaca scarf around his neck. "Should I tell my folks we'll be joining them for Christmas brunch?"

"Absolutely," Kelly said before draining her mug. "Are you sure it's all right to bring Carl? I know he's trained now, but no telling what he'll do when he sees livestock again."

"Oh, yeah. Carl will be fine. We'll let him roam in the pastures and chase varmints."

"That'll work as long as your dad doesn't decide to cook steaks on the grill. You know, we're gonna weigh a ton after the holidays. Brunch at your parents' house, then Christmas dinner at Mimi's with the whole crowd. I'd better start running extra miles ahead of time." She checked the coffeepot. Empty. *Rats.*

"Hey, speaking of dinner, do we have plans tonight? There's so much going on these last few days, I've lost track." Steve maneuvered around the Christmas tree as he headed to the front door.

"Matter of fact, we do. Thanks for reminding me. Jayleen called last night. We're invited to Curt's for a steak and chili supper." She scooted between the tree's pine branches and the sofa, following after Steve.

"They must have read my mind. I've been thinking about steak. Where're you off to?" he asked, watching Kelly grab her ski jacket.

"Over to the shop. I figure Mimi and Burt can use all the help they can get these last few days before Christmas." Shaking her mug, she added, "Plus, I need coffee."

Steve opened the door before giving her a quick kiss. "I'll be running around doing last-minute stuff the rest of the afternoon, so I'll see you tonight. Six o'clock?"

"Sounds good." Kelly glanced back at the tree. "By the way, where'd that big box come from? I nearly stepped on it trying to get around the tree."

Steve jogged down the steps. "I dunno, must be Santa Claus."

"Riiiight."

He turned and gave Kelly a wink before heading to his truck. "See you later. Say hi to Mimi and Burt."

Kelly started across the gravel driveway then spun around and called, "Oh, yeah, tell your folks if they really want to get in the holiday mood, they should come to the Saint Mark's family service on Christmas Eve. I've got some ideas that will liven up the Nativity scene."

Steve grinned out the window. "I can hardly wait." He revved the big engine, and it came to life with a throaty rumble.

Kelly sped along the stone pathway around the shop to the café's back entrance and raced up the wooden steps. The wind kicked up, whipping her hair into her face. Icy wind, too. Rushing through the doorway, she let out an exaggerated shiver.

"Brrrr! Don't anybody ask if it's cold enough for me," she declared, giving a wave to Burt as he came around a corner. "I've had it with this Colorado hardiness. I'm freezing."

"Hey, Kelly, I was about to call you," Burt said, beckoning her to a nearby table in a quiet corner. "Come on over and warm up with some coffee."

"Thanks, Julie," Kelly said as the waitress refilled her mug with Eduardo's black gold. The scent of bacon and eggs floated on the air. "What's up?" she asked as she joined Burt at the table. She took a deep drink of the dark brew and felt its tangy burn. *Ahhhh.*

"I heard from Dan this morning, and I thought you'd be

interested in the latest police update." He gave her a smile from over the top of his coffee cup.

Kelly sat up straighter. "You bet! Is Dan going to investigate Sheila?"

"He already has. Dan and the guys spent all day yesterday checking out everything we gave them the day before. They started with Detective Watson in Sarasota, then they talked with Manny Ramirez and his guard, Hank, to confirm their records of the motel parking lot. Then they checked out Sheila's hotel parking garage files, and they even contacted Connie at home to take her statement about witnessing Sheila stealing Claudia's car keys. Oh, and they also got a copy of the shop's sales receipt for Sheila's cape."

"Whoa . . ." Kelly breathed. "Dan jumped right on it, didn't he? Good for him."

"You bet he did. That evidence is still circumstantial, but Sheila's motive is a heckuva lot stronger than Claudia's. As you pointed out," he added with a wink. "By the way, Dan says thanks."

Kelly was surprised how good that praise made her feel. She hadn't lost her sleuthing skills during the long layover. Not a bit. She could still pick up clues and piece things together. As Burt said, *You've still got it, Sherlock.*

She'd also forgotten how good that rush of discovery felt. What a sense of satisfaction she had after she'd helped solve a puzzle the professionals had missed. It felt good. Really, really good.

"You tell him Junior Detective Flynn is happy to help

anytime," she joked. "What will Dan do now? When's he going to question Sheila?"

Burt glanced over his shoulder before speaking. No customers were seated in this section of the café. "Matter of fact, Dan will probably be over here sometime this morning. First, he needs a search warrant in order to take Sheila's cape in for testing."

"Did Sheila finally bring it in?"

"Oh, no." Burt shook his head. "After you and I talked, I called Sheila and told her not to bring the cape in yet. Claimed that we were so swamped at the shop we couldn't even send it out, and if it sat around here one of our temporary helpers might accidentally sell it." He gave Kelly a sly smile. "So I told her to wait until I called."

Kelly was already following Burt's drift. "And that way, the cape never leaves Sheila's possession, right?"

"You got it."

"Do you think she'll try to destroy the cape?" Kelly mused out loud.

Burt shook his head. "I'm guessing she won't. After all, she promised she'll sell it to that Michigan buyer. She has no reason to be suspicious."

"Well, I figure she's already discovered blood on the cape. I mean, that's got to be why she's selling it. What if she tries to wash off the blood?"

"She can try, but she won't get it all off. There will still be traces of Juliet's blood on the fibers. Wool is very absorbent, as you know. It absorbs everything we do to it."

Kelly knew that for a fact. Wool was wonderful for that

reason. Its natural elasticity made it flexible. "Forgiving," fiber folk called it. Whenever her stitches started to tighten, all she had to do was make a little stretching motion with the needles to let the wool breathe. Kelly swore she could almost feel the yarn sigh as it loosened.

"I won't relax until Sheila's cape is in police custody," she said, taking another deep drink of coffee.

"Well, Dan's pretty confident that he'll get the search warrant, so I figure he'll be questioning her pretty soon. Matter of fact, I told him I'd ask Sheila to come over to the shop and help us this morning." He gave Kelly another sly grin. "That way Dan will know where Sheila is when he wants to talk with her."

"Won't she think that's kind of funny? Your calling her in to help?"

"I pleaded overwhelmed shopkeepers sending out a distress signal. All hands on deck sort of thing," he joked. "In fact, I told her she would be helping you bag up fibers in the basement and wind skeins of yarn."

"Sounds good, I'll—"

The rest of Kelly's sentence stayed on her tongue when she saw Sheila walk around the corner, coat over her arm, coffee mug in hand, clearly headed toward the shop. Ready to work. Meanwhile, there sat Kelly and Burt drinking coffee. Not bagging fibers, winding yarns, or rushing around taking care of customers. Boy, were they ever busted.

Sheila did a double take and marched up to their table. "I thought you said you needed all hands on deck," she declared in a skeptical tone. "Have all the customers left? I have my cape in the car. I can bring it in now. It looks like everything has slowed down."

"Uhhhh," Kelly began.

Burt stepped in. "We're just taking a well-deserved break during a temporary lull, Sheila. Believe me, customers were pouring in this morning. The lines stretched all the way into the next room. Sit down and join us, enjoy your coffee. We'll all head back to the shop in a few minutes."

Sheila settled into the chair beside Kelly and sipped her coffee. "What is it you want us to do, again? Bag up fibers or something?"

"And wind and weigh yarn skeins, too. We've sold out of so many, we have to bring up new stock all the time. But the staff is so busy at the register, they don't have time to work in the basement. I really appreciate your helping, Sheila," Burt said with a believable sigh. "I only have two hands, and I figured both you and Kelly had helped at the bazaar and at the church, so maybe you'd help us here."

Sheila's frosty attitude melted slightly, Kelly noticed. "Of course I'll help. It's the holidays."

"And don't forget to come to the Christmas Eve family service," Kelly suggested, in an attempt to continue the melt. "Jennifer and I are in charge of the—"

Once again, Kelly was interrupted, but this time it was the sight of Mimi racing from the shop and heading their way. But instead of looking harassed and overwhelmed, Mimi looked exuberant. She was grinning from ear to ear.

"You'll never guess the good news!" she said as she rushed

up to them. "Claudia just called and said Fort Connor police are allowing her to return to Florida to face those car theft charges against her."

Kelly glanced at Burt for a response, but he was studiously examining his coffee mug. "Wow . . . that is good news," she said, trying not to sound too surprised.

Why would Fort Connor police allow Claudia to return to Florida? Had they already taken her off their suspect list, or simply moved her down a notch?

"What?!" Sheila erupted. "How could they do that? Why would the police let her go to Florida for those—those vehicle charges when she's killed somebody right here in Fort Connor?"

Mimi gave Sheila a polite smile. "Claudia told me the police said they've gotten all the statements they need from her. If they need to ask more questions, then the Florida police can take her written statement."

"That's—that's ridiculous! She's a murderer!" Sheila spewed again.

This time, Mimi's smile disappeared completely. "Well, I just spoke with Claudia's attorney, and he says the police are not going to charge her in Juliet Renfrow's death."

"*What?!*" Sheila nearly shouted. "That's—that's ridiculous! She's a *killer!*"

"Sheila, try to keep your voice down," Burt said at last.

"But—but that's an outrage! She killed that woman. The police found the woman's blood and fibers from her clothes on Claudia's car. How can they just let her go like that? She's guilty of murder."

"According to Claudia's attorney, the police have another 'person of interest' they're considering. Isn't that the right term, Burt?" Mimi said, her tone frosty now.

"Yes, it is," Burt said, clearly not about to get between Mimi and Sheila in this debate.

Sheila drew back, staring at Mimi, obviously incredulous at what she heard. "That's absurd. Claudia's the guilty one. Why are the police wasting their time on some unknown person?"

"You'll have to ask them," Mimi replied tartly. "Excuse me, I have to return to the shop now. Customers are waiting." She executed a turn with almost military precision and walked away.

"This is insane." Sheila continued her rant. "The police are not doing their jobs. Are they incompetent or something? They've got the killer right here, and they're letting her go!" Her hand jerked out in emphasis.

Kelly sensed the emotional temperature of Sheila's tirade was red hot about now. Perhaps, with a little more prodding, the controlled, tight-lipped woman would let something slip. It was worth a try.

"Who knows what the police found, Sheila?" Kelly offered with a shrug. "Claudia's motel is right next to the interstate. Maybe some guys stole her car and went carousing around town. Burt said there was a wild college party going on that night. Maybe some guy confessed that he was drinking and didn't see Juliet on the street."

Sheila gave a disgusted snort. "Some drunken driver wearing a red cape? That's ridiculous."

Kelly and Burt exchanged glances. The only way Sheila

would know about the red cape was if she was the driver. Kelly had been scrupulously careful not to tell anyone else at Lambspun, and she was certain that Mimi hadn't mentioned it, either. And Claudia certainly wouldn't reveal details about her case. That would only add fuel to the gossip fire.

Burt ran his finger around the edge of his coffee mug. "How did you know the hit-and-run driver wore a red cape?"

Sheila darted a glance his way, then back to her coffee. "I heard it here at the shop. Everyone's been gossiping about this murder since it happened."

Burt took a sip of coffee. "I don't think that particular piece of information was released by the police."

"Well, it got out anyway. Because I'm certain I heard it around the table." She gestured toward the shop. "Apparently some guy was driving by and saw Claudia in that red cape."

Kelly's pulse raced. The passing motorist was also part of the information police had kept from the public. Once again, wily, scheming Sheila had tripped herself up. Tangled in her own lies.

A man stepped from the shop into the hallway beside the café, a uniformed police officer behind him. Kelly recognized Burt's old partner, Dan. She looked at Sheila and decided to give her just another little nudge.

"You really hate Claudia, don't you, Sheila?" Kelly barbed.

Sheila shot her a glare. "Of course I do. She's an evil, wicked woman. Who's gotten away with murder countless times. And I cannot believe the Fort Connor police are about to let her off again. What is the matter with them? Are they blind?"

"Well, you can ask them yourself," Burt said, glancing over his shoulder as his old partner approached. "Sheila, this is Detective Dan Patterson of the Fort Connor Police Department."

Sheila jerked around in her chair, clearly surprised. "Well, it's about time the police showed up. I hope you're here looking for Claudia Miller," she snapped.

Kelly had to hand it to Sheila. Strike first. Best defense is a strong offense.

"You're Sheila Miller?" Dan asked politely.

"Yes, I am, and I'll be glad to tell you anything you'd like to know about Claudia Miller. She's gotten away with murder three times already in other states, and you have no business letting her get away—"

"Actually, we're here to ask *you* some questions, ma'am," Dan explained in a low voice. "If you'll accompany us to the department, please, we'd appreciate it."

Sheila went rigid, her face contorting in a scowl of disbelief. "*Me?* Why do you want me to come to the police department? I can answer your questions right here. You should be taking Claudia Miller to jail instead of sending her to Florida."

"I think it's better if you come with us, Ms. Miller. We have more than a few questions for you. Plus, we've executed a search warrant for your hotel room and your car." Dan flipped open the notebook in his hand and studied it. "We've identified a vehicle parked outside this shop, a 2005

Pontiac, Florida license number 456457, registered to Sheila Miller, 222 Azalea Drive, Sarasota, Florida. That is your car, is it not, Ms. Miller?"

"Of course it's my car," she retorted. "Why on earth would you want to search my car?"

Dan withdrew a piece of paper from his jacket pocket. "We've just confiscated a package from your vehicle that contains a woolen cape. The cape had a tag pinned on it with your name and Florida address. That is the same woolen cape you purchased from this shop, Lambspun, on December eighth this month, is it not?"

Sheila's eyes narrowed. "Why do you ask?"

"Just for confirmation. We have the receipt signed by you, Ms. Miller. That is your signature, is it not?" He held the receipt out for Sheila to read.

Instead, Sheila stared back at him, not answering. Her face was growing paler.

"That is your signature, isn't it, Ms. Miller? We have signed statements that you purchased the cape on that date from this shop."

"Why . . . why do you want the cape?"

"We want to send it to the state crime lab for analysis for traces of blood."

Sheila drew back, staring at the detective for a long moment before she spoke again. "That's impossible. I just bought it."

"That's what the crime lab will determine, Ms. Miller. We have a statement from the night watchman at the Happy Traveler Inn stating that your car was parked in that motel lot for over two hours the night of Juliet Renfrow's death. During that same time period, Claudia Miller's car was missing."

All color drained from Sheila's face. "That . . . that's not possible . . . I was at my hotel the entire time."

Dan flipped the pages in his notebook. "We also have records from your hotel showing that you drove out of the parking garage at eight oh two p.m. and did not return to the garage until eleven fifty-eight p.m."

Sheila's gaze darted from Dan to Burt to Kelly. "What are you saying? Are you suggesting I had something to do with that woman's death? You're crazy!"

"Why don't you come down to the department, and you can explain everything to us there," Dan suggested again.

Sheila's features froze into an icy mask. "I want to speak to an attorney. Right now."

"You'll be able to contact your attorney as soon as we get to the department." Dan stepped to the side and gestured toward the café's back door. "We can leave by this door, if you'd prefer."

Sheila hesitated just a minute before she pushed back her chair. In that minute, Kelly thought she glimpsed a hint of fear flash through Sheila's eyes. Then it was gone. Sheila grabbed her coat and stalked out of the café without so much as a backwards glance.

Dan, however, gave a silent goodbye wave to Burt and Kelly before following the officer who had hastened after Sheila.

Kelly stared at the nearly empty café, grateful that there

weren't many customers to witness this unpleasant ex-
change.

"What do you think, Burt? Will Sheila confess or try to
stonewall like she has so far?"

Burt drained his coffee. "I think Sheila's going to 'lawyer
up.' Dan won't get one more word out of her. She is as hard
as they come."

Kelly swirled the last of the coffee in her mug. "Well, let's
hope Sheila's Christmas cape will do the talking for her."

Kelly walked Carl across the driveway and down the stone
path leading around the knitting shop, putting her dog
through his paces. Carl's *sits* and *heels* and *stays* were still
sharp.

Spotting Jayleen's truck pull into the driveway, Kelly
walked Carl back along the pathway and waited for Jayleen
to approach. Carl sat obediently by her side. "Hey, Jayleen,
what are you doing here? I thought you'd be helping Curt
with dinner." Pointing at the darkening sky, she added, "It's
getting close to dinnertime."

Jayleen shifted the large white plastic bag in her arms.
"Curt's got it covered. Besides, Mimi called and said she
needed more fleeces. I swear, you folks are about ready to
sell the wool right off the sheep, you're so busy."

Kelly laughed. It felt good to be outside in the fresh air,
even though it was cold. The twilight sky was turning a
silky blue over the foothills. "You're right about that."

"You taking a break from helping in the shop?"

"Actually, I thought I'd give Carl a workout while I waited for Claudia to show up. A Florida court revoked her bond and has ordered her back to face those car theft charges. She and her police escort have a flight out of Denver tonight. Claudia told Mimi she wanted to stop by and say goodbye on the way out of town."

Jayleen stared toward the empty, desolate golf course. "I sure am sorry Claudia's having to go through that ordeal, but it could be a blessing in disguise."

"How do you figure that?"

"Sounds like this will be the first time Claudia hasn't had some man show up to rescue her. So now it's up to her. Maybe this time, she'll discover that she has to rescue herself."

Kelly nodded. "Let's hope so."

Car headlights pierced through the dusk as a police car pulled up in front of Lambspun. A uniformed policewoman stepped out of the cruiser and opened Claudia's door.

"Kelly, how sweet of you to stay and say goodbye," Claudia said as she approached, a white shopping bag dangling from her arm. "And, Jayleen, so good to see you. Thank you both for being here." She glanced over her shoulder at the attractive policewoman standing right behind her. "Officer Johnson was nice enough to let me stop by on our way out of town. I didn't want to come earlier in the day. Too many people in the shop."

Kelly noticed that Claudia's voice wasn't breathy or gasping or panicked. Claudia actually sounded calm. She guessed that answering to car theft charges in Florida was a lot less threatening than being a murder suspect in Colorado. Amazing how perspective altered things.

"I just wanted to tell you that we'll be thinking of you, Claudia. We won't forget you, I promise." She grinned. "You're pretty unforgettable, as a matter of fact. Take care of yourself, okay? Tell your lawyer to keep Marty posted." She reached over and gave Claudia a big hug.

Claudia held on to Kelly for a minute before letting go. Kelly saw some moisture glisten on Claudia's face, even in the twilight. "Thank you, Kelly, so much. For everything you and Burt have done to help me. I'll never forget you."

"Do you want me to take that package into the shop for you, Mrs. Miller?" Officer Johnson asked, pointing to the bag over Claudia's arm.

"No, I'll take it, Officer. I want to say goodbye to Mimi and Burt and all the others." She glanced toward the brightly lit shopwindow looking into the front room, customers still browsing.

"You're gonna be all right, Claudia," Jayleen suddenly said. "No matter what that Florida judge rules, you're gonna be okay. You know that. Deep down inside, you know that. You're stonger than you think you are, woman. Now, you latch on to that strength. And it'll get you through those tough times, you hear?"

Claudia stared back at Jayleen. "Thank you for saying that, Jayleen. No one's ever said that to me before."

"I'm only telling you the truth," Jayleen said with her good-natured grin. "Take care of yourself, Claudia."

"I will," Claudia said as she turned toward the shop.

Kelly's curiosity got the better of her. She had to know. "What's in the bag?" she called as Claudia and Officer Johnson walked away.

Claudia paused on the brick steps. "It's my Christmas cape. I heard Mimi needed one to send to a customer in Michigan. I certainly won't have need of a woolen cape in Florida." She gave a little smile that Kelly could see from the driveway. The old playful Claudia was still in there.

Twenty

"**Should** we save you and Jennifer a seat?" Steve asked as he settled into the pew beside Megan and Marty. Burt, Mimi, Curt, and Jayleen were already seated across the aisle.

"No, Jen and I will be supervising our troops," Kelly said, standing in the aisle. "Hey, Marty, slide down a little more, would you? I think I spotted Greg and Lisa."

Marty waved his camera as he and Megan slid across the wooden pew. "My photographer fees are astronomical, but I can be bribed. Those gingersnap cookies will work."

"Forget about it," Steve said. "Kelly already took them to the shop. They're probably in Pete's café with the rest of the food."

Kelly glanced about the crowded pews of Saint Mark's Catholic Church, which were filled with excited children

and chattering adults, proud parents and indulgent relatives. The church was packed. Any latecomers would have
to stand in the back. Kelly was glad to see that her friends
had all heeded her advice and arrived earlier. Hilda and
Lizzie were stationed in the front pew. The better to keep
watch.

The fresh scent of evergreen hung in the air, mixing with
the aroma of scented candles. Lighted candles were nestled
in all the evergreen boughs. The entire church seemed to
shimmer with a soft golden light.

"Wish us luck," Kelly said, holding up crossed fingers to
her friends before heading down the aisle.

The vestibule, which separated the front doors of the
church from the sanctuary, was the perfect place to gather
antsy, nervous teenagers. Jennifer was stationed there, rounding up the cast. Fortunately their depiction of the Nativity
would occur early on in the service. Kelly had already noticed
performance jitters the last time she'd checked on the troops.

"Hey, you got in under the wire," Kelly teased Lisa and
Greg as they met in the center aisle. "Marty's saving a place
for you. Fifth pew from the front, right side."

"You know, the last time I was in a church was for my
grandmother's funeral a few years ago," Greg said. "So this
better be good. That service took forever as I recall."

"This service should be shorter. We hope," Kelly joked.
"Say a prayer that the kids stay in character." She held up
crossed fingers.

Lisa glanced about the church. "Wow, it's beautiful in
here. I've never been to Saint Mark's for a Christmas service
before. It's gorgeous with all the decorations. Look, even the

chandeliers have evergreens and candles." She pointed to the vaulted ceilings.

"Let's hope the hot wax doesn't start dripping," Greg teased as he tugged at Lisa's hand, guiding her toward the front.

Kelly hastened down the aisle. Burt waved to her, brandishing his camera. Curt gave Kelly a thumbs-up as she passed. She noticed both Curt and Jayleen were attired in corduroy rather than denim. Jayleen's jacket sported long fringe, too. Colorado Cowgirl Deluxe.

Pushing open the doors to the vestibule, Kelly spotted her teenage cast clustered about Jennifer, each one colorfully dressed in his or her version of biblical garb, be it peasant or king.

Joseph wore a long dark robe, plain and unadorned, completely in character. Mary was dressed in a long navy blue tunic, which Jennifer had obviously accessorized as promised. A shimmering sapphire blue shawl was draped across the pretty teenager's head and shoulders, providing a stunning contrast with her burnished auburn hair. Mary looked both innocent and beautiful.

The Three Wise Guys, on the other hand, had gone for glitz. They appeared to be wearing velvet bathrobes that were trimmed in faux fur, satin ribbons, and something else. Something that sparkled. The shepherds were more modestly dressed in what looked like hooded fleece sweatshirts turned inside out. No logos, just soft gray and fuzzy. Gray sweatpants completed their matched look. Shep Two even held a tall walking stick with a curved hook on the end. Clearly, his version of a shepherd's crooked staff.

Angel had gone for glamour. Not a surprise. Her blonde curls clustered perfectly on the shoulders of her long-sleeved snow white gown, which draped gracefully to the floor. Was that satin? Kelly wondered. A silvery halo of tinsel-like sparkles rested on her head. But the highlight of the outfit was the delicate, feathery wings that curved upward and out from behind her shoulders. She truly did look angelic.

Narrator, however, had gone for suave elegance. He wore a midnight blue velvet smoking jacket, trimmed with black satin collar. A white silk scarf was tucked neatly at his neck. He even had his hair gelled into a fifties-style pompadour. Pipe in one hand, leather-bound book in the other, he looked as if he'd stepped off the set of *Masterpiece Theatre*.

Kelly figured if they looked that good, their parents would forgive any flubs. "Good job! Everybody's here on time," she said as she joined the cluster. Nodding to the Three Wise Guys, she added, "Looking good, you guys. O'Leary, what's up with your robe? It sparkles."

"Just my personality, Coach," O'Leary replied, striking a pose, eliciting groans from the others. "Actually, it's glitter. Hey, we're the Three Kings, right? Kings gotta glitter."

"Got that right," Caspar agreed.

"Check it out." Balthazar turned around and spread his robe. A ferocious eagle was outlined in glitter, diving toward prey, claws outstretched.

"That really works for Christmas," Angel said sarcastically.

"Angel, that outfit is gorgeous. Your mom is one heckuva designer," Kelly said as she fingered Angel's wing tips. Strips of fluffy white mohair were hand-stitched to the cloth-covered wings, creating the ethereal visual appearance of feathers.

"Thanks," Angel said with a big smile. "She loves to sew for me."

"You guys look *great*. All of you," Jennifer said, dressed like Kelly in dark wool slacks and a bright sweater. Jennifer in shamrock green, Kelly in fire engine red. Turning to Narrator, Jennifer added, "But I gotta give the award for originality to this guy."

Narrator stepped forward and gave a deep bow. "Thank you very much," he said, imitation-Elvis style, while the others snickered.

"Please tell me you're not going to channel Elvis during the reading," Kelly joked, hoping to relax the cast. They joined in teasing Narrator. Humor to the rescue once again.

"Okay, now that we've got all hands on deck, I want to capture this moment forever." Jennifer pulled out her cell phone and flipped it open. "Who knows? Maybe I'll turn it into my screen saver."

"Okay, everyone, huddle up," Kelly said, waving the kids to a corner of the vestibule so Jennifer could snap photos. Churchgoers were still traipsing through the doors.

The teenagers clustered about in an untidy and rowdy semicircle, while Jennifer captured cheesy smiles and last-minute goofing off. "That's great, you guys," she said, pocketing her phone. "And just to let you know, I'll be recording the Nativity scene. So stay sharp and stay in character."

"Hey, will ya e-mail us the video?" O'Leary asked.

"Oh, I'll do better than that," Jennifer said with a wicked grin. "I'll e-mail the entire video file to my niece, and she'll upload it to her Web groups. She'll have you guys all over YouTube. With enough hits, you'll be Internet stars by tomorrow."

Kelly had to laugh, watching the mixed reactions explode from the cast. From Mary's look of horror to the Wise Guys' whoops of glee. Angel and Narrator looked delighted. Shep One and Shep Two looked amused. Joseph looked skeptical. Jennifer's brilliant scheme had sent an electric charge throughout the cast that was guaranteed to override any nervousness.

From the corner of her eye, Kelly noticed a familiar figure hovering in the stairwell. Lucy, cradling Baby David in her arms. Kelly sent her a big smile. Now it was time for the first of her two contributions to this production. Aside from providing muscle and playing straight man to Jennifer.

"Is someone saving you a seat?" Kelly asked as she approached mother and child.

"Oh, yes," Lucy replied, over the sound of organ music billowing from the sanctuary. "Oh, Come, All Ye Faithful" rose along with voices. "I just fed him, so he should stay asleep the whole time. But I'll be in the front row with Hilda and Lizzie in case you need me."

"You're a sweetheart, Lucy. Let's go over and meet the stage parents," Kelly said, beckoning Lucy over to the teenagers.

Jennifer had already lined them up in order of procession. Narrator was in front, followed by Angel. Ready for her walk into stardom. Shep One and Shep Two would be right behind. Mary and Joseph would follow, walking side by side. The Wise Men would bring up the rear, which was perfect placement for any spontaneous showing off to occur.

Kelly noticed the mischievous expression on Shep Two's face and hoped he wouldn't use that shepherd's staff to trip Angel during her promenade down the aisle. Shep Two was looking for trouble, Kelly could tell. No telling what an inventive teenage mind could come up with.

Fortunately, Kelly had planned for such an occurrence. She glanced toward the front door, people still entering. Sure enough, she glimpsed someone else she recognized standing outside. Kelly smiled and held up her hand, giving a wait signal to the woman.

"Hey, Lucy, how's the little guy?" Jennifer said, joining them.

"Sleeping soundly," Lucy said with a smile. "Are your kids ready?"

"Let's find out," Kelly said, escorting Lucy toward Mary and Joseph. "Hey, guys, I thought we'd add a bit of realism to this whole scene. This is David, who's six months old, and his mom, Lucy, has agreed to let him participate."

Mary stared, eyes wider than wide. "What? You mean *hold* him?"

"He's sound asleep. He won't be any trouble," Lucy assured her, placing the snoozing David into a surprised Mary's arms.

"But . . . but what if he cries? I used to babysit my baby brother and he cried a *lot!*" Mary protested.

"Don't worry, you'll be fine," Jennifer said, giving Mary a reassuring pat on her shoulder. "You already know how to do this." Mary stared back at Jennifer, looking only slightly less fearful.

Kelly pointed to the surprised and still skeptical Joseph. *Your turn, Joe.*

"Okay, Joseph, your job during this whole thing is to take care of Mary and the baby. That was the original Joseph's role, and he did a pretty good job of it, too. If he hadn't, we wouldn't all be here today celebrating."

A spark of engagement flickered in Joseph's eyes. "Okay," he said, nodding.

"Good. There are a lot of steps leading up to where you two are sitting, and we don't want Mary to trip. Her hands are full, so she can't pick up her skirt."

"Got it covered," he said, then turned to Mary. "Listen, if he starts making noise, I'll help. I was the only one who could get my baby sister to sleep."

"Hey, guys, I've gotta run to the front pew before they finish singing," Jennifer said, opening the door to the sanctuary. "You'll do great. Trust me." She hastened up the aisle, cell phone in hand, as the last notes of the chorus echoed out the door.

Okay . . . time for the pièce de résistance. Kelly walked to the front doors and beckoned the woman outside to join them.

"Sorry to make you wait," Kelly said as she held the door open. "You're sweet to do this, Shelly."

Shelly Reynolds stepped inside the vestibule. She, too, was carrying something in her arms, but it wasn't a baby. Not exactly.

"Baaaaaaaah!" Annie announced her entrance.

"I couldn't pass this up, Kelly. It's just too cute. I'll be watching from the back in case she gets too playful," Shelly said as she approached the startled teenagers.

"Guys, meet Annie the Celebrity Lamb," Kelly announced. "She appears at charitable events all over town. And her owner and I thought she'd make a great addition to the scene."

Everyone except Mary and Joseph stared blankly at Kelly. And Annie. Then they all started talking at once.

"Don't look at me, Coach," O'Leary said, holding up both hands.

"You've gotta be kidding!"

"Oh, man!"

"What if it poops?"

"Don't give it to me, I'm allergic to wool."

"Baaaah!"

Kelly took Annie from Shelly's arms and walked to the front of the line, where Shep One and Shep Two stared in disbelief.

"Shep Two, hand off your staff. Annie is yours."

He did a double take. Any hint of mischief evaporated from his expression. "You've gotta be kidding!"

"Hey, you're a shepherd, here's a sheep." Kelly handed over the fuzzy bundle. Annie bleated once, then licked Shep Two's chin.

"What if she . . . you know, poops up there?"

"Step around it," Shelly said, chuckling.

Kelly glanced over her shoulder and noticed Jennifer giving them the high sign from the front of the church. *Showtime.* She opened the door.

"Okay, guys, this is it. Narrator, start 'em off. Angel, hang back so you can make a big entrance."

Narrator set off, chin high, pipe and composure in hand. Rock-Star-in-Waiting Angel paused until he was halfway up the aisle before starting off, smiling and angelic at the same time.

"*Oh, man . . .*" Shep Two complained as Annie nibbled at his inside-out fleece.

"Listen, it'll be fine. Annie's a bigger ham than you are. You can let her walk around when you're up there, but keep track of her. We don't want her chewing the scenery."

"Okaaaay . . ." he said doubtfully.

Noticing Angel's progress, Kelly pointed up the aisle. "Shep One, you're on. Shep Two, you and Annie lag behind. Milk the audience reaction for all it's worth." She gave him a wink.

Something in Shep Two's eyes flickered, and Kelly wondered if she'd set more in motion than she'd planned.

Shep Two paused then set off, Annie bleating at appropriate intervals, which caused a stir throughout the entire congregation. Heads turned all over the church. Even the priests were grinning. Parents, relatives, visitors, all grabbed their cameras and cell phones and clicked away. Kelly noticed Shep Two slow down, clearly taking his time. Annie bleated as he showed her off to everyone.

If Annie had elicited smiles and laughter, it was nothing to the oohs and aahs heard when Mary and Joseph walked down the aisle, Baby David still asleep. Not only did Joseph help Mary up the steps, but he also moved a cushion for her to sit on. Kelly smiled to herself. *Good job, Joseph.*

O'Leary and the Wise Guys made the most of their entrances, displaying their finery, causing chuckles and laughter to ripple around the church. Kelly noticed O'Leary had added his jersey number to the back of his kingly robe. Number 43. King in the making. So far, so good, Kelly thought as she stood at the rear of the sanctuary. Now, if they can just stay in character.

She shouldn't have worried. Narrator carried off his reading in a clear voice. Mary sat holding the sleeping babe, looking beatific, while Joseph knelt beside them. The Three Wise Men had scattered themselves around the altar steps after presenting their gifts. Angel stood on the top step, smiling radiantly, arms outstretched, flanked by both shepherds. Annie bleated periodically, causing Narrator to repeat himself while the audience chuckled.

Kelly sighed with relief. They were a hit.

Suddenly the chuckles got louder. Kelly noticed Jennifer hold her cell phone at an angle, aiming its camera toward Angel. Kelly peered closer at the scene, and noticed that Shep Two had maneuvered himself close enough to Angel to enable Annie to indulge her favorite pastime—nibbling.

Annie had stopped bleating. She was too busy nibbling Angel's fluffy wings. Shep Two had that troublemaker grin on his face again. Meanwhile, Angel continued to beam at the assemblage, blissfully unaware.

Once again, Annie had managed to steal the show.

"**Where's** that chocolate mint fudge?" Marty demanded as he surveyed the knitting table. "I swear I saw it a minute ago. Now it's gone."

"Rosa's in charge of the fudge," Mimi said from across

the table, where she and Burt sat surrounded by the rest of Lambspun's family and friends. Every inch of the knitting table was covered with holiday food. Plates spilled over with delectable treats.

Brownies, both butterscotch and chocolate, rum cake, cherry cake, meringues, divinity, toffee bars, chocolate rum balls, and cookies of all kinds—Mexican wedding cakes, spritz cookies, sugar cookies shaped like Santas and candy canes frosted with icing. Kelly's gingersnaps were almost gone. So was the pumpkin nut bread Megan made.

Two huge punch bowls dominated both ends of the table. One with Burt's deadly wassail and the other with milder eggnog. And an urn of coffee was also perched on a side cabinet. Mimi made sure all her guests could drive safely when they left.

"But I haven't had any fudge yet!" Marty complained dramatically. "I saw Greg chowing down."

"She only let me have one piece," Greg replied before he took a bite of toffee bar. "Man, Rosa, you're brutal."

"Have to be, with you guys around," Rosa said, hovering over the foil package of fudge while she enjoyed a slice of cherry walnut cake. "You two are worse than my dogs at home, and they gobble up everything."

Burt chortled. "Now, that's a picture."

"May I please have a piece of fudge, Rosa?" Marty asked politely, palm outstretched. "Oh, and put my name on your list for seconds, okay?"

Rosa grinned and handed over a fat piece of fudge. "I'm not sure there will be any."

"Dude, give it up."

"Hey, Marty, any word about Claudia?" Jayleen said, leaning over the table to snare a gingersnap. "Didn't you find her a Florida lawyer?"

Marty didn't answer at first. Instead, he made several loud humming sounds of pleasure. Sugar delight. "Yep, I heard from him right before the service. Claudia is settled into the Sarasota jail. Her hearing is scheduled for this Friday."

"Poor Claudia," Mimi said before sipping her wassail. "I cannot imagine how she's going to hold up if she's sentenced to prison. She just might fall apart."

"Don't be so sure," Jayleen said, cup of coffee in hand. "I've got a hunch Claudia's a lot stronger than she lets on. She may come out of this a whole lot tougher than before."

Burt sipped from his cup. "I hope you're right, Jayleen."

Steve leaned over the table and snatched some chocolate rum balls, popping first one, then another into his mouth. "Mmmm, you gotta try these," he told Kelly as he sat beside her.

"I already did, and they're deadly. Almost as deadly as that chocolate mint fudge," she said, sipping eggnog. Burt's wassail was also a potent brew.

"I cannot believe that baby is so good," Rosa said, glancing to Lucy, who was seated in the corner beside Curt and Jayleen.

"He's a sweetheart." Lucy cooed to her son, who had captured Curt Stackhouse's index finger in his fat baby fist.

"What a cutie," Jayleen said, caressing Baby David's soft hair.

As if on cue, Annie trotted up and nuzzled David's baby blanket, then bleated. Lucy, Jayleen, and Curt laughed as

David discovered Annie. A little baby fist reached out for Annie to sniff.

Kelly watched the tableau. Lambspun's own Madonna and Child.

"Who made the fudge?" Lisa asked from the other end of the table. "It was here last year, too."

Mimi shrugged her shoulders. "I have no idea. It suddenly shows up for the holidays. Whenever we have a gathering like this, the fudge magically appears."

Curt snorted. "Magic? Somebody's pulling your leg, Mimi. You ought to cut off their wassail until they confess."

"Not a bad idea," Megan said from another corner, her plate overflowing with goodies. "Okay, fess up, someone. Who made the fudge?"

"Not me."

"Don't look at me, I only do gingersnaps."

"Are you kidding?"

All around the room, the same negative responses.

"Come on, somebody had to make it," Connie said from the archway.

"I told you," Mimi said with a smile. "It's magic. Maybe Santa Claus makes it."

That caused another round of laughter.

"I bet Pete made it," Jennifer said, giving him a poke as they both sat side by side at the table. "It's good enough to be Pete's." She took a bite of toffee.

Pete shook his head. "It's not mine. I don't do candies, just pies and cakes," he said with a broad smile, clearly enjoying the cranberry bread.

"Maybe it's a satisfied customer who slips it on the table

when we're not looking," Kelly suggested, snagging a rum ball. The fermented flavors of rum and chocolate melted on her tongue.

"Maybe so," Burt mused out loud. "The shop was open today until right before we headed to the church."

Kelly waited for the surrounding voices to rise before she leaned toward Burt. "Any word on Sheila? Have you heard from Dan or anything?"

Burt nodded as he leaned his head beside hers. "I called Dan this afternoon. Sheila has retained counsel here in Fort Connor after consulting with her Florida attorney. Dan says she's been advised that she's the prime suspect in the vehicular homicide of Juliet Renfrow and warned not to leave the area."

"When will they hear back from the state crime lab?"

Burt shrugged. "They don't know, but hopefully, they'll hear within a week. Without any blood evidence on the cape, the case against Sheila is entirely circumstantial. And you never can tell what a jury will do with that."

"Well, we did our part, Burt." She volunteered a smile. "It's up to the justice system now."

"Absolutely, Kelly, it's—hey, it's *snowing*!" Burt's face broke into a grin.

"You're kidding!"

"At last!"

"About time."

"Uh-oh. My tires are bad."

Kelly turned around and saw the fat white flakes outside the shop's windows. Flurries of white outlined against the black night.

"Now it's officially winter," she declared, pushing back her chair. "Come on. It's the first snowfall of the season." She grabbed Steve's hand. "Outside, everybody. Let's celebrate."

"Kids," Curt said with a wry smile. "Wait'll they have to shovel out from the first blizzard."

"Got that right," Jayleen agreed with a chuckle as Kelly and all her friends tumbled from the shop, laughing and threatening each other with snowball fights.

"Whoa, look at this!" Kelly skipped down the steps and danced into the driveway. She stared above into the flurry of snow. Flakes were falling faster and thicker.

"Good thing you finished my scarf," Steve teased as he caught her about the waist.

Kelly looked around at her friends, cavorting like she was in the snowfall. Megan and Marty were laughing and catching snowflakes on their tongues, while Greg was scraping snow together into a snowball. Lisa was right behind him, though, hands already filled with snow. Jennifer held her face up to the heavens, into the flurries. Pete stood beside her, laughing. Even Mimi and Burt were watching from the shop doorway, arms about each other's waists.

Despite the frigid air, Kelly felt warmth all around her. She slid both arms around Steve and pulled him close.

"I want to take a sleigh ride. I haven't done that since I was a kid and Helen and Jim took me out there in the pastures." She glanced toward the golf course. Pasture no more.

"We can do that. How about the day after Christmas? I know just the place. They have horse-drawn sleighs, complete with bells, blankets, and hot chocolate afterwards."

"Just the two of us?"

"Yeah, why don't we spend the day in the mountains? Take a snowshoe hike and a sleigh ride, then come home and warm up by the fireplace."

Kelly smiled at the picture he'd painted. "That sounds fantastic. Mountains, sleigh rides. Only one thing. We don't have a fireplace."

"We don't need one," Steve said with a grin, then leaned down to kiss her.

HOLIDAY KNITTING PATTERNS

Lambspun Easy Cozy Mittens

SIZES:

Children 7–10 (Instructions for adult size are shown in parentheses.)

MATERIALS:

3–5 ounces bulky yarn or 2 strands worsted weight yarn, to be knit as one bulky strand

1 set of #9 or 10 7-inch, double-pointed needles or size to obtain gauge

Tapestry needle

Approximately a ½ to 1 ounce of accent color yarn, for decoration

GAUGE:

3 sts and 5 rows = 1 inch

INSTRUCTIONS:

Cast on 22 (26) stitches. Arrange stitches evenly on 3 needles for knitting in the round as follows: 7 (9) sts on the first needle, 8 (8) sts on the second needles, 7 (9) sts on the third needle. Join your round and begin knitting, taking care not to twist your cast-on stitches.

Decorative Cuff (Optional):

Knit 7 rounds of the main color. Pick up the second yarn (a thin decorative mohair, angora, novelty, etc.) and knit 10–12 rounds or until the cuff measures the desired length.

Another option: Purl 1 or 2 rounds to end the decorative portion of the cuff.

Mitten Body:

Continuing on the *right* side of work, knit 10 more rounds or until the mitten is the desired length to the base of thumb. Try the mitten on, leaving it on the needles, to determine thumb placement.

Thumb Opening:

Child's Mitten Thumb:

Knit 9 stitches (7 from the first needle and 2 from the second needle) and place the next 4 stitches on a stitch holder or piece of scrap yarn. Cast-on 4 stitches on the needle with 2 stitches (the second needle) and then knit the 2 remaining stitches and continue knitting the round. Knit a total of 18 rounds or until the mitten reaches the last joint of the middle finger. Begin decrease rounds.

Adult's Mitten Thumb:

Knit 11 stitches (9 from the first needle and 2 from the second needle) and place the next 5 stitches on a stitch holder or piece of scrap yarn. Cast-on 5 stitches on the needle with 2 stitches (the second needle) and then knit the 1 remaining stitch and continue knitting the round. Knit a total of 18 rounds or until the mitten reaches the last joint of the middle finger. Begin decrease rounds.

Decrease Rounds:

Round 1: Knit together the first 2 sts on the first needle (k2tog), and knit until 2 stitches remain on the needle and knit these 2 together (k2tog). Repeat this process for needles 2 and 3. Total sts decreased = 6.

Round 2: Knit 1 round even.

Repeat Rounds 1 and 2 until 10 (14) stitches remain. Break or cut the yarn, leaving a 12-inch tail. Thread the tapestry needle with tail and slip it through the remaining stitches twice. Remove the needles, and pull the yarn tight. Tie off and weave in the end on the wrong side of the work.

Thumb: (Use contrasting color if desired.)

Leaving a 6-inch tail (which marks the start of your thumb round), join a ball of yarn, using a crochet hook to create (or "pick-up") one stitch at the left side of thumb opening. Transfer the new st to a needle. Repeat this step to create 4 (5) stitches above the thumb opening. Pick-up 1 stitch at the right side of the thumb opening. (You will have picked-up a total of 6 stitches.) Transfer the sts that were on the stitch holder or piece of yarn to a needle. You now have 10 (12) stitches. Distribute the sts evenly among 3 needles as follows: for a child's size: 3, 4, 3; for an adult size: 4, 4, 4. (For a smaller child's size, knit together the center 2 stitches on the second needle (the one with 4 stitches) for 9 stitches total.) Knit around until work reaches the tip of the thumb (approximately 9 (11) rows).

Thumb Decrease:

Round 1: Knit 2 together at beginning of each needle. 7(9) stitches remain.

Round 2: Repeat Round 1. 4(6) stitches remain.

Break or cut yarn, leaving an 8-inch tail. Using the darning needle, thread through the remaining stitches once. Tie off and weave in the end on the wrong side of the work.

Finishing:

Weave in all loose yarn ends on wrong side of work. At the base of the thumb, use the yarn end to close any holes or loose spots.

Embellishing:

Use your imagination and embroider your mittens with fun colors and fine yarns. Suggested embroidery stitches: Blanket Stitch * Stem Stitch w/Leaves * Feather Stitch * Daisy Flower Stitch * French Knots.

Felting:

If desired, you can felt your mittens (before embroidering) by rubbing them in warm, sudsy water while wearing them. Mittens will pull in, tighten, and shrink up. Shrink to fit and rinse in clear warm water. Dry flat.

Notes for Knitting Bulky Chenille Mittens:

Use #9 needle.

Use 6-ounce chenille.

For adult-size mittens with bulky chenille, use children's-size pattern.

Pattern courtesy of Lambspun of Colorado, Fort Collins, Colorado.

Sweetheart Gloves

You will love this simple pattern for knitting with 2 needles.

YARN:

1 ounce of Lambspun Summit Silk
100 yards KiwiWool or worsted weight yarn of the color of your choice

MATERIALS:

US #3 knitting needles
1 darning needle

1st Glove:

CO 49 sts
Work in k1, p1 rib until cuff measures 3 inches or desired length.
Ending with the right side facing, work 3 rows in stockinette.
You will now be caring the yarn through charts 1, 2, and 3.
Row 4 (WS): p10, start chart 1, p18, work chart 2, p6, work chart 3, p12.
Row 5: work in stockinette following the charts.
Row 6: work in stockinette following the charts.

271

Row 7: work 27 sts, make 1*, k1, make 1, work to end of row not forgetting the charts (51 sts).

Rows 8, 9, and 10: work in stockinette with charts.

Row 11: work 27, make 1, k3, make 1, work to end of row.

Repeat rows 8 through 11 until you have 61 sts.

Work one row in order to finish on a WS row and be ready for the next RS row.

(* to make 1, knit in the bar before the next stitch)

All 3 charts are now complete: chart 1 and 2 on row 9 and chart 3 on row 15.

Make thumb:

Row 1: k40, turn. Leave the rest of the sts unworked.

Row 2: p13, CO 4, turn (you now have 17 sts).

Work these 17 sts for 16 rows (or desired length for thumb) in stockinette.

Next row: k2tog (k1, k2tog) 5 times.

Next row: purl.

Next row: (k2tog) 5 times, k1.

Next row: purl.

Break yarn, threat ends through remaining sts, draw up, and fasten securely. Sew seam.

With right side facing PU 5 sts from CO sts at base of thumb. Knit to end of row (you now have 53 sts).

Begin with a purl row, work 17 rows even in stockinette stitch ending with RS facing for next row.

Make 1st finger:

Next row: knit 34, turn.

Next row: p15, turn, CO 2, turn (17 sts).

Work 18 rows in stockinette.

Next row: (k2, k2tog) 4 times, k1.

Next row: purl.

Next row: (k1, k2tog) 4 times, k1.

Next row: purl.

Break yarn, threat ends through remaining sts, draw up, and
    fasten securely. Sew seam.

Make 2nd finger:

PU 3 sts, knit 7, turn.

Next row: p17, CO 2 (19 sts), turn.

Work 20 rows in stockinette.

Next row: (k2, k2tog) 4 times, k3.

Next row: purl.

Next row: (k1, k2tog) 5 times.

Next row: purl.

Break yarn, threat ends through remaining sts, draw up, and
    fasten securely. Sew seam.

Make 3rd finger:

PU 3 sts, knit 7, turn.

Next row: p17, CO 2, (19 sts), turn.

Work 18 rows in stockinette.

Next row: (k2, k2tog) 4 times, k3.

Next row: purl.

Next row: (k1, k2tog) 5 times.

Next row: purl.

Break yarn, threat ends through remaining sts, draw up, and
fasten securely. Sew seam.

Make 4th finger:
PU 3 sts, knit 5, turn.
Next row: p13, turn.
Work 14 rows in stockinette.
Next row: (k1, k2tog) 4 times, k1.
Next row: purl.
Next row: (k2tog) 4 times, k1.
Next row: purl.
Break yarn, threat ends through remaining sts, draw up, and
fasten securely. Sew seam.

2nd Glove:
Work the same as the 1st glove but start with the 2 little
hearts instead.
Row 4 (WS): p12, work chart 3, p6, work chart 2, p18,
work chart 1, p10.
Row 5: work in stockinette following the charts.
Row 6: work in stockinette following the charts.
Row 7 (RS): work 26 sts, make 1, k1, make 1, work remain-
ing sts.
Rows 8, 9, and 10: work in stockinette with charts.
Row 11 (RS): work 27 sts, make 1, k3, make 1, work to end
of row.
Repeat rows 8 through 11 until you have 61 sts.
Work 1 row in order to finish on a WS row and be ready for
the next RS row.

chart 1

	1	2	3	4	5	6	7	8	9	10	11	12	13	14
row 15					k	k			k	k				
row 14			p	p	p	p		p	p	p	p			
row 13			k	k	k	k	k	k	k	k	k	k	k	
row 12			p	p	p	p	p	p	p	p	p	p	p	
row 11			k	k	k	k	k	k	k	k	k	k	k	
row 10			p	p	p	p	p	p	p	p	p	p	p	
row 9			k	k	k	k	k	k	k	k	k	k	k	
row 8				p	p	p	p	p	p	p	p	p		
row 7					k	k	k	k	k	k	k			
row 6						p	p	p	p	p				
row 5							k	k	k					
row 4								p						

charts 2 and 3

	1	2	3	4	5	6	7	8	9	10	11	12	13	14
row 9						k	k		k	k				
row 8						p	p	p	p	p				
row 7						k	k	k	k	k				
row 6						p	p	p	p	p				
row 5							k	k	k					
row 4								p						

k = knit	
p = purl	

Keep working and finish the same way as making the 1st glove.

If you wish for the thumb and fingers to be shorter or longer, subtract or add 2 rows at a time before the decreases.

Pattern courtesy of Lambspun of Colorado, Fort Collins, Colorado. Designed for Lambspun by Melina Bernhardt.

Ribbed Hat

This hat takes about 3 hours to make and will give years of joyful wear. By doing the ribbing with a size smaller needle than the rest of the hat, you will have a snug but comfortable fit. This hat can be made small enough for a child, who is sure to love its soft, fluffy yarn. Wear with the ribbing folded up. On a cold day, the ribbing can be a welcome cover for ears.

MATERIALS:
2.5 ounces chinchilla chenille
1.5 ounces lambspun yarn

NEEDLES:
1 US #8 16-inch circular needle
1 US #9 16-inch circular needle
1 set of US #9 double-point needles

GAUGE:

4 sts to 1 inch in stockinette st.

PATTERN:

Cast on 72 sts (or a multiple of 6 to give the right size) with the #8 16-inch circular needle. Join and work in k2, p2 ribbing for 2.5 inches or longer, if desired. Change to #9 circular needle and knit around until hat measures 9 inches including ribbing.

TIP:

Try the hat on a person the size of the person who will wear it and check for length. Depending on age and size, the hat can be easily made longer or shorter at this point.

Switch to double-point needles for decrease rds as follows:

DECREASE RDS:

#1: k2tog, k5, repeat around
#2: k2tog, k4, repeat around
#3: k2tog, k3, repeat around
#4: k2tog, k2, repeat around
#5: k2tog, k1, repeat around
#6: k2tog, repeat around

Cut yarn leaving a 10-inch tail. Thread a tapestry needle and pass the needle and yarn through the remaining sts, removing needles as you go. Pass yarn through needles once more, pulling the circle tight. Pass the needle through the center of the circle and weave in the end on the inside of the hat. Cut off excess yarn.

Weave in yarns from the cast on edge. Place hat over a hat form, bowl, or tissue paper, wet the crown and shape. Let dry.

POM-POM (OPTIONAL):
Cut 2 pieces of cardboard in a perfectly round shape (3 or 4 inches diameter). Cut a perfectly round hole in both of them (1 or 1½ inches diameter). Place the 2 discs on top of each other and wrap the yarn around them while held together, until no yarn fits through the hole anymore. Cut around the external border of the discs, making sure your scissors slip between the 2 cardboard discs. Then, cut a 6–7 inch piece of yarn and wrap it around between the 2 discs and tie it in several knots to secure the pom-pom well. You can now re-move the 2 cardboard discs or tear them off. Your pom-pom is ready to be sewn onto your hat!

Pattern courtesy of Lambspun of Colorado, Fort Collins, Colorado. Designed for Lambspun by Laura Macagno-Shang.

Striped Christmas Stocking

This is a fun, decorative Christmas stocking that could be used as part of a holiday centerpiece, stuffed with candy canes, small packages, or other goodies.

MATERIALS:

4 ounces each of 2 colors:

Knitting worsted yarn (use 3 strands) *OR* bulky yarn (use 2 strands) *OR* chunky yarn (use a single strand)

NEEDLES:

US #17 or size to obtain gauge

Size K crochet hook

GAUGE:

2 sts = 1 inch

INSTRUCTIONS:

Using #17 needles and color A, cast-on 20 sts. Knitting every row, alternate 2 rows of each of colors A and B until there are 10 stripes in all. Break off yarn. Slip first 7 sts to a holder, join yarn, and knit center 6 sts; slip last 7 sts to a holder. Continue in striping pattern on center 6 sts until 4 more stripes are completed. Slip the first 7 sts from the holder to a free needle, join color A and knit these sts. Pick-up and knit 4 sts along side or instep, slip maker on needle, knit across 6 instep sts, slip marker on needle, pick-up and knit 4 sts on other side of instep, knit 7 sts from holder. Working with color A only, knit next row. Next row: Dec one st before and after each marker (4 sts dec). Knit next 5 rows, repeat dec row, knit next row, bind off.

FINISHING:

Sew back and bottom seam. Join color B to top of stocking at back seam and with right side facing you, using K hook, work 1 row sc around top edge, join with sl st, ch 1 turn. Work 1 row loop st. Repeat last 2 rows until there are 3 loop rows; end off.

Pattern courtesy of Lambspun of Colorado, Fort Collins, Colorado. Designed for Lambspun by Jani Fellows.

Blue Angel Christmas Stocking

MATERIALS:

MC = Ciniglia navy chenille	2 50 g skeins
CC = Variegated novelty yarn	1 50 g skein
A = White metallic (use doubled)	.2 ounce

ACCENTS:

Yellow pima cotton	.1 ounce
Yellow angora (use doubled)	.2 ounce
Green angora	.2 ounce
Burgundy viscose chenille	.1 ounce
White/Gold double-strand metallic	.1 ounce
Tan alpaca	5 yards
White curly mohair	5 yards
Brown angora	2 yards
Black silk	1 yard

Cuff:

Using CC cast-on 64 sts. Join circle and work in K1, P1 rib for 3 inches. Leave out lace round, you will not need to fold or sew this cuff.

Leg:

Switch to MC and St st. Work in the round for 1 inch then begin working flat at the beginning of the round and start graph on row 1 as follows: Knit 4 sts MC then start graph so back of wing will appear on the front of the stocking. Burgundy sash will wrap slightly around to the back of the other side. Join and begin knitting in the round after the last row of the chart (see main pattern). Knit for 1 more inch in MC then start heel in CC. Knit foot in MC and toe in CC.

Finishing:

After stocking is knitted, duplicate stitch with A single stitches placed randomly on the blue background to create "starry night" look. Embroider face, hand, and stars with outline stitch as indicated on graph. Knit 5 inches of I-cord and sew loop onto back of cuff for hanger. Sew together the seam up the back of stocking. Cold block lightly.

Pattern courtesy of Lambspun of Colorado, Fort Collins, Colorado.

	=	Dark blue chenille
●	=	Yellow pima cotton
○	=	Yellow angora
■	=	Green angora
×	=	Burgundy viscose
+	=	Double-strand metallic
▲	=	Tan alpaca
✕	=	Curly white mohair

BLUE ANGEL CHRISTMAS STOCKING PATTERN

Outline stars with white metallic, left hand with tan alpaca, face with brown angora, mouth with red angora, eye is French knot with black silk.

Lambspun Knitting Pattern Abbreviations

BO	Bind off
CO	Cast-on
Dec	Decrease
in	Inches
Inc	Increase
k	Knit
k1	Knit 1 stitch
k2tog	Knit 2 stitches together
oz	Ounces
p	Purl
p1	Purl 1 stitch
p2tog	Purl 2 stitches together
Rnd/Rnds	Round/rounds
RS	Right side of work
sl	Slip
ssk	Slip one stitch as if to knit, slip the next stitch as if to knit, and knit the 2 slipped stitches together
st st	Stockinette stitch (knit on the right side, and purl on the wrong side)
st/sts	Stitch/stitches
WS	Wrong side of work
YO	Yarn over

Maggie's Cinnamon Rolls

Dough:

- 1 package active dry yeast
- 3½–4 cups all-purpose flour
- 1 cup whole milk
- ⅓ cup butter
- ⅓ cup sugar
- ½ teaspoon salt
- 1 beaten egg

Lemon Cream Cheese Frosting:

- 4 ounces cream cheese, softened
- 2 tablespoons butter, softened
- 1 tablespoon lemon juice
- 2 cups confectioners' sugar
- half-and-half (if needed)

Filling:

- 2 tablespoons melted butter
- 1 cup packed dark brown sugar
- 3 teaspoons ground cinnamon

Optional:

- ½ cup walnuts, pecans, or raisins

Stir together the yeast and 1½ cups of flour in large mixing bowl and set aside. In a saucepan over medium-low heat, combine milk, butter, and sugar. Add salt and heat till warm and butter has melted. Slowly add to flour mixture with beaten egg, stirring until well-blended. Beat with electric mixer 3 minutes, stirring in as much remaining flour as possible. Place dough on lightly-floured surface and knead until smooth and elastic (5 minutes). Shape dough into a ball and place in a lightly-greased bowl, turning once. Then cover and let rise in a warm place until doubled (about 1½ hours).

Make frosting. Combine softened cream cheese and butter. Stir until light and fluffy. Add lemon juice. Beat in confectioners' sugar gradually until well-blended and smooth. If needed, add half-and-half until desired consistency. Set aside.

Punch the dough down and turn onto a lightly-floured surface. Cover and let rest 10 minutes. Grease a cookie sheet or large baking pan(s) and set aside. Roll dough into a 10×18-inch rectangle. Spread with melted butter. Stir together dark brown sugar and cinnamon and sprinkle over dough. Add nuts or raisins, if desired. Tightly roll up dough from the long side. Pinch and seal ends. Cut dough into 1-inch sections and place on prepared baking sheet or pan. Cover and let rise until double (40–60 minutes). Brush rolls with melted butter. Bake in 350° oven for 25 to 30 minutes until golden brown. Remove rolls to wire rack and frost while still warm. Makes approximately 12 rolls.

** Warning: This yeast sweet dough recipe is very sensitive to heat. Try a lower oven temperature the first time. Because I live in Colorado at a higher altitude, I set my oven for 325° and bake the rolls for 23 minutes. *For best results, please adjust baking time and temperature accordingly.*

Pumpkin Nut Bread

2 cups all-purpose flour

I cup packed light or golden brown sugar

I tablespoon baking powder

I teaspoon ground cinnamon

¼ teaspoon salt

¼ teaspoon baking soda

¼ teaspoon ground nutmeg

¼ teaspoon ground cloves

I cup canned pumpkin

½ cup milk

2 eggs, slightly beaten

⅓ cup butter

½ cup chopped walnuts (more if desired)

In a large mixing bowl, combine 1 cup of the flour, then add the brown sugar, baking powder, cinnamon, salt, baking soda, nutmeg, and cloves. Then add the pumpkin, milk, eggs, and butter. Beat with electric mixer or by hand with wooden spoon until well-blended, at least 2 minutes. Add remaining flour and beat well. Stir in nuts.

Pour batter into a greased 9 × 5 × 3-inch loaf pan. Bake in a 350° oven for 60 to 65 minutes or until a knife inserted near the center comes out clean. Cool for 10 minutes on a wire rack. Remove from the pan and cool completely on wire rack. Wrap and store in refrigerator at least overnight before slicing. Makes 1 loaf.

Aunt Helen's Gingersnaps

This is one of my family's favorite holiday cookies. They're meant to be soft and chewy, not crispy.

  2½ cups all-purpose flour
  1 tablespoon plus 2 teaspoons ground ginger
  2 teaspoons ground cinnamon
  2 teaspoons baking soda
  ½ teaspoon salt
  1½ sticks (¾ cup) unsalted butter, softened
  1 cup firmly packed dark brown sugar
  1 large egg, room temperature
  ¼ cup unsulphured molasses
  2 tablespoons freshly grated lemon peel
  ¼–½ cup granulated white sugar

Heat oven to 350°. Lightly grease cookie sheets. Mix flour, ginger, cinnamon, baking soda, and salt in a small mixing bowl. Cream butter and brown sugar together in a medium bowl, mixing well for at least 2 minutes until well blended, pale, and fluffy, scraping bowl with rubber spatula. Beat in egg, then molasses and lemon peel until blended. Slowly add half the flour mixture, mixing with wooden spoon just until blended, then add remaining flour mixture, mixing it in well.

Cover bowl with plastic wrap and chill for 15 minutes. Then take out and roll rounded tablespoons of dough into 1¼-inch balls (approx.). Roll balls in granulated sugar and place 2 inches apart on prepared cookie sheets(s). Bake just until puffed and cookies look dry—anywhere from 9 minutes to 14 minutes, depending on your oven. (Do not overbake or cookies will become hard.) Carefully remove with metal spatula to wire rack to cool. Makes approximately 32 cookies.

I usually double this recipe when I make it, because those amounts are easier to work with. But, be prepared to make a lot of cookies. ☺

Chocolate Pecan Rum Balls

2 cups crushed vanilla wafers
2 cups confectioners' sugar
3 cups chopped pecans
4 tablespoons cocoa
4 tablespoons light corn syrup
½ cup dark rum
½ cup fine granulated sugar

Combine crushed wafers and confectioners' sugar, then add chopped pecans and cocoa. Mix well. Add corn syrup then rum and mix well. Shape into 1-inch balls. Roll in granulated sugar. Then place in covered container and store in refrigerator until ready to serve—or mail as presents. Makes approximately 4 dozen. (Storing in airtight container allows the flavors to become stronger and even more delicious.)

Enjoy!

Burt's Wassail (Hot Mulled Wine)

6 cups Burgundy or claret

1 cup dry sherry

Peel of two oranges and two lemons

6 sticks cinnamon (broken into 1 inch pieces)

2 whole nutmegs, crushed

10 whole cloves

2 tablespoons white sugar

Mix all ingredients in a saucepan or pot and simmer gently from 5 to 10 minutes. **Do not boil.** Strain to remove the spices and serve hot in a punch bowl or serving bowl with ladle.

Enjoy, and make sure you have a "designated driver" for the evening.

Maggie's Chocolate Mint Fudge

This recipe is an old favorite I remember from childhood. I've seen varia-tions of it over the years in newsletters, magazines, cooking shows—everywhere there are chocolate lovers. My contribution has been to substitute peppermint extract for vanilla. Family and friends have loved it ever since. Enjoy!

I medium-to-large jar of marshmallow crème
I can evaporated milk
I stick butter (use regular salted butter—not a butter substitute)
I teaspoon salt
3 cups granulated white sugar
2 12-ounce packages of semisweet chocolate chips/morsels
I tablespoon peppermint extract

A large thick-bottomed pot is recommended to keep the fudge from burning.

Line two 8 × 8-pans with aluminum foil. Grease lightly with butter (not oil or margarine).

Place marshmallow crème in pot over medium heat, then stir in evaporated milk, stirring slowly. Cut stick of butter into 8 pieces and drop into simmering mixture. Stir in salt. Adjust heat to medium-high and add sugar, a ½ cup at a time, stirring well after each addition. Continue stirring as sugar mixture starts to bubble. Cook for 5 minutes, no more, STIRRING CONSTANTLY. I cannot emphasize this enough.

Remove from heat and immediately stir in the packages of semisweet chocolate chips/morsels, 1 package at a time, stirring vigorously. Add peppermint extract, stirring well until blended. Pour fudge into the 2 pans. Let cool on counter for several minutes, then place pans in fridge to set up and cool completely.

Makes two 8 × 8-pans of fudge.

Carl's Doggy Christmas Cookies

1 pound beef or chicken livers
2 cups water
1 package active dry yeast
¼ cup warm water
1 cup beef broth
1½ cups whole wheat flour
1½ cups toasted wheat germ
1 egg, slightly beaten
1 teaspoon milk

Optional:
1 teaspoon garlic powder
cornmeal

Dissolve yeast in ¼ cup warm water. In a 2-quart pot, bring liver and 2 cups water to a boil over high heat. Cover, reduce heat, and simmer until liver is no longer pink in center (about 10 minutes). Strain and cut liver into 1-inch pieces.

Put in blender with 1 cup of beef broth. Blend until smoothly pureed. Scrape liver into a bowl, add dissolved yeast, wheat germ, and whole wheat flour. Stir until well-moistened. On a lightly floured board, roll out dough ¼ inch thick. Cut into shapes (bones, rectangles, circles, whatever). Place cookies on greased cookie sheet, brush with egg and milk glaze. Bake at 350° for 20 minutes or until brown. Refrigerate when cool in airtight container for up to 2 weeks.

Cookies must be refrigerated. You can add 1 teaspoonful of garlic powder to mixture or sprinkle cornmeal over finished cookies, if desired. Dogs love both flavors.

This recipe comes from Lambspun knitter and spinner Jill Koenig. Jill breeds llamas and Navajo-Churro sheep on the outskirts of Fort Collins, Colorado.